Sergeant O'Brien, a tall thin man with hard eyes and a flock of freckles, came out of the lounge. 'Found anything?' Bardin asked. 'Some slugs, nothing else. No finger-prints that aren't accounted for. It's my guess the killer just walked in, shot down everyone in sight and then walked out again without touching a thing.'

James Hadley Chase hits this peak in the opening pages of his new thriller, hots up evermore the furious pace, and ends up with an almost underplayed, infinitely deadly double-take climax on the very last page.

By the same author

JAMES HADLEY CHASE

This Way for a Shroud

GRAFTON BOOKS

A Division of the Collins Publishing Group

LONDON GLASGOW
TORONTO SYDNEY AUCKLAND

Grafton Books
A Division of the Collins Publishing Group
8 Grafton Street, London W1X 3LA

Published by Grafton Books 1965
Reprinted 1967, 1969, 1973, 1975, 1977, 1978, 1980,
1984, 1986

First published in Great Britain by
Robert Hale Ltd 1953

ISBN 0-586-02836-6

Printed and bound in Great Britain by
Collins, Glasgow

Set in Intertype Plantin

CHAPTER ONE

THE telephone bell rang sharply as Janey Conrad came briskly down the stairs. She was wearing her new evening dress: a strapless, sky-blue creation, the bodice of which was covered with silver sequins. She was looking her best, and she was aware of it.

At the sound of the telephone bell she stopped in mid-stride. Her animated expression turned to exasperated anger: a transformation as swift and as final as the turning off of an electric lamp.

'Paul! Don't answer it,' she said in the cold quiet voice that always came with her anger.

Her husband, a tall, loose-limbed, powerfully built man in his late thirties came out of the lounge. He was wearing a tuxedo and carried a soft black hat in his hand. When Janey had first met him he had reminded her very sharply of James Stewart, and the resemblance had been the main reason why she had married him.

'But I've got to answer it,' he said in his soft, drawling voice. 'I may be wanted.'

'Paul!' Her voice rose a little as he walked over to the telephone and picked up the receiver.

He grinned at her, motioning with his hand for her to be quiet.

'Hello?' he said into the mouthpiece.

'Paul? This is Bardin.' The Lieutenant's voice boomed against Paul's ear and spilt into the quiet tense hall.

As soon as Janey heard the voice, she clenched her fists and her mouth set in a hard, ugly line.

'You'll want to be in on this,' Bardin went on. 'There's been a massacre up at Dead End: June Arnot's place. We're knee deep in corpses, and one of them is June's. Brother! Is this going to be a sensation! How soon can you get out here?'

Conrad pulled a face and looked at Janey out of the corners of his eyes. He watched her walk slowly and stiffly into the sitting-room.

'I guess I'll be right over,' he said.

'Swell. I'll hold everything until you get here. Snap it up. I want you here before the press get on to this.'

'I'll be right over,' Conrad said, and hung up.

'Goddamn it!' Janey said softly.

She stood with her back to him, facing the mantelpiece.

'I'm sorry, Janey, but I've got to go. . . .'

'Goddamn it, and you too,' Janey said without raising her

voice. 'This always happens. Whenever we plan to go out, this happens. You and your stinking police force!'

'That's no way to talk,' Conrad said. 'It's a damn shame, but there's nothing we can do about it. We'll go tomorrow night, and I'll make certain we do go.'

Janey leaned forward and with the back of her hand she swept the ornaments, photograph frames and the clock off the mantel-piece, to crash into the hearth.

'Janey!' Conrad came quickly into the room. 'Now stop that!'

'Oh, go to hell!' Janey said in the same cold, quiet voice. She stared at Conrad's reflection in the mirror, her eyes hostile and glittering. 'Go and play cops and robbers. Never mind about me, but don't expect to find me here when you get back. From now on, I'm going to have fun without you.'

'June Arnot's been murdered, Janey. I've got to go. Now look, I'll take you to the Ambassador's tomorrow night to make up for this. How would you like that?'

'You won't take me so long as there's a telephone in this house,' Janey said bitterly. 'I want some money, Paul!'

He looked at her.

'But, Janey . . .'

'I want some money now: at this minute! If I don't get it I'll have to hock something, and it won't be anything belonging to me!'

Conrad shrugged. He took a ten-dollar bill from his billfold and handed it to her.

'All right, Janey. If that's the way you feel about it. Why don't you give Beth a call? You don't want to go alone.'

Janey folded the bill, looked up at him and then turned away. It was a shock to him to see how impersonal and indifferent her eyes were. She might have been looking at a stranger.

'You don't have to worry about me. Go and worry about your silly little murder. I'll get along fine on my own.'

He started to say something, then stopped. When she was in this mood there was no reasoning with her.

'Can I drop you anywhere?' he asked quietly.

'Oh, drop dead!' Janey said violently, and walked over to the window.

Conrad's mouth tightened. He went across the hall, opened the front door and walked quickly down to his car, parked at the kerb.

As he slid under the driving-wheel he was aware of a tight feeling across his chest that restricted his breathing. He didn't want to admit it, but he knew Janey's and his sands were running out. How long had they been married now? He frowned as he trod down on the starter. Just under three years. The first year had been pretty good, but that was before he had become Chief Investigator to the District Attorney's office. That was when he kept regular hours and could take Janey out every night.

She had been pleased enough when he had got promotion: overnight his salary had doubled, and they had moved out of the three-room apartment on Wentworth Street and had taken a bungalow on the swank Hayland's Estate. This was a big move up in the social scale. Only people earning five-figure incomes and more were accepted on Hayland's Estate.

But Janey wasn't so pleased when she began to realize that he was on call any time of the night and day.

'For heaven's sake,' she had said, 'anyone would think you were a common policeman instead of a Chief Investigator.'

'But I am a policeman,' he had explained patiently. 'I am the D.A.'s special policeman, and if a big case breaks I have to represent him.'

There had been quarrels which at first didn't seem to Paul to amount to much: just natural disappointment when a sudden emergency call spoilt an evening out. It was understandable, he had told himself, but he wished she would be more reasonable. He had to admit that emergency calls always seemed to turn up just when they were going out, but that was something they both had to put up with.

But Janey wouldn't put up with it. The quarrels developed into rows, and rows into scenes, and now he was getting tired of it.

But this was the first time Janey had asked for money to go out on her own. This was a new development, and it worried Conrad more than all the rows, the breakages and scenes of the past.

Janey was far too attractive to go out by herself. Conrad was aware of the reckless streak in her. From some of the things she had let slip in off-guarded moments, he had gathered she had led a pretty hectic life before they married. He had decided that what had happened in her past was none of his business, but now, remembering some of the stories she had told him of wild parties, and the names of past boy friends she had sometimes taunted him with when she was in a rage, he wondered uneasily if she were going on the war-path again. She was only twenty-four, and sex seemed to mean much more to her than to him, and this surprised him, for he had the normal appetites of the male. Then there were her looks. With her forget-me-not blue eyes, her silky blonde hair, her perfect complexion and her cute *retroussé* nose she was a temptation to any man.

'Oh, goddamn it!' he muttered under his breath, unconsciously repeating her cry of exasperation.

He raced the engine, engaged gear and swung the car away from the kerb.

II

For the past three years June Arnot had been rated the most popular actress in motion pictures, and she was said to be the richest woman in Hollywood.

She had built for herself a luxurious home on the promontory of the east arm of Tammany Bay, a few miles outside Pacific City and some ten miles from Hollywood.

The house itself was a show piece of luxury and blatant ostentation, and June Arnot, who was not without a sense of humour, had named it *Dead End*.

As Conrad pulled up outside the small creeper-covered guard-house where all visitors had to book in before going on up the mile-long drive to the house, the bulky figure of Lieutenant Sam Bardin of the Homicide Bureau loomed out of the darkness.

'Well, well,' he said when he caught sight of Conrad. 'You didn't have to dress up like that for my benefit. Was that what kept you so long?'

Conrad grinned.

'I was about to take the wife out to a party when you called. This has put me in the dog-kennel for weeks. McCann shown up yet?'

'The Captain's in San Francisco, worse luck,' Bardin said. 'He won't be back until tomorrow. This is a hell of a thing, Paul. I'm glad you're here. We'll want as much help as we can get before we're finished.'

'Let's make a start, then. Suppose you tell me what you know and then we'll take a look around.'

Bardin wiped his big red face with his handkerchief and pushed his hat to the back of his head. He was a tall, heavily built man, ten years older than Conrad, which made him around forty-five.

'At eight-thirty we got a call from Harrison Fedor, Miss Arnot's publicity manager. He had a business date with her for tonight. When he arrived here he found the gates open, which is unusual as they are always kept locked. He walked into the guard-house and found the guard shot through the head. He telephoned the house from the guard-house, but could get no reply. I guess he lost his nerve. Anyway, he said he was too scared to go up to the house and see what was wrong, so he called us.'

'Where's he now?'

'Sitting in his car fortifying himself with whisky,' Bardin said with a grin. 'I haven't had time to talk to him properly yet, so I told him to stick around. I've been up to the house. The five servants have been wiped out: all shot. I knew Miss Arnot was somewhere on the estate as she had this business date, but she wasn't in the house.' He took out a pack of cigarettes, offered one to Conrad and lit his own. 'I found her in the swimming-pool.' He made a little grimace. 'Someone ripped her wide open and hacked her head off.'

Conrad grunted.

'Sounds like a maniac. What's happening now?'

8

'The boys are up at the house and at the swimming-pool doing their stuff. If there's anything to turn up, they'll turn it up. Want to have a walk around and see for yourself?'

'I guess so. Can Doc fix the time?'

'He's working on it now. I told him not to move the bodies until you arrived. He should have something for us before long. Let's have a look at the guard-house.'

Conrad followed him through the doorway into a small room equipped with a flat-topped desk, a chair, a padded settee and a battery of telephones. On the desk was a big leather-bound Visitors' book open at that day's date.

The guard, in an olive-green uniform and glittering jack boots, lay half under the table, his head resting in a crimson halo of blood. He had been shot at close quarters, and one quick glance at him was enough for Conrad.

He moved over to the desk and bent to look at the Visitors' book.

'The killer isn't likely to have signed himself in,' Barden said dryly. 'Just the same, the guard must have known him or he wouldn't have unlocked the gates.'

Conrad's eyes took in the almost empty page.

15.00 hrs. Mr. Jack Belling, 3 Lennox Street. By appointment.
17.00 hrs. Miss Rita Strange, 14 Crown Street. By appointment.
19.00 hrs. Miss Frances Coleman, 145 Glendale Avenue.

'This mean anything?' he asked. 'This girl Coleman was here about the time of the killings.'

Bardin shrugged his shoulders.

'I dunno. We'll check on her when we've got the time. If she had something to do with it you can bet she would have ripped out the page.'

'That's right: unless she forgot.'

Bardin made an impatient gesture.

'Well, come on; there are lots of other pretty sights for you to look at.' He moved out into the growing darkness again. 'May as well run up in your car. Take it slowly at the second bend. The gardener was shot there.'

Conrad drove up the drive, flanked on either side by giant palms and flowering shrubs. When he had driven three hundred yards or so, Bardin said, 'Just round this bend.'

They came upon a parked car by the edge of the drive. Doc Holmes, two interns in white coats and a couple of bored-looking patrolmen were standing in a group with the car's headlights lighting up their backs.

Conrad and Bardin walked over and joined them. They were grouped around an old, shrivelled-up Chinese, who lay on his back, his yellow, claw-like fingers hooked in his death agony. The front of his white smock was dyed red.

'Hello, Conrad,' Doc Holmes said. He was a little man with a round pink face and a fringe of white hair to frame his bald head. 'Come to see our massacre?'

'Just slumming,' Conrad said. 'How long has he been dead, Doc?'

'About an hour and a half : not more.'

'Just after seven?'

'About then.'

'Same gun as killed the guard?'

'It's probable. They were all butchered by a .45.' He looked at Bardin. 'This looks like a professional job, Lieutenant. Whoever shot these people knew his business. He killed them instantly with one shot.'

Bardin grunted.

'Doesn't mean much. A .45 will kill anyone whether it's in the hands of a professional or an amateur.'

'Let's go up to the house,' Conrad said.

A three-minute drive brought them to the house. Lights were on in every room. Two patrolmen guarded the front entrance.

Conrad and Bardin walked up the steps and into the small reception room and down into the inner well of the house, a mosaic-paved patio. The rooms of the house surrounded the three sides of the patio which provided a cool and sheltered courtyard in which to sit.

Sergeant O'Brien, a tall, thin man with hard eyes and a flock of freckles, came out of the lounge. He nodded to Conrad.

'Found anything?' Bardin asked.

'Some slugs, nothing else. No finger-prints that aren't accounted for. It's my guess the killer just walked in, shot down everyone in sight and then walked out again without touching a thing.'

Paul wandered to the foot of the broad staircase and stood looking up at it. At the head of the stairs lay the body of a young Chinese girl. She was wearing a yellow house-coat and dark blue silk embroidered trousers. A red stain made an ugly patch in the middle of her shoulder blades.

'Looks like she was running for cover when she was shot,' Bardin said. 'Want to go up and look at her?'

Conrad shook his head.

'Exhibit number four is in the lounge,' Bardin said, and led the way into a lavishly furnished room with leather settees and armchairs that afforded sitting room for thirty or forty people.

In the centre of the room was a large fountain on which played coloured lights, and in its illuminated bowl tropical fish added their charm to the effect.

'Nice, isn't it?' Bardin said dryly. 'You should see my sitting-room, Paul. I must tell my wife about the fish. They might give her ideas : she could do with a few.'

Conrad moved farther into the room. By the casement windows leading to the garden, June Arnot's butler sat huddled up on the floor, his back resting against the tapestry wall. He had been shot through the head.

'Spoilt the tapestry,' Bardin said. 'Pity. I bet that stuff costs a whale of a lot of dough.' He dropped his cigarette into an ash-bowl, went on, 'Want to see the kitchens? There are two more of them in there, a chink cook and a Filipino. They were both running for the exit, but neither of them ran fast enough.'

'I guess I've seen enough,' Conrad said. 'If there's anything to find, your boys will find it.'

'I'll put that little sentiment in my birthday book and show it to you the next time I pass up a clue,' Bardin said. 'Okay, we'll go down to the pool.'

He went over to the casement windows, opened them and stepped out on to the broad terrace. The full moon was rising and shedding its hard, cold light over the sea. The garden was heavy with the scents of flowers. In the far distance an illuminated fountain made a fairy-land scene below them.

'She went for lights and pretty colours, didn't she?' Bardin said. 'But it didn't get her anywhere. It's a pretty crude way to finish your life: having your head hacked off and your belly ripped open. I guess even all this display of wealth wouldn't compensate me for an end like that.'

'The trouble with you, Sam,' Conrad said quietly, 'is you're class conscious. There are plenty of guys who would envy you your way of life.'

'Show them to me,' Bardin returned with a sour smile. 'I'll trade with them any day of the week. It's easy for you to shoot off your mouth. You've got a glamorous wife, and she can take your mind off things. I'd put up with a shabby home and lousy meals if I'd got me a little glamour. You want to look over my garden fence when the washing is hanging out if you're interested in female museum pieces. I bet your wife goes in for those nylon nifties that keep knocking my eye out every time I pass a shop window. That's as close as I'll ever get to them.'

Conrad felt a sudden wave of irritation run through him. He knew Bardin's wife. She wasn't anything to look at; she wasn't smart, but at least she did try to run her home which was more than Janey ever did.

'You don't know when you're well off,' he said curtly, and walked down the gently sloping steps towards the swimming-pool.

III

Close by the forty-foot-high diving-board, Doc Holmes, the two interns, a photographer and four policemen stood on the edge of the swimming-pool, looking down at the water. That section of the water was dyed crimson, the rest of the water was a vivid blue.

As Bardin and Conrad came through the cocktail lounge on to the blue-tiled surround of the pool, Bardin said, 'I've had one look at this, and I can't say I'm looking forward to seeing it again.'

They joined the group under the diving-board.

'Well, there she is,' Bardin went on, and waved his hand to the water.

Paul looked at the headless, naked body that lay on the floor of the shallow end of the pool. The savage way it had been mutilated made his stomach suddenly contract.

'Where's the head?' he asked, turning away.

'I left it where I found it. It was on a table in one of the changing-rooms. Want to look at it?'

'No, thank you. You're sure it's June Arnot?'

'No doubt about it.'

Conrad turned to Doc Holmes.

'Okay, Doc, I've seen all I want to see. You can get busy now. You'll let me have a copy of your report?'

Doc Holmes nodded.

Bardin said, 'Okay, boys, get her out. Careful how you handle her.'

Three of the policemen moved forward reluctantly. One of them pushed a long boat-hook into the water and groped for the body.

'Let's talk to Fedor while this is going on,' Conrad said. 'Have him up to the house, will you?'

Bardin sent one of the policemen to fetch Fedor.

As he and Conrad mounted the steps on their way back to the house, he asked, 'Well, what do you make of it so far?'

'Looks to me as if it was done by someone who is a fairly frequent visitor to the house. The fact he was admitted by the guard puts him out of the stranger class, and the fact he wiped out the whole of the staff who probably could have identified him, points to it too.'

'Unless some maniac got in and ran amok.'

'The guard wouldn't have opened the gates to him.'

'He might have. Depends on the story the guy told him.'

As they reached the house two policemen came through the front entrance, carrying a stretcher on which was a covered body.

'That's the lot, Lieutenant,' one of them said. 'The house is clear now.'

Bardin grunted and walked up the steps and down into the patio.

'Do you think Fedor's in the clear?' Conrad asked as he sat down in a basket chair.

'He's not the type to cut loose like this. Besides, if he did do it, he'd have to have a damned strong motive. She was his only client, and he made a small fortune out of her.'

'A woman like her would have a lot of enemies,' Conrad said, stretching out his long legs. 'Whoever did it certainly hated her guts.'

'She seems to have had some pretty horrible acquaintances,' Bardin said, rubbing his hand across his eyes. 'From the hints I've picked up from time to time, there was nothing too bad for her to dabble in. Did you know she was supposed to be a special friend of Jack Maurer?'

Conrad stiffened to attention.

'No. How special?'

Bardin grinned.

'Thought that would make you sit up. I can't swear to it, but I've heard plenty of rumours. She kept it very quiet, but the story has it they were lovers.'

'I wish I could believe that. This is the kind of job Maurer might pull. He's ruthless enough. Remember that gang massacre he engineered a couple of years back? Seven men machine-gunned against a wall?'

'We don't know for certain Maurer did pull that one,' Bardin said cautiously.

'Who else did, then? Those men were muscling in on his territory. He had everything to gain by getting rid of them.'

'The Captain wasn't convinced. He thought it was Jacobi's mob trying to hang something on Maurer.'

'He knows what I think of that cockeyed theory. It was Maurer, and this killing could fit Maurer too.'

'You've got a bug about Maurer,' Bardin said, shrugging. 'I believe you'd sell your soul to get him behind bars.'

'I don't want him behind bars,' Conrad said, a sudden savage note in his voice. 'I want him in the chair. He's been in the world a damned sight too long.'

A policeman came to the patio door, coughed and jerked his thumb expressively.

'Here's Mr. Fedor, sir.'

Conrad and Bardin got to their feet.

Harrison Fedor, June Arnot's publicity manager, came across the mosaic-paved floor with a bouncing little rush. He was a small thin man with steady hard eyes, a rat-trap of a mouth and lantern jaws. He grabbed Conrad's hand and shook it violently.

'Nice to see you here. What's been happening? Is June all right?'

'Far from it,' Conrad said quietly. 'She's been murdered: she and the whole staff.'

Fedor gulped and his face sagged, then he got hold of himself and sat down in one of the basket chairs.

'You mean she's dead?'

'She's dead all right.'

'For God's sake!' Fedor took off his hat and ran his fingers through his thinning locks. 'Dead, eh? Well, goddamn it! I can't believe it.'

He stared first at Bardin, then at Paul. Neither of the men said anything. They waited.

'Murdered!' Fedor went on after a pause. 'What a sensation this is going to be! Phew! I don't know whether to laugh or cry.'

'What does that mean?' Bardin growled, his face heavy with disapproval.

Fedor grinned wryly.

'As you didn't have to work for her for five interminable years you couldn't know what it means.' He leaned forward and jabbed his forefinger in Bardin's direction. 'I'll be damned if I'll cry. Maybe I've lost my meal ticket, but I've also lost a goddamned pain in the neck. That bitch has been riding me to death. It was either her or me in the long run. I've got an ulcer because of her. You don't know what I've had to put up with from that woman!'

'Someone hacked her head off,' Conrad said quietly. 'Not content with that, he ripped her as well. Can you think of anyone who would do that to her?'

Fedor's eyes popped.

'Good grief! Hacked her head off! For God's sake! Why did he do that?'

'For the same reason he ripped her: he didn't like her. Know anyone who'd dive off the deep end like that?'

Fedor's eyes suddenly shifted.

'Can't say I do. Hell! Have the press got this yet?'

'No, and they won't get it until I have some more facts to work on,' Bardin said grimly. 'Now look, if you do know someone who might fit, you'd better spill it. The quicker we shut this case down, the better for everyone, including you.'

Fedor hesitated, then shrugged.

'I guess that's right. Ralph Jordan was her current lover. They have been having some mighty awful quarrels recently. This picture he's making with June is his last. Pacific Pictures have torn up his contract. They've had more than enough of him.'

'Why?' Conrad asked, lighting a cigarette.

'He's been living on a diet of reefers for the past six months, and boy! does that guy hit the roof after a reefer session!'

'In what way?'

'He runs amok.' Fedor took out his handkerchief and blotted his face with it. 'He set fire to one of the studios the week before last. Then last week, at Maurice Laird's swim party, he started something that took Laird everything he had to hush up. Jordan had some kind of acid he went around splashing on the girl's swim-suits. The stuff started burning, and Bingo! there were no swim-suits. You've never seen anything like it. Some thirty of our best-known stars were running around without a stitch on. Okay, it was pretty funny for us guys, and we appreciated the joke until we found the stuff hadn't only taken off the swim-suits. It took off a few yards of skin as well. Five girls had to go to hospital. They were in a terrible state. If Laird hadn't paid up handsomely Jordan would have been prosecuted. Next morning Laird tore up his contract.'

Conrad and Bardin exchanged glances.

'Sounds as if we might go along and talk to this guy,' Bardin said.

'For the love of mike don't tell him I said anything about him,' Fedor said feverishly. 'I've enough on my hands without having to cope with him.'

'Apart from Jordan,' Conrad said, 'does anyone else come to your mind who might have done this?'

Fedor shook his head.

'No. Most of June's friends were pretty rotten, but not all that rotten.'

'Is there anything in the story that she and Jack Maurer were lovers?'

Fedor suddenly looked down at his hands. A cold, remote expression came over his face.

'I wouldn't know.'

'You could make a guess. Did she ever mention Maurer to you?'

'No.'

'Did you ever hear his name coupled with her?'

'I guess not.'

'Did you ever see him with her?'

'No.'

Conrad looked across at Bardin.

'Isn't it wonderful that as soon as Maurer's name is mentioned everyone clams up? You'd think the guy didn't exist.'

'Don't get me wrong,' Fedor said hastily. 'If I knew anything I'd tell you. I don't know a thing about Maurer except what I've read in the papers.'

'The same old song and dance,' Conrad said in disgust. 'One of those days, with any luck, I'll come across someone with a little guts who isn't scared of Maurer, and who knows something: one of these days but, God knows when.'

'Take it easy,' Bardin said. 'If the guy doesn't know he doesn't know.'

Sergeant O'Brien came down the steps of the patio.

'Can I have a word, Lieutenant?'

Bardin took his arm and walked with him into the lounge.

'Stick around,' Paul said to Fedor, and went after them.

'He's found the gun,' Bardin said, his heavy face more cheerful. He held out a .45 Colt automatic. 'Look at this.'

Conrad took the gun and examined it. Engraved on the butt

were the initials R.J.

'Where did you find it?' he asked O'Brien.

'In the shrubbery about thirty yards from the main gate. I'll bet a dollar it's the gun. It's empty; it's been fired very recently, and it's a .45.'

'Better get it checked, Sam.'

Bardin nodded. He handed the gun to O'Brien.

'Take it down to headquarters and have it checked against the slug you've found.' He turned to Conrad. 'R.J. That's easy, isn't it? Looks like I've got me an open and shut case. Looks like Jordan's got some talking to do. Coming?'

IV

According to Fedor, Ralph Jordan had a penthouse apartment on Roosevelt Boulevard. He had taken the apartment soon after June Arnot had got rid of her Hollywood home, and although he had kept on his own luxurious home in Beverly Hills, he seldom lived there.

Conrad swung the car up the circular drive leading to Jordan's apartment block and pulled up in the shadows. Near by was a row of garage lock-ups. A big black Cadillac, parked half in and half out of one of the lock-ups attracted his attention.

'Someone wasn't looking where he was driving,' he said as he got out of the car. He walked over to the lock-up. Bardin followed him.

The Cadillac's off-side wing had crashed against the side of the lock-up, splintering the wood. The wing was pushed in and the off-side headlamp was smashed.

Bardin opened the car door and inspected the registration tag.

'Might have guessed it,' he said. 'Jordan's car. Who said he wasn't hopped to the eyebrows?'

'Well, at least he's home,' Conrad returned, and walked over to the entrance to the apartment block. He pushed through the revolving doors into the lobby, followed by Bardin.

A stout pink-and-white reception clerk in a faultlessly fitting tuxedo rested two small white hands on the polished top of the reception desk and raised his pale eyebrows at Conrad with a touch of hauteur.

'Is there something I can do?'

Bardin pushed his bulk forward. He flashed his buzzer and scowled. When he wanted to, he could look tough and ferocious, and he was looking tough and ferocious now.

'Lieutenant Bardin, City police,' he said in a grating voice. 'Jordan in?'

The reception clerk stiffened. His small hands fluttered.

'If you mean Mr. Ralph Jordan; yes, he is in. Did you wish to see him?'

16

'When did he get in?'

'Just after eight o'clock.'

'Was he drunk?'

'I'm afraid I didn't notice.' The shocked expression on the clerk's face made Conrad grin.

'What time did he go out?'

'Just after six.'

'He's on the top floor, isn't he?'

'Yes.'

'Okay. We're going up. Keep your hands off the telephone if you know what's good for you. This is a surprise visit. Anyone up there with him?'

'Not as far as I know.'

Bardin grunted, then tramped across the pile carpet that covered the half-acre of lobby to the elevator.

'So he went out just after six and got back at eight. That would have given him plenty of time to get to Dead End, do the job and get back again,' he said as the elevator took them swiftly and silently to the top floor.

'Keep your eye on him,' Conrad cautioned as the elevator doors slid back. 'If he's still hopped up he may be dangerous.'

'He won't be the first hop-head I've had to handle, and I bet he won't be the last – worse luck.'

Bardin paused outside the front door to the apartment.

'Hello: the door's open.'

He thumbed the bell-push. Somewhere in the apartment a bell rang sharply. Bardin waited a moment then shoved the front door wide open with his foot and looked into the small lobby.

A door facing them stood ajar.

They waited another moment or so, then Bardin walked into the lobby and pushed open the inner door.

They looked into a big, airy lounge, ablaze with lights. Wine-coloured curtains covered the windows. The walls were grey. There were armchairs, settees, a table or two and a well-equipped cocktail-bar. A television set and a radiogram stood side by side, and on the mantelpiece were glass ornaments, beautifully fashioned and blatantly obscene.

Bardin stood looking round, breathing heavily through his nostrils.

'Isn't it wonderful how these punks live?' he said savagely. 'The guy who said virtue is its own reward should take a look at this joint.'

'Your time will come when you get to heaven,' Conrad said with a grin. 'You'll be given a gold-plated revolver and diamonds on your badge. Doesn't seem to be anyone around.'

'Hey! Anyone here?' Bardin bawled in a voice that rattled the windows.

The silence that greeted his shout was as solid and as engulfing as a snowdrift, and as cold.

They exchanged glances.

'Now what?' Bardin said. 'Think he's hiding up some place?'

'Maybe he went out again.'

'That queen would have seen him go.'

'Then let's take a look.'

Conrad crossed the room, rapped on a door to the left, turned the handle and looked into a big airy bedroom. The only furniture except for a white pile carpet was a twelve-foot-wide bed that stood on a two-foot-high dais and looked as lonely as a lighthouse.

'No one here,' Conrad said as he walked into the room.

'Try the bathroom,' Bardin said, his voice sharpening.

They crossed the room to the bathroom door and opened it. They looked into the most elaborately equipped bathroom they had ever seen, but their eyes had no interest for the luxury nor the glittering plumbing. Their attention became riveted on the sunken bath.

Ralph Jordan lay in the waterless bath, his head sunk on his chest. He was wearing a wine-coloured dressing-gown over a pair of pale blue lounging pyjamas. The walls of the bath and the front of his dressing-gown were stained red. He held in his right hand an old-fashioned cut-throat razor. The blood on the thin blade looked like scarlet paint.

Bardin pushed past Conrad and touched Jordan's hand.

'Deader than a joint of beef: chilled beef at that.'

He took hold of a long lock of Jordan's hair and lifted his head.

Conrad grimaced as he caught sight of the deep gash across Jordan's throat: so deep it had severed the wind-pipe.

'Well, that's that,' Bardin said, stepping back. 'Like I said: an open and shut case. He went out there, knocked her off, then came back here and cut his throat. Very considerate of him. It makes a nice tidy job – for me, anyway.' He groped for a cigarette, lit it and blew a cloud of smoke into the dead man's face. 'Looks like Doc Holmes is going to have a busy night.'

Conrad was moving around the bathroom. He discovered an electric razor on the wall.

'Odd he should have a cut-throat razor. You'd have to go to a good many homes these days to find one, and you wouldn't have thought Jordan would have kept one so handy.'

Bardin groaned.

'Now don't start lousing up the issue. Maybe the guy cut his corns with it: people do.' He pushed open a door by the head of the bath and looked into an elaborately equipped dressing-room. On a chair was a suit, shirt and silk underwear. A pair of brogue shoes and socks lay near by.

Conrad walked into the room, then came to a sudden standstill.

18

'Now this will make you really happy, Sam,' he said, and waved to a blood-stained object on the floor.

Bardin joined him.

'Well, I'll be damned! A machete!' He knelt beside the razor-sharp knife. 'I bet it's the murder weapon. It's just the thing to cut someone's head off with, and it would lay a belly open like you open a door.'

'It wouldn't interest you to wonder why a guy like Jordan should have a South American jungle knife in his possession?'

Bardin sat back on his heels. His grin made him look like a wolf.

'Maybe he picked it up as a souvenir. I bet he's been to South America or the West Indies: probably the West Indies. It's the murder weapon all right, and I'll bet the blood on it is June Arnot's blood.'

Conrad was turning over the clothes on the chair.

'There's no blood on these. I shouldn't have thought it possible to cut off someone's head and not get blood on you.'

'For crying out loud!' Bardin said impatiently. He stood up and stretched his big frame. 'Do you have to lean so hard on your job? Maybe he had a coat on or something. Does it matter? I'm satisfied; aren't you?'

'I don't know,' Conrad said frowning. 'It's all very pat, isn't it? The whole set-up could be a plant, Sam. The gun with Jordan's initials on it, the smashed car, Jordan's suicide and now the murder weapon. Everything cut and dried and laid out ready for inspection. It smells a little to me.'

'It smells because you're over-anxious to earn a living,' Bardin said, lifting his massive shoulders. 'Forget it. It convinces me, and it'll convince the Captain. It would convince you if you didn't yearn to get Maurer into the chair. That's it, isn't it?'

Conrad pulled at his nose thoughtfully.

'Maybe. Well, okay. I guess there's nothing here for me. Want me to drop you off at headquarters?'

'I'll call them from here. I'll want the boys to look this joint over. As soon as I get them working, I'll go back to Dead End and give the press the story. You're going home?'

Conrad nodded.

'May as well.'

'Lucky guy. No late work, a nice little home and lots of glamour to keep you warm. How is Mrs. Conrad?'

'Oh, she's fine, I guess,' Conrad said, and was annoyed to hear how flat and unenthusiastic his voice sounded.

V

Driving just below the speed limit, Conrad cut through the back streets to avoid the theatre traffic. He wondered uneasily if Janey had made good her threat and had gone out, and if she had, whether she was back yet. He didn't want to think about her just now, but inevitably, whenever he headed for home, she forced herself into his thoughts.

He slowed down to light a cigarette. As he flicked the match through the open window his eye caught the name-plate of the street: *Glendale Avenue*.

It was not until he had nearly reached the end of the street that he remembered the girl, Frances Coleman, who had called on June Arnot at seven o'clock this night, had given her address as 145 Glendale Avenue. His foot trod down hard on the brake and he swung the car to the kerb.

For a moment he sat still, staring through the windshield at the dark empty street. Doc Holmes had said June Arnot had died around seven o'clock. Was it possible this girl had seen something?

He got out of the car and peered at the nearest house. It was numbered 123. He walked for a few yards until he came to 145.

It was a tall, shabby, brown-stone house. Some of the windows showed lights; some didn't.

He climbed the flight of steep stone steps and looked through the glass panel of the front door. Beyond was a dimly lit hall with stairs going away into the darkness.

He turned the door knob and pushed. The door opened and a violent smell of frying onions, virile tomcats and ripe garbage jostled past him as if anxious to reach some fresh air.

He tipped his hat to the back of his head, wrinkled his nose and moved farther into the hall. A row of mailboxes screwed against the wall told him what kind of house it was. The third mail-box belonged to Miss Coleman: that put her on the third floor.

Conrad climbed the stairs, passing shabby doors from which came the blare of radios playing swing music as if the listeners were stone deaf but determined to hear something.

The door facing the head of the stairs on the third floor told him this was where Miss Coleman lived. A neat white card bearing her name was pinned to the panel with a thumb tack.

As he closed his hand into a fist to knock, he saw the door was ajar. He knocked, waited a long moment, and then stepped back, his eyes suddenly wary.

Was this going to be another body behind a half-open door? he wondered.

Already he had looked at six bodies this night, each of them in its own particular way, horrible and pathetic. He felt his nerves crawl under his skin and the hair on the nape of his neck move.

He took out a cigarette and pasted it on his lower lip. As he set fire to it he noticed his hands were steady enough, and he suddenly grinned.

He leaned forward and pushed the door open and peered into darkness.

'Anyone in?' he said, raising his voice.

No one answered. A solid silence came out of the room on a faint perfume of Californian Poppy.

He took two steps forward and groped for the light switch. As the light went on, he drew a deep breath of expectancy, but there were no bodies, no blood, no murder weapons: just a small, box-like room with an iron bedstead, a chest of drawers, a chair and a pinewood cupboard. It looked as comfortable and as homely as a Holy man's bed of nails.

He stood looking round for a moment or so, then he moved forward and opened one of the cupboard's doors. Except for a far-away smell of lavender the cupboard was empty. He frowned, reached for one of the drawers in the chest and pulled it open. That, too, was empty.

He scratched the back of his neck with a forefinger, stared around some more, then lifted his shoulders and walked out into the passage.

He turned off the light and then walked down the stairs, slowly and thoughtfully. Back again in the hall, he inspected Miss Coleman's mail-box. It was unlocked and empty.

A notice on the wall caught his attention. It read: *Janitor. Basement.*

'What have I got to lose?' he thought, and went along a passage and down a flight of dirty stairs into darkness.

At the foot of the stairs he collided with something hard and he swore under his breath.

'Anyone at home?' he called.

A door swung open and the light of a naked electric lamp flowed out, making him blink.

'No vacancies, pally,' a mild oily voice oozed from the doorway. 'This joint's fuller than a dog with fleas.'

Conrad looked into a small room that contained a bed, a table, two chairs and a worn rug. At the table sat a large fat man in shirt sleeves. In his mouth he held a dead cigar. Spread out before him on the table was a complicated patience game.

'You've got a vacancy on the third floor, haven't you?' Conrad said. 'Miss Coleman's moved out.'

'Who says so?'

'I've just been up there. The room's empty. Clothes gone. All the little knick-knacks that make up a home gone too.'

'Who are you?' the fat man asked.

Conrad flashed his buzzer.

'City police.'

The fat man curled his upper lip into a complacent sneer.

'What's she been up to?'

'When did she leave?' Conrad asked, leaning against the door post.

'I didn't know she had left,' the fat man said. 'She was here this morning. Well, that's a relief off my mind. I would have had to put her out tomorrow : saves me a job.'

'Why?'

The fat man wheezed as he pushed a fat finger into his ear and massaged it briskly.

'The usual reason. She was three weeks behind on her rent.'

Conrad rubbed the back of his neck thoughtfully.

'What do you know about her? When did she come here?'

'A month ago. Said she was a movie extra.' The fat man swept the spread-out cards into a little heap, picked them up and began to shuffle them. 'Couldn't get anything cheap in Hollywood: anyway, cheap enough for her. She was a nice girl. If I had a daughter I'd like her to be like her. Nice way of talking, nice looks, quiet, well-behaved.' He lifted his fat shoulders. 'But no money. It's the bad ones who have the dough, I guess. I told her to go home, but she wouldn't listen. She promised to have the money for me by tomorrow morning for certain. Looks like she didn't get it, doesn't it?'

'That's the way it looks,' Conrad said. He suddenly felt tired. Why should an out-of-work movie extra call on June Arnot, he wondered, except for a touch? She probably never got farther than the guard-house. It was unlikely June Arnot would have seen her.

He glanced at his watch. It was just after midnight.

'Well, thanks.' He pushed himself away from the door post. 'That's all I want to know.'

The fat man asked, 'She isn't in trouble, is she?'

Conrad shook his head.

'Not as far as I know.'

The night air felt cold and fresh after the fusty smells of the apartment house. Conrad drove home. Bardin had said he was convinced that Jordan had done the job. Why should he bother? He would talk to the D.A. tomorrow. If only he knew for certain that Maurer and June had been lovers. If they had been then there might be a chance that Maurer had engineered the job; might even have done it himself.

'Oh, the hell with Maurer!' Conrad thought as he walked up the path to his front door. 'I've got him on my mind like a junkie's got dope.'

He sank his key into the lock and moved into the dark little hall.

The house was very still and silent.

He went along the passage to the bedroom, pushed open the door and turned on the light. The twin beds had an empty and forlorn look about them.

So Janey had gone out and she wasn't back yet.

He began to strip off his clothes. As he walked into the bathroom for a quick shower, he said aloud, 'And the hell with her too!'

CHAPTER TWO

CHARLES FOREST, District Attorney, sat behind his big, flat-topped desk, a cigarette between his thick fingers and a brooding expression in his eyes.

Forest was a short, bulky man with a fleshy hard face, searching green eyes, a thin mouth and a square jutting chin. His thick white hair was seldom tidy as he had a habit of running his fingers through it when he was working on a knotty problem, and he seemed to spend most of his working hours solving knotty problems.

'McCann seems satisfied it was Jordan,' Forest said, waving his hand to the pile of newspapers that lay in an untidy heap on the floor. 'On the face of it, Paul, he's got a watertight case. I've read Bardin's report, and that seems pretty conclusive. What's worrying you?'

Conrad sank lower in the armchair. One leg hung over one of the arms of the chair and he swung it backwards and forwards irritably.

'It's too damned pat, sir,' he said. 'Doc Holmes said it looked like a professional job, and I think so too. I think a hop-head would have to be very lucky to kill six people with six shots, especially when he's using a .45. Those guns kick, but each time he hit a bull's eye. It seems to me the killer was a crack shot, and I wouldn't be surprised if he hadn't killed before.'

'I know,' Forest said mildly. 'I thought those five shots good shooting. I've checked on Jordan. He was a crack shot. He could hit a playing-card edge on at twenty yards, and that wants some doing.'

Conrad grimaced.

'I should have checked that myself,' he said, annoyed with himself. 'Well, all right, that takes care of that. There is another thing: he uses an electric razor. From the look of him he hasn't put a razor blade against his skin for years, and yet he had a cut-throat razor in his possession. Doesn't that strike you as odd?'

'Not particularly. It would be something if we knew for a fact that he didn't own such a razor, but we don't know that. People cut their corns with razors, you know.'

'That's what Bardin said, but I asked Doc Holmes. Jordan hadn't any corns. And another thing, there was no blood on his clothes.'

Forest nodded.

'Well, go on: what's on your mind?'

'Bardin said he'd heard rumours that June Arnot was Jack Maurer's mistress,' Conrad said quietly. 'Suppose Maurer found out she was cheating on him with Jordan? What would he do? Send them his congratulations? If I know Maurer as well as I think I do, he would have gone up there and ripped her wide open and then cut her head off to teach her not to double-cross him in the future.' He sat forward, his eyes intent. 'The moment I saw the set-up I wondered if it wasn't a gang revenge. It would explain the professional touch and the ruthless slaughter to make sure there were no witnesses. Maurer has the imagination to leave a set of clues to lead the investigation away from him and to incriminate Jordan.'

Forest stared at his blotter, his brows drawn down.

'Do we know for certain she was Maurer's mistress?' he asked after a long pause.

'No, but we might find out if we dug deep enough.'

'If we could prove she was his mistress beyond any reasonable doubt, then I would think you're on to something, Paul.' Forest reached out and stubbed his cigarette out into the ash-bowl. He looked up and his cold green eyes probed Conrad's face. 'I don't have to tell you that the only reason why I accepted office was because I was determined to nail Maurer. I know how you feel about him yourself: that makes the two of us. Up to now we've got exactly nowhere. He's never stepped out of turn, never made a wrong move, never given us anything we can use against him. We've nailed four of his best men during the past two years, and that was an achievement, considering the opposition we came up against. But in spite of keeping after him, we're no further to nailing Maurer now than we were when I took office.' He leaned forward and poked a finger in Conrad's direction. 'I'm not going to discourage any hunches, any leads or any ideas that might give me a chance – no matter how remote – to throw a hook into Maurer. Okay, you think Maurer could be at the back of this killing. He could be. I don't say he is, but he could be, and that's enough for me. Go ahead and make some inquiries, but don't let anyone know what you're doing. The only way we're going to corner Maurer is to surprise him, and make no mistake about it, surprising Maurer is my idea of a modern miracle. He has ears everywhere. He knows every move we make as soon as we make it. But go ahead and start digging. I don't give a damn if it is a waste of public money. We've got to gamble on hunches or we'll get nowhere. Don't make any written reports. Keep this between your staff and myself. Don't bring police headquarters into it unless you have to. I'm pretty certain someone at headquarters talks.'

Conrad's face lit up with a triumphant smile. He had hoped Forest would react in this way, but knowing the amount of work the office had to handle, he didn't think Forest would give him an okay to go ahead on the flimsy evidence he had to offer.

'That's fine, sir. I'll start right away. Van Roche and Miss Fielding are okay. I'll need them, but apart from them I'll keep this under my hat. I'll see if I can dig up some dirt on June Arnot. If I can link her with Maurer we've really got something to work on.'

'I'll leave it to you, Paul,' Forest said. 'As soon as you think you've got something, let me know.' He glanced at his wristwatch. 'I've got to be in court in ten minutes. Don't take up too much time on the investigation. We've got a lot on our hands, but this comes first, understand?'

'Yes, sir,' Conrad said happily, and got to his feet.

'There's just one other little thing,' Forest said, and looked up. 'This isn't my business, but I'm going to mention it because I like you and because I take an interest in you. If I'm talking out of turn, say so and I'll shut up, but sometimes a word at the right time can be helpful.'

'Why, sure,' Conrad said, puzzled. 'What's wrong, sir?'

'Nothing yet,' Forest said. He looked down at his smoking cigarette, then looked up again. 'Are you looking after that pretty wife of yours properly, Paul?'

Conrad's face tightened. This was unexpected, and he felt blood mount slowly to his face.

'I don't think I understand, sir.'

'Someone told me your wife was at the Paradise club last night on her own,' Forest said quietly. 'She wasn't exactly sober. I don't have to tell you that Maurer owns the club, nor do I have to tell you a lot of people, including Maurer and his mob, know she is the wife of my Chief Investigator.' He got to his feet and came around the desk. 'That's all, Paul. I don't know if you knew, but if you didn't, it's time you did. See what you can do about it, will you? It's not good for business, and I don't think it's good for your wife.' He smiled suddenly, and his hard face softened a little. He put his hand on Conrad's shoulder. 'Don't look as if the end of the world has come. It hasn't. Young women as pretty as your wife often try to kick over the traces. Maybe she's finding life a little dull: especially when you get called out suddenly. But have a word with her. She'll listen to reason.' He patted Conrad's shoulder, picked up his brief-case and made for the door. 'I must be going. I'll expect some news of Maurer from you in a day or so.'

'Yes, sir,' Conrad said woodenly.

II

Conrad's staff consisted of his secretary, Madge Fielding, and his leg-man, Van Roche. Neither of them appeared to have any other interests except the work of the department, and when Conrad came into his office he found them waiting impatiently for him.

'What's the verdict, Paul?' Van Roche demanded as Conrad crossed the room to his desk.

'We go after Maurer,' Conrad told him, pulling out his chair and sitting down. 'The D.A. says he isn't going to pass up the remotest chance, and although he isn't entirely sold on the evidence, he thinks we should at least do some preliminary work.'

Van Roche grinned and rubbed his hands together. He was tall and thin, dark-complexioned with a pencil-lined moustache.

'That's terrific!' he exclaimed. 'You certainly must have dug it into him! What's the preliminary work?'

Conrad glanced over at Madge Fielding who sat at her desk, toying with a pencil, her big grey eyes thoughtful. She was around twenty-six or seven, small, compact and durably put together. She had no claim to beauty. Her small features, her snub nose and her strong, firm mouth gave her face interest, but nothing more. Instead of beauty, she had an astonishing stamina for hard work, boundless enthusiasm and energetic efficiency.

'Well, what's your reaction, Madge?' Conrad asked, smiling at her.

'I was thinking that if you two are going to dig into Maurer's past you'd better buy yourselves a couple of bullet-proof vests,' she said quietly. 'And I'm not kidding.'

Van Roche gave an exaggerated shudder.

'How right she is. Trust our little Madge to put her finger on the weak spot. Well, I guess I'll take out an insurance policy to cover my funeral. I'd like to be put away in style.'

Conrad shook his head.

'That's the least of our worries. Maurer's got beyond shooting cops. Ten years ago he wouldn't have hesitated, but not now. He's too much of a business man, and he has too much to lose to take chances. He knows shooting cops is about the one thing no one gets away with. No, I don't think we have much to worry about on that score. We'll be all right; it's our witnesses we'll have to protect, if we ever find any witnesses.'

'Well, that's a relief,' Van said, lighting a cigarette. 'How do we start? What's the first move?'

'Nothing very exciting, I'm afraid,' Conrad returned. 'Our first job is to make a review of the work we have in hand and see what can be shelved and what has got to be done. The D.A. said Maurer comes first, but we can't just sling the other work into the trash-basket. Suppose we see what we've got? If we put our backs into it, we should be able to have a clear run by tomorrow morning. Madge, will you make a list of the important items and then we'll get down to it?'

Madge nodded and went briskly over to the filing cabinets. While she was getting out the more urgent files, Van went over to his desk and hurriedly inspected the files that lay in his pending tray.

'What's our first move against Maurer, Paul?' he asked as he flicked through the files.

'Before we can hope to hook him up with June Arnot, we must prove they knew each other,' Conrad said. 'We'll have to work from June's end. It might be an idea if you went down to Dead End tomorrow and checked every house and everyone you meet on the way. Make out you're checking on Jordan. Try and get a description of anyone who went to see June regularly. With any luck we might get a description of Maurer along with the rest of them. Whatever you do, don't mention Maurer's name. We'll tip our hand if we ask direct questions about him, and that's the last thing we want to do.'

Madge came over with a pile of files.

'There's more than I thought,' she said, putting them on Conrad's desk, 'but some of them aren't immediately urgent.'

'Let's get at it,' Conrad said, slipping out of his coat. 'Come on, Van, let's see how hard you can work.'

It wasn't until nine-fifteen that night that the more urgent work had been cleared, and Conrad felt satisfied that he had at least four days ahead of him free to concentrate on Maurer.

With a soft whistle of relief, he pushed back his chair.

'I guess that's it,' he said. 'That's the last one, isn't it?'

Madge nodded. She took the file from Conrad, placed it on the top of the others and carried them over to the safe.

Van Roche got up from behind his desk and stretched.

'I don't want another day like this,' he said feelingly. 'Comrade Maurer would be flattered if he knew we'd worked this hard just for a chance of throwing a spanner in his works.'

Conrad glanced at his watch.

'Well, I'm going home. See you two here at nine tomorrow. We'll get the plan working and see what we can do.' He picked up his hat and stood up. 'Be seeing you, and get some sleep; you may need it.'

It wasn't until he got into his car and started the engine that his mind turned to Janey. He had ruthlessly refused to let himself think of her during working hours, but now he turned his attention to her.

Why had she gone to the Paradise Club of all places? he thought angrily as he sent the car shooting along the deserted street. She knew Maurer owned the club, and she knew how Conrad felt about Maurer. Had she gone there deliberately to annoy him?

And who had been the kind friend who had told Forest? Conrad wondered, his face hardening. 'She wasn't exactly sober.' That was a pretty nice thing to hear about your wife, and from your boss, too. 'Have a word with her,' Forest had said. 'She'll listen to reason.' He certainly didn't think Janey justified that observation. Listening to reason wasn't Janey's strong point, and Conrad wasn't kidding himself he could persuade her to do something she didn't want to do.

When he opened the sitting-room door, he found Janey in

an armchair flicking through a magazine. Her face was cold and sullen, and he saw at once how tense she was.

Although he was a light sleeper, he hadn't heard her come in the previous night, and when he got up in the morning, she hadn't moved, although he was sure she had been awake.

He decided to come to the point right away. There was bound to be a row: that was inevitable.

He came over to the empty fireplace, and sat down in an armchair opposite to where Janey was sitting.

'Janey . . .'

'Well, what is it?' she said in her cold, flat voice. She didn't look up.

'You were seen at the Paradise Club last night.'

He saw her stiffen and a sudden wary expression cross her face. She recovered immediately and looked up, her eyes plainly hostile.

'So what? You were lucky I didn't go to the Ambassadors. The Paradise is a lot cheaper.'

'That's not the point. You know as well as I do that Maurer owns the Paradise Club. What were you thinking of, Janey?'

'Now look here, Paul, I've put up with a lot from you, but I'll be damned if I'll let you lecture me!' Janey said with violence. 'You're a nice one to preach! You come home at any hour and you sneak out at any hour. I don't complain. Don't imagine I don't know what goes on in your office. That Fielding woman may be nothing to look at, but anyone can see she's a sexy little bitch, and with a face like hers I suppose she lets you do what you like to her!'

'Now look, Janey,' Conrad said sharply, 'we're not going to have that old red herring brought up again. I fell for it the first time, but not again. You're trying to side-step the issue. Why did you go to the Paradise Club?'

'That's my business!' Janey flared. 'And I'm not going to be cross-examined by you!'

'But you can't go there!' Conrad said, his voice suddenly angry. 'You know as well as I do it's Maurer's headquarters. You're making the department a laughing-stock by going there. Can't you see that?'

Janey giggled, but immediately her face hardened again as she pointed her chin at him.

'Do you think I care a damn about your stupid department? If I want to go to the club, I'll go!'

'It was Forest who told me you have been there. Some kind person told him, and added you were drunk. How long do you imagine I'll keep my job if you're going to behave like that?'

Janey suddenly went white, and her eyes flashed.

'So your dirty little police force has started to spy on me, has it?' she cried. 'I might have expected that. Well, you can tell your smug, blue-nosed boss from me to mind his own business!

Neither he nor you nor anyone else is going to tell me what to do! And if you don't like it you can go to hell!'

She turned and went out of the room, slamming the door behind her.

III

As the City Hall clock was striking nine, Conrad walked briskly along the corridor to his office. He pushed open the door and entered, hanging his hat on the hat-stand without pausing on his way to his desk.

Madge and Van Roche were already at their desks. Madge was typing busily. Van was scribbling notes on a pad, a cigarette in his mouth, his eyes screwed up to avoid the smoke as it spiralled past his face.

'You've got a visitor, Paul,' he said, pushing the pad aside. He jerked his thumb to the door to the little ante-room that was used for interviews. 'And you'll never guess who.'

Conrad put his brief-case on the desk and reached for a cigarette from the box that stood by the telephone.

'I don't want to see any visitors this morning. Who is it?'

'Flo Presser.'

Conrad looked up sharply, his eyebrows climbing.

'You kidding?'

Van grinned.

'Go ahead and see for yourself. Come to that you've only to take a sniff at the keyhole to have the fact confirmed. I reckon she must have had a bath of Last Night's Kiss or whatever the stuff's called. She fairly hums with it.'

'Flo Presser? At this hour? What does she want?'

'She's lost her boy friend. She wants you to find him.'

'Why the hell didn't you tell her I was busy? Get rid of her, Van. I've got other things to do than to bother my head about her. Tell her to go to the police.'

'Know who her boy friend is?' Van asked, his face suddenly serious.

'No. Who is he?'

'Toni Paretti.'

Conrad frowned. The name sounded familiar.

'Well, what about him?'

'He happens to be Maurer's chauffeur and bodyguard,' Van said quietly. 'I thought maybe you'd want to talk to her.'

Conrad took a long drag at his cigarette, then blew smoke to the ceiling.

'That's right; of course he is.' He got to his feet. 'Did she give you any details?'

'They had a date the night before last. He called her around five o'clock and told her he had a job to do. He said he would meet her at eleven o'clock at Sam's Bar on Lennox Street. She waited until two o'clock, and then went home. Yesterday morning she kept calling his apartment, but couldn't get a reply. She went round there in the afternoon. He wasn't there. She asked around, but no one had seen him. She went to Sam's Bar in the evening and waited, but he didn't show up. This morning she decided something must have happened to him, so she's come here.'

'What does she expect us to do?'

'She wants us to find him.'

'Didn't it cross her mind he's tired of her and has walked out on her?' Conrad asked.

'Didn't seem to, and it didn't occur to me either. I can't imagine a rat like Paretti walking out on Flo. She's a gold mine. It's not as if she's like the usual run of tarts. She makes money, Paul from what I hear: good money, and I can't imagine Paretti passing up an income as good as she can provide.'

'He could have found another girl,' Conrad returned. 'But what foxes me is why should she come here. Why didn't she go to the police?'

Van concealed a grin.

'That's exactly what I asked her, and she said you were a gentleman and she trusted you. I won't tell you what she said about the police.'

Conrad sighed.

'Well, I'm not going to waste much time on her.'

He crossed the room, opened the sound-proof door that led into the ante-room.

A blast of cloying perfume enveloped him as he stepped into the room, and he grimaced.

Flo Presser was pacing up and down, a cigarette between her scarlet lips. She was a good-looking girl, around twenty-five, with a provocative figure, brassy blonde hair and big money-hungry eyes.

She swung around as Conrad came in. Her full skirt swirled out and then moulded itself for a brief moment around her long slender thighs.

'Hello, Flo,' Conrad said. He had met her often enough in the court room. She was regularly arrested for soliciting, and she had got to know most of the officials connected with the court. 'What's on your mind?'

'Gee! Mr. Conrad,' Flo said, coming over to him. 'I didn't think you'd mind me coming like this. I'm worried stiff. I know I shouldn't be bothering you. I know how busy you are. I thought I'd go nuts last night wondering about Toni, and this morning ...'

'Okay, skip the song and dance,' Conrad said impatiently. He sat on the edge of the table. 'You shouldn't have come here, Flo, but now you're here, let's keep it brief. What makes you so sure Toni hasn't walked out on you?'

Flo's big brown eyes opened wide.

'Walked out on me? Why, Mr. Conrad, he wouldn't do that. Besides, I know he hasn't.'

'How do you know?'

She hesitated, looking at him out of the corners of her eyes.

'You'll keep this to yourself, won't you, Mr. Conrad? If Toni knew I'd come to you, he would skin me.'

'How do you know he hasn't walked out on you?' Conrad repeated.

'I'm looking after his bank roll,' she said after a pause. 'I shouldn't be talking about it, but Toni wouldn't go off leaving me with five grand, not that he ever would leave me.'

Conrad looked at her, a sudden thoughtful expression in his eyes. She was right. He knew a little of Paretti's record. If Paretti were going to leave Flo, he would make sure he collected his money first.

'Do you imagine anything's happened to him?'

She nodded.

'Something must have. He might have been run over or something.'

'He was going to meet you the night before last: is that right?'

'Yes. He called me around five and said he couldn't meet me as arranged. He had a job to do.'

'What was the job?'

She shook her head.

'He didn't say.'

'He told you he had a job to do and nothing else? What were his exact words?'

'He said, "The boss wants me to do a job. I'll see you at Sam's Bar at eleven." That's what he said, and I haven't seen him since.'

'What time were you going to meet him before he put you off?'

'Seven o'clock.'

He studied her.

'Why did you come to me, Flo?'

Her eyes shifted away from his direct stare.

'There wasn't anyone else I could go to. I wouldn't get any sense out of the coppers. They don't like Toni anyway. I asked around and no one could tell me anything, and I got more and more worried and I thought of you. You've always been nice to me, Mr. Conrad, and I thought . . .'

'Okay, skip it,' Conrad said. 'Toni works for Maurer, doesn't he?'

A blank, remote expression came into Flo's eyes. She half turned away to drop her cigarette into the trash-basket.

'I don't know who Toni works for. He's never told me.'

'Don't give me that stuff. It's Maurer, isn't it?'

She swung round to face him, her face hard.

'I tell you I don't know! Don't start acting the copper with me, Mr. Conrad. I've always looked on you as a friend.'

Conrad shrugged.

'Okay, Flo. I'll make some inquiries. I can't promise anything, but I'll see what I can do. Where can I reach you?'

Her face brightened.

'I knew you would, Mr. Conrad! I said to myself . . .'

'Where can I reach you?' Conrad repeated impatiently.

'23c 144th Street. Why don't you come up one night and see me, Mr. Conrad? I'll give you a good time: honest I will, and it won't cost you a thing.'

Conrad laughed.

'That's no way to talk to a respectably married man, Flo,' he said, edging her to the door. 'But thanks for the offer just the same.'

'First time I've ever heard a married man was respectable,' she returned. 'And I should know.' She paused in the doorway that led directly into the passage. 'You'll let me know as soon as you find out something, won't you, Mr. Conrad?'

'Sure. I'll be in touch with you before long.' He edged her into the passage. 'Be seeing you,' and he closed the door.

'Pretty nearly gassed, weren't you?' Van asked as Conrad came back into his office.

'Yeah, pretty strong.' There was a hard, tense light in Conrad's eyes. 'Madge, have we got a file on Paretti?'

'Yes.' Madge got up and went over to the filing cabinet. She found the file and brought it over to Conrad.

'Thanks.'

He opened the file and settled down to read its meagre contents while Van watched him with alert interest.

'Not much here,' Conrad said after a few minutes. 'He's had two convictions; neither of them amounted to much, and believe it or not, he's been arrested twenty-seven times. Listen to this: seven arrests for homicide, twelve arrests for assault and robbery, four arrests for being in possession of drugs, one arrest for malicious mischief, one arrest for consorting with known criminals and one arrest for juvenile delinquency. He's beaten the rap each time except for the juvenile delinquency and consorting with known criminal charges, and those two convictions stuck before he hooked up with Maurer.' He looked up to stare at Van. 'There's a note here that's interesting. Paretti is a crack shot with a .45. That mean anything to you?'

Van pursed his lips into a soundless whistle.

'Are you trying to tie him up with the Dead End massacre?'

'Work it out for yourself,' Conrad said quietly. 'He had a date with Flo for seven o'clock the night before last: the night of the killing. Suddenly he cancels his date with Flo, telling her he has a job to do for his boss. We know who his boss is. At around seven on that night, eight people get wiped out: six of them by a .45.'

'I can't see Paretti hacking June's head off,' Van said doubtfully. 'That's not his line.'

'I'm not suggesting he killed June. I think he drove Maurer out to Dead End, and while Maurer was taking care of June, Paretti took care of the staff.'

'For crying out loud! Maurer wouldn't be so crazy as to kill June *himself*! He's got dozens of thugs who'd do it for him.'

'It's my bet it was Maurer who did the job himself,' Conrad said, leaning forward, his elbows on the desk, his face in his hands. 'I think he found out June was cheating on him, and he went haywire. I think he took Paretti and went up there and did the job.' He stubbed out his cigarette. 'And I'll tell you why I think so. He knew the risk he was running. Up to now he hasn't made a wrong move. He hasn't done a thing we can use to pin on him. Up to now every murder he's planned has been carried out by one of his thugs who gets his instructions from some other thug so the trail will never lead back to Maurer. Okay, this time Maurer gets the bit between his teeth. This time he wants to even the score in person. This is a personal thing between June and him. He takes Paretti and goes up to Dead End. He's known there, and he knows there must be no witnesses, no one must be left alive on the estate who can link his name with June's or who might have seen him arrive. Paretti takes care of the staff while Maurer goes down to the pool, surprises June and hacks off her head.' He pointed a finger at Van. 'Then what happens? There is still one witness left alive after the slaughter – Paretti. Isn't that like Maurer? He wouldn't trust his own mother. Paretti has worked for him for fifteen years, but he doesn't trust him. So he takes care of Paretti, and it's my bet Flo knows Maurer has taken care of him, and that's why she came here. She's too scared of Maurer to mention his name, but she's no fool, and she must have hoped that by coming to me with this story, I'll get around to what she's driving at.'

Both Van and Madge were sitting tense and silent while Conrad talked. When he paused, Van slammed his fist down on his desk.

'I bet that's it!' he said excitedly. 'It fits Maurer, and it does explain why Flo came here. It's her way of getting even with Maurer for ironing out her boy friend! And now we've got to prove it.'

'And that won't be easy,' Conrad said quietly. 'Here's what we do. Your first job, Van, is to go to Paretti's apartment and turn it inside out. Go over the place as if you were looking for gold nuggets. I'm not saying you'll find anything, but you might, so get over there and snap it up.' He scribbled an address he took from Paretti's file and tossed it to Van. 'That's where he hangs out. Take a gun with you, and watch out. Don't let anyone know who you are unless you have to. If you have to break in, break in. I'm going to the Pacific Sudios and see if I can dig up some information about June. I'll be back here at one o'clock, and we'll see how we've got on.'

Van opened his desk and took out a .38. He checked the magazine, tossed the gun into the air with a theatrical gesture, then stowed it away in his hip pocket.

'I want you to take notice of this,' he said, looking at Madge. 'I get sent on a job where I can get a skinful of slugs, but the Master Mind over there picks himself a soft one: among the movie stars, glamour, legs and the rest of the trappings. Just make a note of it. I'm not saying it's unfair, but just record it for the sake of the underdog.'

'Get moving!' Conrad snapped. He wasn't in the mood for banter. 'And let's have some results!'

IV

Conrad followed a pert, orange-haired girl along a maze of rubber-floored corridors, past innumerable doors on which were easy to remove signs bearing the names of directors, producers and movie executives.

The orange-haired girl appeared to be deeply affronted that she had to conduct Conrad to so lowly a person as Harrison Fedor, and when they came upon his office in the remotest part of the building, she didn't bother to stop, but waving her hand disdainfully, said without turning, 'That's it; go right ahead,' and she continued on her way, swinging her hips contemptuously.

Conrad rapped on the door and pushed it open.

'Come right in,' Fedor said.

He sat behind a desk, a cigar in his mouth, a relaxed, contented expression on his thin, hatchet face.

'Did that orange-haired hip-swinger bring you up here?' he asked, opening a drawer and producing a pint bottle of *Four Roses* and two tot-glasses which he placed on his blotter. 'She has a surprise coming to her. Tomorrow, when the news breaks, she'll stop that fanny-waving routine of hers and show me some respect.'

Conrad pulled up a chair and sat down.

'What news?'

Fedor rubbed his hands together and beamed.

'Laird's promoted me to general publicity manager with a salary that'd knock your right eye out. I had to talk him into it, but he finally came across this morning. Tomorrow I move into an office that'd make the President green with envy, and on the first floor. How do you like that?'

Conrad offered his congratulations and accepted one of the tot-glasses. They drank solemnly, then Fedor sat back and raised his bushy eyebrows.

'What's on your mind? I don't want to rush you, but I have a busy day ahead of me.'

'I'm tying up a few loose ends connected with Miss Arnot's death,' Conrad said smoothly. 'Is there anyone here she confided in, would you know? Did she have a dresser or a secretary or someone like that?'

Fedor's eyes became wary.

'What did you want to know?'

'The inquest's tomorrow. I have to have a reliable witness who'll testify that Miss Arnot and Jordan were lovers. I didn't think you would want to be bothered.'

'You're damn right I don't!' Fedor said, squirming forward on his chair. 'I have a hell of a big day on my hands tomorrow. Is that all you want to know?'

'That's all.'

Fedor thought for a moment.

'You'd better talk to Mauvis Powell. She was June's secretary. She'll know the details.'

'Where do I find her?'

'She has an office just down the corridor. I'll call her and tell her you're on your way.'

'That's fine. One other thing: how about someone to cover Jordan's end of it?'

Fedor frowned.

'You're pretty thorough, aren't you? I thought this was an open and shut case.'

Conrad grinned disarmingly.

'We want to keep it shut. We never know what kind of questions a coroner will ask, and we have to be prepared. Is there anyone within reach who would know what Jordan did in his spare time?'

Fedor scratched his aggressive chin.

'There's Campbell, his dresser. He might know. You'll find him downstairs, clearing up Jordan's dressing-room. Anyone will tell you where to find him.'

'Okay. I'll have a word with him. Would you tell Miss Powell I'm on my way?'

'Sure.' Fedor reached for the telephone. He called a number. After a moment's delay, he said, 'Mauvis? This is Fedor. I have Paul Conrad here. He's from the D.A.'s office. He wants to talk to you about June. Tell him all he wants to know, will you?' He listened, then said, 'Good girl. He'll be right along.' To Conrad, he said, 'Okay, brother. Help yourself. Last office along the corridor.'

Mauvis Powell was a tall, dark woman in her late thirties; neatly dressed in a black tailored costume with a white silk shirt and severe collar. She looked up as Conrad came in and gave him a cool, distant smile.

'Come in,' she said, and waved him to an armchair. 'What can I do for you?'

Her desk was a litter of unopened letters and glossy photographs of June Arnot.

Conrad sat down.

'We may need a witness at the inquest, Miss Powell,' he said. 'Just to tie up the loose ends. Is it a fact Miss Arnot and Jordan were lovers?'

She surveyed him with tired, bored eyes.

'I wouldn't want to swear to it,' she said with a contemptuous smile. 'Miss Arnot often told me of her experiences with Mr. Jordan, together with a wealth of detail, but she may have been lying. As I never saw them together as lovers, I can't be explicit.'

'That's understood, but you did gather from her conversation that they were lovers?'

'That's putting it mildly.'

'Did she have any other lovers except Mr. Jordan?' Conrad said casually.

He saw a sudden alert expression come into her eyes.

'Is it necessary to ruin what reputation Miss Arnot may have left after the inquest?' she asked, her voice suddenly cold.

'I hope not, but the question is important, and I would like an answer.'

'She had other lovers: Miss Arnot had her own code of ethics.'

'In confidence, can you give me any names?'

He saw her stiffen, and anger chased the wary expression from her eyes.

'I have no intention of taking part in any smear campaign the District Attorney may be considering,' she said sharply. 'If that is all you wish to know, Mr. Conrad, perhaps you will excuse me. I have a lot of work to do.'

'This is not a smear campaign,' Conrad said quietly. 'I am investigating a murder, Miss Powell. We're not entirely satisfied that Jordan did kill Miss Arnot.'

She sat very still, looking at him.

'Then I must have misread the newspapers.'

'I said we were not *entirely* satisfied,' Conrad said patiently. 'On the face of it, it would seem pretty obvious that Jordan did kill her, but we have learned not to accept the obvious. Is it a fact that Miss Arnot and Jack Maurer were lovers?'

She stiffened, and her mouth set in a hard line.

'I don't know,' she said in a flat, cool voice that was so final Conrad knew he would be wasting his time to press the question.

'Okay, if you don't know, you don't know,' he said, shrugging. 'I give you my word this is in confidence. You won't be asked to make a public statement.'

'I don't know,' she repeated woodenly.

He looked at her, and she looked at him, and he knew there

was nothing more he would get out of her on that angle.

'Do you know Frances Coleman, Miss Powell? I believe she is an out-of-work extra?'

He saw surprise in her eyes.

'I know of her. She had a small part in Miss Arnot's last picture.'

'Do you know why she called on Miss Arnot on the night Miss Arnot was murdered?'

'I didn't know she had called on Miss Arnot.'

'Her name was in the Visitors' book.'

She looked puzzled.

'She hadn't an appointment. She must have called on the off-chance of seeing Miss Arnot.'

'What would be the chances of Miss Arnot seeing her?' She lifted her elegant shoulders in a shrug.

'It would depend on Miss Arnot's mood. I should say the chances were practically non-existent. Miss Arnot never liked to be bothered by people she didn't know. I've never known her to see anyone without an appointment.'

'That wouldn't apply to Jordan, of course?'

Mauvis Powell shook her head.

'Oh, no. He had the run of Dead End.'

'And Jack Maurer would have the run of it too?'

She looked at him, her mouth tightening.

'I have already told you, I know nothing about Mr. Maurer.'

'But you have heard of him?'

'Who hasn't?' she said, shrugging. 'If that's all, Mr. Conrad . . .' Her hand went out to hover over a packet of unopened mail.

'There is just one other thing. Miss Coleman has left her apartment house. You wouldn't know how I could get in touch with her?'

'Have you tried the Central Casting Agency or the Union Offices? They will have her new address.'

Conrad nodded.

'Thanks. I'll try them. You wouldn't have a photograph of her, would you?'

She gave him a for-heaven's-sake-when-are-you-going-to-stop-pestering-me look, swung round in her chair, opened a filing cabinet and took out a bulky file.

'There may be one amongst these stills of Miss Arnot's last picture. I'll see.'

Conrad watched her slim fingers flick through a big batch of glossy prints, saw her fingers hesitate over a print, flick it out and look at it more carefully.

'Here she is. She stood-in for Miss Arnot occasionally, and this still was taken to see how Miss Arnot's costume would photograph.'

Conrad took the 7" × 5" plate and looked at it. The girl in the picture was about twenty-three, dark, with large serious eyes that looked right at him and gave him an odd, creepy feeling that crawled up his spine and into the roots of his hair.

It was, he found himself thinking, an unforgettable face: a face that could haunt a man's dreams. Her hair was parted in the exact centre of her head and framed her face, reaching almost to her shoulders. She had a straight-cut fringe which half concealed an unusually broad forehead. But it was her eyes that attracted him. He liked the serious and yet half-humorous curiosity he fancied he found in them, as if she were looking out on to a world she found exciting, novel and unexplored.

'Most men appear to get struck all of a heap when they see her,' Mauvis Powell said dryly.

The sound of her voice made Conrad start.

'Why, yes,' he said a little blankly. 'She is unusual, isn't she?'

'But she couldn't act worth a cent,' Mauvis Powell said scornfully. 'She's wasting her time in pictures.'

Conrad took out his billfold and slipped the photograph into one of the compartments.

'I'll be glad to keep this if you can spare it.'

She smiled, and her direct look embarrassed him, to his annoyance.

'Keep it by all means.'

Conrad found he had to make a slight effort to concentrate; his mind was still occupied with the photograph.

'Well, thanks for your help. I'll let you know if we want you at the inquest. Sorry to have taken up so much of your time.'

'You're welcome,' she said indifferently, and reached out for a packet of mail.

Outside in the corridor, Conrad took out his billfold and had another long look at Frances Coleman's photograph. The girl's face drew him like a magnet. He couldn't understand it, and he couldn't remember ever having had such a feeling of intense interest for a girl as he was now feeling for this girl.

'What's the matter with me?' he thought. 'I'm behaving like a goddamn schoolboy.'

He put the photograph away, pushed his hat to the back of his head and swore softly under his breath. Then he walked quickly along the corridor to the row of elevators, jabbed the nearest button and waited. While he waited he caught his hand going towards his inside pocket for his billfold again, and he had to make a conscious effort to change its direction and fish out a pack of cigarettes.

v

The hands of the City Hall clock stood at five minutes past one o'clock as Conrad swung his car to the kerb outside a drug store. He crossed the sidewalk, pushed his way past the crowd besieging the quick-lunch counter and shut himself into a pay booth.

Madge answered his call.

'Is Van there?' Conrad asked.

'He's just come in. Hold a moment.'

Van's voice came on the line.

'Did you have any luck?' Conrad asked.

'Yeah.' Van's voice sounded excited. 'I've got something that ties Paretti in with Jordan. I found an old envelope in the trash-basket. On the back of it was a sketch-plan of Jordan's apartment. How do you like that?'

Conrad let out a soft whistle.

'You're sure it's Jordan's apartment?'

'You bet! I thought from your description the lay-out looked familiar. On my way back here I dropped into Jordan's place and checked. There's no doubt about it.'

'That's really something,' Conrad said. 'Did you find anything else?'

'A cut-throat razor strop, but no razor. There's a chance the razor found in Jordan's hand belongs to Paretti. It's worth checking. I also found sixteen hundred bucks hidden around the apartment.'

'Nice work. This checks with my idea that Maurer rubbed Paretti out. Paretti wouldn't skip into hiding and leave all that money, plus his roll with Flo. He just wouldn't do it.'

'That's the way I figure it too. Did you turn up anything your end?'

'I sure did. Campbell, Jordan's dresser, talked. He's tied Maurer in with June. He says Jordan knew June was Maurer's mistress and Jordan was scared stiff Maurer would find out he was playing around with June. He was always talking to Campbell about Maurer, especially when he was drunk. This puts Maurer out on a limb. I've got a sworn statement from Campbell. We can start something now, Van.'

'But Campbell's statement won't stand up in court, will it, Paul? You'll need supporting evidence.'

'I'm going after it now,' Conrad said, his voice hardening. 'I'm going to bring Flo Presser down to the office and she's going to talk. She knows Paretti worked for Maurer, and she's damn well going to make a statement if I have to slap it out of her. I'm on my way down to her place now. I want you to tell the D.A. we've got enough evidence to start an investigation. The police will have to be brought into it; we can't do it alone. Ask him if he'll call a meeting for this afternoon or as soon as he can fix it so I can let him examine the evidence for himself. McCann should be there. Find out when the D.A. can hold the meeting, then call McCann and ask him to attend. Don't give him any details over the telephone. We don't want any of this to leak out until we're ready to jump Maurer. Okay?'

'I'll take care of it.'

'Right. Be seeing you around half-past two,' Conrad said and hung up.

He paused long enough at the quick-lunch bar to grab a ham sandwich and a cup of coffee. He bolted them down, then ran out to his car.

144th Street was a side turning off the exclusive Lawrence Boulevard, the main shopping centre of Pacific City. 23c was a top-floor apartment above a florist shop and two empty offices.

Conrad left his car outside the florist shop, entered the side-door entrance and mounted a steep flight of stairs. At the head of the stairs was a sign-board; the only card in the otherwise empty slots read: *Miss Florence Presser. 4th floor. Apartment C.*

There was no elevator, and Conrad started his long climb. As he reached the third-floor landing, his foot on the bottom step of the flight that led to the top floor, he heard a sudden wild scream that came from above.

A voice he recognized as Flo's cried out: 'No! Don't touch me! Keep away!'

Another blood-curdling scream rang out which was suddenly cut short.

Conrad shot forward and tore up the rest of the stairs, cursing himself for not bringing a gun with him.

As he reached the landing, he saw a front door that stood half open. He was half-way across the landing when the door jerked fully open and a big, thick-set man came out. His swarthy, brutal face, under a pulled-down black slouch hat, tightened when he saw Conrad, and his right hand slid inside his coat.

Conrad took off in a flying tackle. His right shoulder slammed against the big man's thighs, and they went down together in a heap on the floor.

The big man had got his gun out and he took a side swipe with the barrel at Conrad's face, but Conrad saw it coming, got his shoulder up in time and took a numbing blow on the fleshy part of his bicep that made him wince.

He grabbed hold of the big man's wrist with his left hand and drove his right fist into the big man's face. His knuckles smashed against teeth that gave under the impact, and the big man cursed.

Conrad swung the big man's hand against the wall and hammered it against the plaster, trying to break the grip on the gun. He got a bang on the side of his head that sent bright lights swimming before his eyes, and then the big man heaved himself away and kicked Conrad in the chest as Conrad grabbed at him.

The big man scrambled to his feet, raising the gun. Conrad squirmed forward, grabbed the big man's ankles and heaved. The big man went over backwards, the gun going off with a roar that rattled the windows. A shower of plaster from the punctured ceiling came down on top of them.

Conrad was half up as the big man heaved himself off the floor. The gun crashed again. The gun-flash burned Conrad's cheek; the slug zipped past his ear. Conrad sent over a long, looping right with all his weight behind it. It caught the big man on the side of his jaw with a devastating impact.

The big man grunted, his eyes rolled back, the gun dropped from his hand. He tried to regain his balance as he swayed on the top stair. Conrad jumped in and drove his left fist into the big man's belly.

The big man came forward with a rasping gasp, then straightened up and went straight back down the long flight of stairs to land on the back of his head and neck with a crash that shook the building.

Conrad stood for a second looking down at the big man as he lay, his arms and legs thrown wide, on the lower landing. He didn't bother to go down. No one of that weight could fall as the big man had fallen without breaking his neck.

As Conrad turned to Flo's apartment he heard the wail of approaching police sirens.

He walked into a long, narrow room, gaudily furnished as a sitting-room. Across the divan bed, wearing only a pair of black nylon stockings held up by a pair of pink, rose-decorated garters, lay Flo.

An ice-pick had been driven with tremendous force into the side of her neck. He didn't have to touch her to know she was dead. The job had been done expertly; a professional job. The point of the ice-pick had punctured her spinal cord.

He swore softly under his breath, rubbed his sore shoulder, then groped for a cigarette.

He was still looking down at Flo when two prowl boys, guns in hand, burst into the room.

CHAPTER THREE

CAPTAIN HARLAN McCANN of the Police Department was a bull of a man whose close-cropped, bullet-shaped head sat squarely on a pair of shoulders as wide as a barn door. His brick-red, fleshy face looked as if it had been hewn out of granite. His restless, small eyes were deep-set, and when he was in a rage, which was often, they glared redly, and struck a chill into the toughest mobster or policeman who happened to cross his path.

This night he was out of uniform. He wore a dark brown lounge suit and a slouch hat pulled well down over his eyes. He drove his Lincoln along Lawrence Boulevard, his big hairy hands gripping the wheel as if he had someone hateful to him by the throat.

He swung the car into Pacific Boulevard and drove along the sea front, passing the brilliantly lit hotels, the Casino, the night spots, the neon-plastered Ambassadors' Club until he reached the far end of the front where the Paradise Club, hidden from casual passers-by by its fifteen-foot walls, overlooked the moon-lit ocean.

He swung the car down a narrow lane that ran alongside the east wall and drove for a quarter of a mile, his headlights stabbing the thick darkness that now lay around him. From time to time he glanced in his driving mirror, but he could see no lights of any following car behind him. Ahead of him iron gates suddenly appeared in the glare of his headlights, and he slowed down, reached forward and flicked the lights on and off four times; twice fast, twice slow.

The gates opened and he drove through, pulling up by the guard-house.

A thick-set man wearing a peak cap peered through the window at him, raised his hand in a casual salute and waved him to drive on.

McCann engaged gear and followed the circular road to the club. He pulled up at a side door and got out. Another man in a peak cap slid into the driving seat and drove the car to a nearby garage.

McCann walked up the stone steps to a massive door, rapped four times, twice fast, twice slow, on the bronze knocker, and the door opened.

'Good evening, sir,' a voice said out of the darkness.

McCann grunted and moved forward. He heard the door shut behind him, then lights sprang on. He continued down a long passage without looking back, paused outside another massive door and knocked again, using the same signal.

Louis Seigel, Maurer's personal bodyguard and manager of the Paradise Club, opened the door.

Seigel was tall and dark, and notorious for his good looks. Ten years ago he had been known to the police and to his fellow mobster as 'Louis the Looker', but since hooking up with Maurer he had acquired more dignity, and the tag had been dropped. He was around twenty-nine to thirty years of age, square-jawed, blue-eyed and sun-tanned. An old razor scar that ran from his left eye to his nose gave him a swashbuckling appearance, and his carefully cultivated smile that showed big, gleaming teeth, was a devastating weapon against women, and women were Seigel's principal interest in life.

'Come in, Captain,' he said, showing McCann his teeth. 'The boss will be out in a minute. What'll you drink?'

McCann looked at Seigel out of the corners of his hard little eyes.

'A Scotch, I guess.' He found it difficult to be civil to this smooth, good-looking hood. He glanced around the luxurious room, lavishly furnished in excellent taste, and moved ponderously over to the mantelpiece and set his great shoulders against it.

Seigel walked to the bar, fixed a Scotch and soda and brought it over.

'The boss was a little surprised at your message. He had to cancel a theatre date. No trouble, I hope, Captain?' he said, handing the glass to McCann.

McCann gave a short barking laugh.

'Trouble? That's not the half of it! If you guys don't handle this right, the whole goddamn lid's coming off – that's how bad it is!'

Seigel raised his eyebrows. He disliked McCann as much as McCann disliked him.

'Then I guess we'll have to handle it right,' he said, and moved back to the bar. As he was pouring himself a whisky, he added with a sneering little smile, 'We usually do handle things right, Captain.'

'There's always a first time not to handle it right,' McCann growled, annoyed he hadn't scared Seigel.

A door by the bar opened and Jack Maurer came in, followed by Abe Gollowitz, his attorney.

Maurer was a short, squat man around fifty. He had put on some weight during the past three or four years. His swarthy fleshy face showed a heavy beard shadow. His thick, oily black hair was turning grey at the temples, but the greyness didn't soften his face, which reminded McCann of a photograph he had once seen of the death mask of Beethoven. At first glance Maurer would strike anyone as no different from the thousand rich, powerful business men who vacationed in Pacific City, but a closer examination would show there was a difference. He had the flat snake's eyes of the gangster; eyes that glittered and were as cold and as hard as frozen pebbles.

Gollowitz, one of the most brilliant attorneys on the Coast, was built on the same lines as Maurer, only he was fatter, older and going bald. He had thrown up his lucrative practice to handle Maurer's business and legal affairs, and had succeeded so brilliantly that he was now Maurer's second-in-command.

'Glad to see you, Captain,' Maurer said, crossing to shake hands. 'You've got all you want – a cigar, perhaps?'

'Sure,' McCann said, who believed in never refusing anything.

Seigel offered a cigar box and McCann took a fat, torpedo-shaped cigar, sniffed at it and nodded his head. He bit off the end, accepted the light which Seigel held out to him, puffed smoke to the ceiling and nodded his head again.

'A damn fine cigar, Mr. Maurer.'

'Yes. I have them made for me.' Maurer looked over at Seigel. 'Have a thousand sent to the Captain's home, Louis.'

'Why, no; I can't accept a present like that,' McCann said, his thin mouth widening into a pleased smile. 'Good of you, all the same.'

'Nonsense,' Maurer said, and walked over to an armchair. He sat down. 'I insist. If you don't want them, give them away.'

Gollowitz was watching this by-play with increasing impatience. He took the Scotch and soda Seigel offered him, then sat down near Maurer.

'Well, what's the trouble?' he asked abruptly.

McCann looked at him. He didn't like Gollowitz. He wasn't exactly scared of him, but he knew he was dangerous, not in the same way as Maurer was dangerous, but he was too full of legal tricks and too close to the politicians.

McCann leaned forward and stabbed with his cigar in Gollowitz's direction.

'I'll give you the facts, then you can judge the trouble for yourself,' he said in his hard barking voice. 'Three nights ago, June Arnot, together with six of her staff, was murdered. June Arnot had her head hacked off and she was ripped. A gun was found in the garden with Ralph Jordan's initials on it. Bardin and Conrad went around to Jordan's apartment and found him in the bath with his throat cut and a razor in his hand. The murder weapon was found in his dressing-room.'

'You don't have to tell us all this,' Gollowitz said impatiently. 'We've seen the reports in the press. What's it to do with us? Jordan killed her and then killed himself. It's plain enough, isn't it?'

McCann showed his teeth in a snarling smile.

'Yeah, it looked plain enough. Bardin was satisfied; so was I; so was the press, but Conrad wasn't.' His little red eyes looked at Maurer, who sat smoking his cigar, his swarthy face expressionless, his flat gangster eyes staring at the carpet with patient indifference.

'Does it matter to us what he thinks?' Gollowitz demanded, moving irritably. 'Does it matter to us?'

'I guess so,' McCann said. 'Conrad's a trouble-maker, and he's smart, make no mistake about that. He's got one set idea on his mind: to make trouble for you, Mr. Maurer.'

Maurer glanced up; his thick, almost negroid lips twisted into an amused smile.

'Sure he's a smart guy,' he said, 'but there's enough room in this town for both of us.'

'There may not be,' McCann said ominously. 'He thinks Jordan was murdered.'

Maurer's smile widened.

'And of course he thinks I'm behind the murder. A cat can't get run over without him thinking I'm responsible. So what? It happens every day.'

McCann pulled on his cigar. His eyes went from Maurer to Gollowitz, who was watching him with an alert expression in his black eyes.

'This is different. He's got hold of a rumour that you and Miss Arnot were special friends,' he said, shifting his eyes back to Maurer. 'This is the way he figures it: you found out Miss Arnot and Jordan were lovers. You went up there with Paretti. You killed her while Paretti took care of the staff. Then Paretti went around to Jordan's apartment, cut his throat, left a razor in his hand, planted the murder weapon, took Jordan's car out of the garage and crashed it against the garage door as evidence Jordan was full of dope. Then Paretti reported back to you and you knocked him off to shut his mouth.'

Maurer burst out laughing. His white plump hand came down on his knee with a loud smacking sound.

'What do you think of that, Abe?' he said. 'The guy's a trier, isn't he? Did you ever hear such a story?'

McCann sat back; a look of relief and surprise chased across his brick-red face.

Gollowitz rubbed his jaw and raised his bushy eyebrows. He didn't look anything like so amused as Maurer: he didn't look amused at all.

'What's his case?' he asked sharply.

'Don't be so damned stupid, Abe,' Maurer said easily. 'He hasn't got a case, and he knows it.'

Gollowitz ignored the interruption.

'What's his case?' he repeated, staring at McCann.

Seigel was listening to all this. He stood by the bar, behind Maurer and Gollowitz; there was a sick expression in his eyes that began to worry McCann.

'He's got evidence that Mr. Maurer and Miss Arnot were special friends, and that Jordan was scared of Mr. Maurer,'

McCann said slowly. 'He has a sworn statement to that effect.'

'Whose statement?' Gollowitz asked sharply.

'Jordan's dresser.'

McCann and Gollowitz looked at Maurer, who continued to smile.

'So what?' Maurer said carelessly. 'Who else has said so?'

'Just one statement,' McCann said.

Maurer shrugged and spread his hands, smiling at Gollowitz.

'That's nothing,' Gollowitz said. 'What else?'

'Flo Presser called on Conrad this morning. She reported that Paretti was missing. She said he had to do a job for Mr. Maurer at seven o'clock on the night of the murder, and Miss Arnot was murdered around seven o'clock.'

Gollowitz slightly relaxed.

'A streetwalker's testimony is about as effective as a handful of feathers,' he said. 'What else?'

'Flo was stabbed to death a couple of hours after she had seen Conrad,' McCann said, his eyes going to Seigel. He saw Seigel grimace uneasily.

'Who killed her?'

'Ted Pascal, one of the Brooklyn boys.'

Maurer shrugged.

'I don't know him. What's the excitement about? Can I help it if some whore gets knocked off?'

McCann's little eyes began to turn red. It had been a severe shock to him when he had listened to Conrad's report at the D.A.'s meeting, and Maurer's careless, indifferent attitude and his unconcern flicked his anger into life.

'Where's Paretti, Mr. Maurer?' he barked.

'Toni's in New York,' Maurer said smoothly. 'I sent him to collect a gambling debt. That was the job he had to do. He caught the seven o'clock plane.'

'Then you'd better get him back quick,' McCann said grimly. 'Conrad wants to see him. A sketch-plan of Jordan's apartment was found in Paretti's apartment.'

Gollowitz stiffened and shot a hard, searching look at Maurer, who waved his hand airily.

'I don't believe it,' he said. 'Who found it?'

'Van Roche.'

'Any witness?'

'No.'

'Obviously a plant,' Maurer said, and laughed. 'Abe can take care of that, can't you, Abe?'

Gollowitz nodded, but his eyes showed a growing uneasiness.

'If Toni shows up today or tomorrow,' McCann said, 'half Conrad's case will be knocked cold. You'd better get to Toni fast, Mr. Maurer.'

There was a long pause as Maurer studied the pattern on the carpet, then he said, without looking up, 'Supposing I couldn't get hold of Toni? Suppose he had decided to skip with the money I had sent him to collect? It is a big sum: twenty thousand dollars. I don't say he has skipped, but suppose he has?'

McCann's face suddenly turned purple. His big, hairy hands closed into knotted fists.

'He damn well better not have skipped!' he said through clenched teeth.

'Take it easy, Captain,' Maurer said, looking up and smiling. 'I don't think for a moment he has skipped, but even if he had, this cockeyed evidence of Conrad's wouldn't stand up in court. What have you got to worry about? I'm not worrying.'

'What else is there?' Gollowitz snapped, sensing that McCann hadn't told them the worst of it.

'The guard who checks in all visitors to Miss Arnot's place enters their names in a book,' McCann said, speaking slowly and deliberately. 'At seven o'clock on the night of the killing a girl named Frances Coleman called to see Miss Arnot. We're looking for her now, and she will be arrested as a material witness. Conrad thinks she may have seen the killer.'

Maurer looked at the glowing end of his cigar. A muscle in his cheek suddenly began to twitch, otherwise his face was expressionless.

There was a tight tension in the room.

Seigel lit a cigarette, his eyes on the back of Maurer's head. He licked his lips as if they had gone suddenly dry.

Gollowitz stared down at his hands, frowning.

McCann's hard little eyes took in each man, watching his reactions, a grinding, rising fury inside him made him feel short of breath.

'Well, say something!' he snarled. 'Is this something Gollowitz can take care of?'

Maurer looked up. The flat snake's eyes glowed as if they were on fire, and under his direct look, McCann's eyes gave ground.

'I want to talk to the Captain,' Maurer said softly.

Gollowitz immediately got up and, followed by Seigel, left the room.

When the door closed behind them, Maurer crossed one short fat leg over the other. He took his cigar out of his mouth, leaned forward and touched off the ash into a cut-glass bowl. He didn't look at McCann.

McCann sat still, his big fists on his knees, his face purple. Sweat gave an oily appearance to his complexion.

'Frances Coleman, did you say?' Maurer said suddenly, keeping his voice down.

'That's right,' McCann said.

'Who is she?'

'Let's get this straight, Mr. Maurer, are you . . .?'

'Who is she?' Maurer repeated without raising his voice, but

47

McCann recognized the danger signals.

'She's an out-of-work movie extra. She checked out of her room on Glendale Avenue on the night of the murder. The Central Casting Agency haven't her new address.'

'Did she know Miss Arnot?'

'She worked with her on her last picture: a bit part.'

'You're looking for her now?'

'Yeah. We should turn her up in a few hours.'

Maurer nodded.

'Got a photograph of her?'

McCann took out a print from his inside pocket. 'I got this from the C.C.A.'

Maurer took the photograph, looked at it, then put the photograph face down on the arm of his chair. He looked up suddenly and smiled.

'You've finished your drink, Captain. Help yourself.'

'No, thanks,' McCann said.

He wasn't fooled by the smile. The atmosphere in the room affected him like the pressure of an approaching electric storm.

Maurer got up and walked across the room to a door near the casement windows. He opened the door and went into the room that McCann knew Seigel used as an office.

McCann sat still, his cigar gripped tightly between his teeth. He was aware that his heart was beating unevenly and his mouth was dry.

Maurer returned from the office carrying a long white envelope. As he crossed the room, McCann got to his feet and faced him.

'I have been meaning to give you this for some time,' Maurer said, smiling. 'A little investment I made in your name came out pretty well.'

McCann took the envelope.

'Fifteen thousand bucks,' Maurer said in a voice scarcely above a whisper.

McCann drew in a slow deep breath. He slid the envelope into his hip pocket.

'Perhaps I can return the favour,' he said woodenly.

'Well, yes,' Maurer said, and moved over to the empty fireplace. 'I should like to be the first to know where Miss Coleman is to be found. Could that be arranged?'

McCann became aware that sweat was running down his face.

'She may not have seen anything,' he said thickly. 'The chances are she didn't. Miss Arnot wouldn't have let her come up to the house. She probably left her name and then went away.'

'Could it be arranged?' Maurer repeated.

'I guess so. I've told my men to report direct to me as soon as they have found her, and to take no action until I give instructions. I've promised to contact the D.A.'s office. They want to see her: they'll take charge of her.'

'I think I should see her first. When you have found her address, please telephone here. Louis will be waiting.'

'The D.A. will be waiting too,' McCann said quietly. 'I have to be careful about this, Mr. Maurer. There mustn't be much of a time lag. I can't give you more than half an hour.'

Maurer smiled. He reached out and patted McCann's shoulder.

'A half-hour will do splendidly.'

'Can't you give me this straight?' McCann said hoarsely. 'Has Conrad got a case? You – you didn't . . .?'

Maurer put his hand on McCann's arm and led him to the door.

'He won't have a case, Captain,' he said softly. 'I promise you that.'

He opened the door and waved McCann to the passage.

'Good night, Captain, and thank you for your co-operation. We shall wait to hear from you.'

It wasn't until McCann was driving down the narrow dark lane away from the club that he gave vent to his pent-up feelings. He swore vilely and obscenely for as long as it took him to reach the bright lights of the sea front.

II

Gollowitz came into the room, closed the door, and walked slowly over to where Maurer was sitting.

There was a long silence. Neither of the men looked at each other. Maurer continued to smoke his cigar, his face thoughtful. Gollowitz waited, his hands clasped behind his back, his mouth hard and set.

'I shouldn't have used Paretti,' Maurer said suddenly. 'That was a mistake. I always thought he was the best man I had. Imagine leaving that sketch-plan where it could be found.'

Gollowitz shut his eyes, opened them and drew in a deep breath.

'Are you telling me you killed that woman – *yourself*?' he said huskily.

Maurer looked up, his heavy eyebrows lifting.

'It gave me a lot of pleasure. I warned her. I told her to keep away from Jordan. She promised, but all the time she was seeing him: a dirty, muggle-smoker like him!'

'Why the hell did you have to do it yourself?' Gollowitz said fiercely. 'Don't you realize this is just what Forest has been waiting for? For years you've kept in the clear. You've never given him an opening. You don't imagine he's going to pass up such an opportunity, do you? If you wanted to get rid of her, why didn't you let Louis handle it?'

Maurer smiled.

'It was a personal thing, Abe,' he said patiently. 'It gave me a lot of satisfaction. You should have seen her face when she saw

49

me. She knew. For all her looks, her poise, her fame, she had no courage. You should have seen her. You should have seen her eyes.' He smiled again; a smile that sent a chill down Gollowitz's fat spine. 'You should have heard her scream. It was a personal thing: I wouldn't have missed doing it for anything in the world.'

Gollowitz rubbed his hand over his sweating face.

'This could sink the organization, Jack,' he said feverishly. 'The Syndicate won't like it.'

'— the Syndicate!' Maurer said, his voice suddenly vicious. 'I've had about enough of the Syndicate! They're not going to tell me what to do!'

Gollowitz turned away, walked over to an armchair and sat down. He didn't let Maurer see the shocked, startled expression that showed for a moment in his eyes.

'If this Coleman girl saw you . . .'

'You don't have to worry about her,' Maurer said indifferently 'She'll be taken care of. Without her, Forest hasn't a case. He can start trouble, but he won't get anywhere. You can handle this, if she's out of the way?'

'Sure. But she's got to be out of the way!'

'She will be. McCann will let us know where she is. He's going to give us half an hour before the police move in.'

Gollowitz thought for a moment.

'We can't take any chances, Jack,' he said abruptly. 'We'll have the yacht stand by. There's going to be a hell of a stink when this girl dies. You'd best be out of the way. A fishing trip where you can't be reached would be an idea. Just until the heat dies down.'

Maurer shrugged.

'I'll have Louis take care of it. The yacht's all ready. I'll go aboard as soon as McCann calls.'

'Who's going to take care of the girl?'

'Get Louis in here. That's his job.'

Gollowitz got up, crossed the room, opened the door near the bar and beckoned to Seigel.

Seigel came in as if he were walking on egg-shells. He was no fool. From what he had heard he knew Maurer had handled June Arnot's killing himself, and he was appalled at the possible consequences. He knew one slip now might upset the whole of the carefully built-up kingdom. He had clawed his way up the ladder during the past ten years until he was now in the highest position he could ever hope to attain, with plenty of money, plenty of women, and every conceivable luxury within reach. The thought of losing what he had gained filled him with a sick, vicious rage.

'Louis, this girl's got to be hit,' Maurer said, coming immediately to the point. 'McCann will let you know where she is. You've got to move fast. We have half an hour before Conrad moves in.'

Seigel stared at him.

'It'll have to be a crude job, Mr. Maurer,' he said. 'We shan't have time to case the joint, and that's bad.'

'I don't care how the job's done so long as it is done. Who's going to do it?'

Seigel thought for a moment.

'Moe and Pete,' he said finally.

'Pete – who?' Maurer asked sharply.

'Pete Weiner. He's okay. He hasn't hit before, but he's got to start some time.'

'Is he the guy with the birth-mark?' Maurer asked frowning.

'That's him. He can talk good. His old man was a minister. We want a guy who can get into her apartment without her making a noise. Pete can do that. If he slips up, Moe can take over, but he won't slip up. He's keen.'

'I don't like using a guy with a birth-mark,' Maurer said. 'He's too easily spotted.'

'I've got no one else who could get into the apartment. I don't know the set-up. If I had a little more time so I could case the joint I wouldn't use him. As soon as he's done the job, I'll get him out of town. There won't be any kick back.'

'There'd better not be,' Maurer said grimly.

A tap sounded on the door and Dutch Feiner, who looked after the club when Seigel was otherwise occupied, came in. He was a big, red-faced man with blond hair and hard ice-grey eyes.

'What is it?' Maurer said impatiently.

'There's a dame just come in, Mr. Maurer. I thought you should know. Seems to me she's Conrad's wife. I may be wrong. She was in the other night, and I thought her face seemed familiar. I'm pretty sure now that's who she is.'

'You mean Paul Conrad's wife?' Seigel said, staring at him.

'That's right,' Feiner said, pleased with the sensation he had caused.

'She's not with Conrad, is she?'

'She's on her own.'

'Check that, Louis!' Maurer said sharply, and got to his feet.

Seigel pushed past Feiner and hurried down the passage that led to the restaurant. He came back after a minute or so, his face excited.

'It's Conrad's wife all right. She's at the bar on her own.'

Maurer waved Feiner away. When he had gone, he looked over at Gollowitz.

'What's the idea? He wouldn't send her here to spy, would he?'

Gollowitz shook his head.

'I can't believe that.'

'Go and talk to her, Louis,' Maurer said. 'Handle her carefully. Don't let her know you know who she is. See if she'll tell you. Try and find out what she's doing here.'

Seigel nodded and went out.

'Do you know anything about her?' Maurer asked as Gollowitz sat down again.

'Not much. She's a looker. I think at one time before she married, she did a bit of singing: small stuff, small fees: you know the kind of thing. They got married about three years ago.'

'What the hell can she be doing here?' Maurer said, pulling at his under-lip.

Gollowitz shrugged. He wasn't interested in Janey Conrad. In a few hours, he was thinking, Maurer would be on the yacht. He would then be in charge of Maurer's kingdom, something he had thought about as a remote possibility for the past three years, and now it was within his grasp. It would be he now who would be the power in the organization. No longer would he have to persuade or even beg to have his advice followed. He would decide something should be done, and it would be done immediately.

His mind shifted from the taking over of Maurer's power to something else that Gollowitz had looked at with envious eyes and frustrated desire ever since he had first met her: Maurer's wife, Dolores.

Just to think of that tall, red-haired, green-eyed woman made Gollowitz short of breath. To his mind there had never been any woman more desirable and intriguing than Maurer's wife, and yet Maurer seemed scarcely to be aware she existed. How could he have had an affair with that Arnot woman when Dolores was his? Gollowitz wondered. How could he?

'What's on your mind, Abe?' Maurer asked sharply, his eyes on Gollowitz's face.

Gollowitz realized he had been practically thinking out loud, and that was highly dangerous.

He shrugged, his face expressionless.

'A hell of a lot of things,' he said, frowning. 'Do you imagine I like this? You walk out of here and leave me holding the can. I've got a hell of a lot of things to think about.'

Maurer nodded.

'I won't be away for long,' he said. 'Just hold everything down until I get back. There's nothing to worry about.'

Gollowitz thought that if anyone should worry it should be Maurer, but he didn't say so.

III

Janey Conrad looked anxiously around the crowded bar. She had got past the doorman by telling him she was expecting friends. The Paradise Club didn't encourage women on their own. The club had its own flock of hostesses, and outside competition wasn't welcomed.

The last time Janey had come to the club she had been picked up almost immediately by a fat, elderly man who had spent the evening buying her drinks and telling her off-colour stories. Janey had found him insufferably dull, but now she hoped feverishly that he would put in an appearance, but there was no sign of him.

In fact there appeared to be no unattached men this night at the club, and Janey began to grow uncomfortable. She realized she couldn't continue to sit alone at the corner table much longer. Already the bartender was looking her way, and two of the hostesses, bright, brassy-looking girls, were eyeing her over with open hostility.

She nervously finished her drink. What a let-down if she had to go! she thought. After spending the whole evening making herself look as attractive as she could, and then wasting a taxi fare to the club. There was nowhere else she dared go. At least none of Paul's stuffy friends ever came to the Paradise Club.

Then just when she was resigning herself that she could stay no longer, she saw a tall man moving towards her, wearing a faultlessly cut tuxedo: a man that set her heart beating rapidly. His lean good-looking face and the white scar that ran from his left eye to his nose set her nerves in a flutter.

He paused at her table and gave her a wide friendly smile. She smiled back, a little uneasily, but she didn't attempt to conceal her hopeful interest.

'Don't tell me he's stood you up,' Seigel said, bending over her. She felt he was trying to look down the front of her low-cut dress, and she drew back, a little alarmed, but excited, too. 'I've been watching you. You've been here quite a time.'

'Well, yes,' she said, and glanced at her wrist-watch. 'He is late, but he'll be along. He – he's always late.'

'Time and woman should wait for no man,' Seigel said, his smile widening. 'Can't I take his place?'

She pretended to hesitate.

'Well, I don't know. I – well, we don't know each other, do we?'

He pulled out a chair and sat down.

'That's easily fixed. I'm Louis Seigel. Who are you?'

'Janey ... Conrad,' Janey said, remembering that Paul had said she was easily recognized and deciding at the last moment not to give her maiden name.

'Well, there you are,' Seigel said. 'We now know each other. Simple, isn't it? Let's have a drink.'

She watched him snap his fingers at the bartender, and saw how quickly the bartender came out from behind his bar to take Seigel's order. She noticed, too, the drinks came with miraculous swiftness, and the martini the bartender placed before her was unrecognizable from the one she had ordered and had to wait for.

'I wish I were a man,' she said, as the bartender went away.

'You get all the service. The last drink I had was disgusting.'

'I'm glad you aren't a man,' Seigel returned, giving her his famous bold look. He had always wondered how Conrad had got hold of such a lovely wife, and now at close quarters he wondered still more. 'Didn't I see you here a few nights ago?'

Janey nodded.

'I look in sometimes. I like this place. Do you know it well?'

'Pretty well,' Seigel said, and laughed. 'It's the best of the night spots in town.' He picked up the martini. 'Here's to a long and beautiful friendship.' He drank the martini, emptying his glass in one swallow. 'Down the hatch with it,' he went on, 'and let's have another.'

Janey was ready to comply, and the bartender immediately served two more martinis without being asked. She was not slow to notice the frank admiration in Seigel's eyes as he looked at her. She was experienced enough to know Seigel was dangerous. He wouldn't be content just to sit and talk. Before very long the inevitable suggestion that they should go somewhere alone together would be made, and Janey's heart beat a little quicker as she tried to make up her mind just how far she would allow him to go. It didn't occur to her that when the time came, she might have no choice. She had plenty of confidence in herself to handle any situation, but then she wasn't to know that Seigel was a difficult man to stop, once he got going.

Talking to him, seeing the way he was looking at her, feeling the effects of the martinis and hearing the dance band in the restaurant, brought back to Janey the exciting days before she married. She had really kicked the can around in those days, she thought. After all, it wasn't all that long ago: three years.

'You have a wicked thought running through your mind,' Seigel said. He had the knack of reading a woman's mind. It was because he invariably knew the right moment to make his advances that his success with women had become a bye-word amongst his friends.

Janey flushed.

'I haven't!' She finished her martini and put the glass down on the table with a defiant little click. 'I don't know what you're talking about.'

Seigel grinned.

'Oh, yes, you do. You're wondering what my next move will be, and if I'm going to suggest you come back to my place to look at a valuable etching I've just bought.'

Janey stared at him, for a moment nonplussed, then she laughed.

'I was thinking nothing of the kind!'

He leaned forward. There was an animal magnetism in his strength and looks that left Janey a little breathless.

'Are you interested in etchings?'

She shook her head.

54

'Not a scrap. Are you?'

'No. I've never found an etching was necessary.' His smile widened. 'A good dinner, a little dancing, discreet lights and soft music are far ahead of any etching.' He pushed his chair back. 'Shall we eat?'

Janey looked at him and hesitated. She suddenly sensed that this big, good-looking man might be taking too much for granted, and he might, as the evening wore on, become much more difficult to handle than she had first imagined. But she knew if she refused his invitation he would leave her flat, and then she would have to go back to the dreary, empty house and the still more dreary television set.

'You're talking in riddles,' she said, 'but I'm hungry, so I will eat.'

'Fine. While you're powdering your pretty nose,' Seigel said, 'I have a phone call to make. Let's meet here in five minutes.'

'It'll take me longer to powder my nose than five minutes,' Janey said, refusing to be ordered about.

'In five minutes,' Seigel said, smiling, and walked quickly across the bar to the lounge where a row of pay booths were discreetly concealed.

He dialled a number, and while he was waiting for the connection, he lit a cigarette.

Janey puzzled him. If he hadn't known who she was, and that she was married to Conrad, he would have been certain that she was inviting seduction. Was she playing with him? he wondered, or was she really a push-over? Was Conrad going to appear suddenly just when Seigel was ready to move in for the kill? Was that the idea? Would Conrad let his wife come here on her own and act like this just for a chance of making trouble for Seigel? Seigel doubted it, but he decided to play his hand carefully.

A click sounded in his ear and Moe Gleb's growling voice snarled, 'Wadyawan'?'

'I've got a job for you,' Seigel said curtly. 'You and Pete are to handle it: the works, understand? Pete will do the hitting, you'll take care of the wheel. Get Pete, and stick to your end of the phone until you hear from me. I'll let you have the address as soon as I get it.'

'Hey! Don't we case the joint first?' Moe's voice sounded startled.

'You won't have time. The job's got to be done within a half-hour of you getting the address; after that the cops move in. It's important; no slipping up, Moe. I'm holding you responsible; understand?'

'Sure,' Moe said.

'Make it a pick job: no noise and quick. I'll call you any time from now on, so stick close,' and Seigel dropped the receiver back on its hook. He walked quickly along the passage

55

to his office and pushed open the door.

Maurer and Gollowitz were still in the room. Dolores, Maurer's wife, had joined them.

Seigel looked at her, feeling his blood quicken; something that always happened to him whenever he saw her.

Dolores was his idea of a woman. No other woman he had ever known excited him as she did. He knew she was as beyond his reach as the snow-capped heights of Everest, but that didn't stop him thinking about her, conjuring up dreams of her and lying awake at nights sweating for her.

She had married Maurer for his money and his power. Seigel knew that, and he knew also she was paying a high price for the position she held.

Maurer by now was sated with women. He had only to lift a finger for any girl to throw herself at him. His control of the movie unions, the night spots along the Californian coast and the big theatres gave him power over the big movie stars as well as the little stars. Even June Arnot, with her fabulous wealth, had thrown herself at him. To him, Dolores was just one more woman, and he treated her as such.

Seigel's eyes went over Dolores as she sat at the bar in a shimmering emerald green evening dress, covered with glittering sequins. She had the most perfect skin he had ever seen on a woman: like old ivory with the texture of cream. Her masses of dark-red hair set off her big, almond-shaped green eyes, and her figure, tall, lush and sensual, turned his mouth dry.

She swung around on the high stool and smiled at him. It was a mocking smile of a woman who knew what was going on in his mind and didn't care.

'Hello, Louis,' she said. 'How's the romance going? I saw you with the blonde. Do you like her?'

Seigel changed colour. He looked quickly at Maurer, then over at Gollowitz. He knew Gollowitz was crazy about Dolores, and he knew Gollowitz stood a chance. If anything happened to Maurer, he knew Gollowitz would not only take over the organization, but he would also take over Dolores. He knew Dolores hated Gollowitz as much as she hated Maurer, but so long as fat old men had money and power, the kind of money and power Maurer had and Gollowitz would have, she chose them.

'Keep out of this,' Maurer said, frowning over his shoulder at Dolores. 'If you can't keep quiet, you'd better get out.'

'Oh, I can keep quiet, Jack,' she returned, smiling. 'Just regard me as part of the scenery.'

Maurer's eyes moved to Seigel.

'What's she doing here?'

Seigel shrugged.

'I don't know. She's having dinner with me. She told me who she was, and she's already a little high. The way she's acting, she's a push-over, but maybe she's playing me for a sucker.'

'Not you, Louis,' Dolores said mockingly. 'Anyone else but you. I'm sure she's just dying to feel your manly arms round her and your passionate breath against her cheek. Who wouldn't?'

Seigel's face went a dusky red and a look of vicious fury jumped into his eyes. He opened his mouth to say something, then stopped himself in time.

'Go away, Dolly,' Maurer said without looking round. 'I've had enough of you tonight. Go home!'

Dolores slid off her stool, picked up her ermine wrap she had thrown carelessly over the back of a chair and walked across the room, trailing the wrap behind her. She moved slowly, a little smile on her red lips, and she swayed her hips slightly, attracting the attention of Gollowitz and Seigel who both watched her with intent expressions. As she passed Seigel, she wrinkled her nose at him.

'Good night, Abe,' she said at the door.

'Good night,' Gollowitz said with a little bow. He was careful not to look at her nor to let Maurer see the anger in his eyes.

'Good night, Louis,' she said.

'Oh, get out!' Maurer exclaimed angrily. 'We're busy!'

'And good night, darling.'

She went out, closing the door behind her.

Maurer made an impatient gesture with his hands.

'Damned women! If that bitch doesn't . . .'

'We shouldn't keep Mrs. Conrad waiting,' Gollowitz put in sharply.

'That's right,' Maurer said. He looked over at Seigel. 'Get friendly with her, Louis. She might be useful, but watch your tongue. Make sure she isn't after information.'

'I'll watch it,' Seigel said.

'Get back to her. I don't have to tell you how to handle her, but handle her right.'

Seigel nodded and stepped out into the passage and closed the door.

Janey was waiting for him in the cocktail bar, and it gave him sadistic pleasure to see how worried she looked as she sat at the table. It was so obvious that she was thinking he had walked out on her, and she was once more alone.

'Well for goodness sake!' she exclaimed when she saw him. 'You said five minutes and you've been a quarter of an hour.'

He grinned at her.

'The number was engaged.' He ran his eyes over her. She was good, but not in the same class as that red-headed devil. Still, she would have to do instead. He would take her somewhere in the dark and imagine she was Dolores. She wasn't going to forget this night with him. He would leave a scar on her mind – a scar in memory of Dolores.

'Come on,' he said, taking her arm possessively. 'Let's eat.'

57

CHAPTER FOUR

MOE GLEB flicked a fried egg on to his plate, added two thick rashers of ham, dropped the hissing fry-pan into the sink and carried the plate to the table.

He was a thickset, undersized youth with a mop of sandy-coloured hair. His small, heart-shaped face was as white as fresh mutton fat; his small, deep-set eyes, his pinched thin mouth were hard and vicious. He looked what he was: a young hoodlum fighting with no holds barred to get into the money, as dangerous and as savage as a treed wild cat.

He sat down at the table, poured himself a cup of coffee, and began to eat ravenously.

From the window, Peter Weiner watched him.

'For cryin' out loud!' Moe snarled, looking up suddenly. 'Wadjer starin' at? Ain't yuh seen a guy eat before?'

'I was admiring your appetite,' Pete said quietly. 'You've eaten twelve eggs and two pounds of ham since nine o'clock last night.'

'So wad? I gotta do somethin' while we wait, ain't I? Why the hell don't yuh eat?'

Pete shrugged.

'I guess I'm not hungry. How much longer do you think we've got to wait like this?'

Moe eyed him; a sudden shrewd expression crossed his face.

This guy was queer, he was thinking. Not that he could blame him. If he had that port wine stain spread over his puss like Pete had, he'd be queer himself.

'Until that bum Louis sez we can go.' He shovelled ham into his mouth, chewed for a moment, reached for his coffee and took a long drink. 'Wad gets up my bugle is why the hell yuh should be the guy to hit the frill. Why pick on yuh? Wad's the matter wid me? I've hit scores of guys. Yuh ain't hit any yet, have yuh?'

Pete shook his head.

'I've got to start some time.' He leaned forward and picked up Frances Coleman's photograph and stared at it. 'I wish it hadn't to be her.'

'Jay-sus!' Moe said, grinning. 'That's right. I could do plenty to her widout hittin' her. Plenty!'

Pete stared at the photograph. The girl's face had a queer effect on him. It wasn't that she was so pretty; she was pretty, but not more than the average girl you saw around Pacific City. There was something in her eyes that moved him: an eager, joyous expression of someone who found life the most exciting adventure.

Moe watched him. He took in the neat grey flannel suit, the brown brogue shoes and the white shirt and neat blue and red stripe tie. The guy, Moe thought a little enviously, looked like a freshman from some swank college: he talked like one, too.

He couldn't have been much older than Moe himself; around twenty-two or three. If it hadn't been for the birth-mark, he would have been good-looking enough to get on the movies, Moe decided, but that stain would have put paid to the best-looking movie actor in the world: bad enough to haunt a house with, Moe told himself.

'Did Seigel say why we had to do this job, Moe?' Pete asked abruptly.

'I didn't ask him. Yuh only ask that bum a question once, and then yuh go an' buy yuhself a new set of teeth.' Moe poured himself more coffee. 'It's a job, see? Ain't nothin' to worry about. Yuh know how to do it, don't yer?'

'Yes, I know,' Pete said, and a frozen, hard expression came over his face. As he stood in the light from the window, his eyes staring down into the street, Moe felt an uneasy twinge run through him. This guy could be tough, he told himself. Sort of crazy in the head. When he looked like that Moe didn't like being in the same room with him.

Just then the telephone bell began to ring.

'I'll get it,' Moe said, and dived out of the room to the pay booth in the passage.

Pete again looked at the photograph. He imagined how she would regard him when she saw him. That lively look of excitement and interest would drain out of her eyes and would be replaced by the flinching, slightly disgusted look all girls gave him when they came upon him, and he felt a cold hard knotting inside him; a sick rage that made the blood beat against his temples. This time he wouldn't pretend not to notice the look; he wouldn't have to force a smile and try to overcome the first impression she would have of him; not that he had ever succeeded in overcoming any first impression; they had never given him the chance.

As if he were some freak, some revolting object of pity, they would hurriedly look away, make some excuse – anything so long as they didn't have to stay facing him, and she would do that, and when she did, he would kill her.

Moe charged back into the room.

'Come on! Let's go! We've exactly half an hour to get there, do the job and get away, and the goddamn joint's the other side of the town.'

Pete picked up a bundle of magazines, checked to make sure the three-inch, razor-sharp ice-pick was in its sheath under his coat, and followed Moe at a run down the dirty rickety stairs and out to the ancient Packard parked at the kerb.

Although it looked old, the Packard's engine was almost as

good as new under Moe's skilful handling, and the car shot away from the kerb with a burst of speed that always surprised Pete.

'Here's what we do,' Moe said, talking out of the side of his mouth. 'I stay wid the heep and keep the engine running. Yuh ring the bell. If she comes to the door, give her the spiel about the magazines, and get her to invite yuh in. If someone else comes to the door, ask for her: Miss Coleman, see? Get her alone. Make out yer coy or something, see? Then give it to her. Hit her hard, and she won't squeal. Then beat it. Use yer rod if yuh have to. Get back in the heep. We beat it to Wilcox an' 14th Street and ditch the heep. Dutch'll pick us up and take us to the club. We take a speed-boat to Reid Key an' an airplane to Cuba.'

'Okay,' Pete said irritably. 'I know all that by heart.'

'Yeah, so do I, but it don't hurt to run over it again. The worse spot'll be getting to the club. If we get there, it's a cinch. Cuba! Gee! Yuh ever been to Cuba? I seen pictures of the dump. Terrific! And the women ...!' He pursed his thin mouth and gave a shrill whistle. 'Brother! Just wait until I get among those brown-skinned honies!'

Pete didn't say anything. He was scarcely listening. He was thinking that he was at last approaching the climax of his life. For months now he had thought about this moment: the moment when he would take a life; when he would inflict on someone something worse than had been inflicted on him, and he felt the cold knot tighten inside him.

'This is it,' Moe said after five minutes' driving. 'Lennox Avenue. She's staying with some frill called Bunty Boyd. I dunno wad yuh do about her. Hit her too if yuh have to.' He slowed down to a crawl and drove the car past a long row of four-storey houses. 'There it is, across the way.' He swung the car across the road and pulled up. 'That's the one; three houses up. I'll wait here. I'll have the heep movin' towards yuh as yuh come out.'

Pete picked up his bundle of magazines, opened the car door and got out. He had a sick feeling inside him, and his hands felt like ice.

'Yuh okay?' Moe asked, staring at him through the car window. 'This is important, Pete.'

'I'm okay,' Pete said. He looked at his wrist-watch. The time was two minutes past half-past ten. He had twenty-one minutes to do the job and get clear.

He walked quickly towards the house, emptying his mind of thought. It would be all right, he told himself, when he saw the look in her eyes. This sick feeling would go away then, and he would enjoy doing what he had come to do.

As he walked up the path that ran between two small lawns, he saw the curtain of one of the ground-floor windows move. He mounted the steps leading to the front door. There were four name-plates and four bells by the side of the door. As he read the name-plates and found Bunty Boyd's apartment was on the second floor, he felt he was being watched, and he looked round sharply in time to see the curtain of the ground-floor window drop hurriedly into place and the dim shadow of a man move away.

Pete rang the second-floor apartment bell, opened the front door and walked across the small hall and climbed the stairs. As he reached the second floor he heard a radio playing swing music. He crossed the landing as the front door of the apartment jerked open.

He felt his mouth suddenly turn dry and his heart skip a beat, then he found himself looking at a blonde-haired girl, wearing a white beach frock, whose young, animated face had a chocolate-box prettiness. She came forward, smiling, but the moment she caught sight of his face she came to an abrupt standstill, and her eyes opened wide and her smile went away.

The look he had come to expect jumped into her eyes, and he knew then it would be all right. He felt a rising viciousness inside him that left him a little breathless.

He forced himself to smile and said in his quiet, gentle voice, 'Is Miss Coleman in, please?'

'Have – have you come to see Frankie?' the girl asked. 'Oh! Then you – you must be Burt Stevens. She won't be a minute. Will you wait just a moment?' She spun around on her heels and ran back into the apartment before he could speak.

He stood waiting, his hand inside his coat, his fingers around the plastic handle of the ice-pick. If she came out on to the landing, he could do it at once. It would be easier and safer than doing it inside where the other girl might not leave them alone. A cold anger and an overpowering desire to inflict pain and fear gripped him.

Through the half-open door he heard Bunty say in a dramatic whisper, 'But he's awful! You can't go with him, Frankie! You simply can't!'

He waited, his heart pounding, blood beating against his temples. Then the door opened, and she came out on to the sunlit landing.

She might have stepped out of her photograph, except she was smaller than he had imagined. She had a beautiful little figure that not even the severe pale blue linen dress could conceal. Her dark silky hair rested on her shoulders. Her smile was bright and sincere, and there was that look in her eyes that had had such an effect on him when he had seen her picture for the first time.

Her fresh young beauty paralyzed him, and he waited for her smile to fade and for disgust to come into her eyes, and his fingers tightened on the ice-pick.

But the smile didn't fade; pleasure lit up her face as if she were really happy to see him. He stood there, staring at her, waiting for the change, and not believing it wouldn't come.

'You must be Burt,' she said, coming to him and holding out her hand. 'Terry said you were going to take his place. It's sweet of you to have come at the last moment. I should have been sunk if you hadn't come. I've been looking forward to this for days.'

His hand came out from inside his coat, leaving the ice-pick in its sheath. He felt her cool fingers slide into his hand and he looked down at her, watching her, waiting for the change, and then suddenly realizing with a sense of shock that it wasn't coming.

II

The girl, Bunty, came out on to the landing, followed immediately by a tall, powerfully built young fellow with a crew hair-cut and a wide india-rubber grin. He was wearing a red-patterned shirt worn outside a pair of fawn slacks, and in his hand he carried a gay red-and-white striped hold-all.

Still holding Pete's hand, Frances turned and smiled at Bunty. 'Are you ready, then, at last?' she asked.

'Buster says if we don't hurry we'll miss the tide.'

'Burt, this is Buster Walker,' Frances said, turning to look at Pete. 'You've already met Bunty, haven't you?'

Pete's eyes moved over the big fellow who pushed out his hand, grinning. There was no disgust, no surprise in the big fellow's eyes, just a desire to be friendly.

'Glad to know you,' Buster said. 'Sorry we couldn't give you longer notice. I don't know what I should have done if I had to have these two on my hands without support. It's as much as I can do to manage Bunty.'

Pete muttered something as he shook hands.

'Would you like to leave those magazines and pick them up when we get back?' Frances asked, and held out her hand for them.

Pete let her take them. He watched her return to the apartment, lay them on the hall table, then shut the front door on the catch lock.

'Now, let's go,' she said, and took his arm.

He allowed her to lead him down the stairs. He didn't know what to do. His mind was confused. He knew he couldn't turn on her now, not in cold blood, not a girl who hadn't flinched away from him and who was actually holding his arm. If only it had been the other girl, the job would have been over by now.

As they walked down the stairs into the hall, Buster said, 'I suppose Terry did tell you where we were going, Burt?'

Pete looked back over his shoulder.

'No . . . he didn't say. . . .'

'Isn't that like Terry!' Buster exclaimed. 'The nut! Well, we're going to spend the day on the beach, and take in the amusement park.'

'Buster imagines he's going to take me on the Big Wheel,' Bunty said, 'but he's quite, quite mistaken. I wouldn't go on that thing for Gregory Peck, let alone Buster Walker!'

Buster laughed.

'You'll come on with me if I have to carry you.' He opened the front door and stood aside to let the girls pass. 'I have a car at the corner,' he went on, falling into step with Pete. 'I got a flat and I left it at the garage to be fixed.'

Out of the corner of his eye, Pete saw the curtain move again in the ground-floor window, and again caught sight of a shadowy outline of a man, drawing back quickly.

'Old nosy-parker's snooping again,' Bunty said scornfully. 'That's all he does, peep through the curtains.'

'Perhaps he's lonely,' Frances said. 'He never seems to go out, does he?'

'Oh, you're hopeless, Frankie,' Bunty said impatiently. 'You always find some excuse for lame dogs. The fact is he's a nasty old drunk who spends all his time spying on people, and that's all there is to it.'

Pete felt blood rise to his face. That was it, he thought. It's pity. She's one of those people who live by pity. That was why she hadn't flinched when she had seen his face. She may have flinched inwardly, but rather than hurt his feelings, she had controlled her expression. Once again he felt the cold knot tighten inside him, and his hand went inside his coat and he touched the handle of the ice-pick.

The Packard was only twenty yards away. If he hit her now, he could reach the car before the other two could recover from the shock.

Again he knew he was deluding himself, for Frances and Bunty were now several yards ahead of him, and Buster was walking by his side.

He saw the Packard move forward and then stop, and he wondered what Moe was thinking. He felt a little chill run up his spine. Perhaps Moe would move into action. Suppose he shot her from the car? The moment the thought dropped into his mind, he quickened his step and closed the gap between himself and Frances, and walked just behind her, covering her back from Moe with his body.

Buster, determined to make conversation, began to talk about the prowess of the Brooklyn Dodgers, and kept up an enthusiastic harangue until they reached the garage where a small, battered sports car with two seats in front and a tiny bucket seat at the back stood waiting.

'There's not much room,' Buster said, 'but it goes all right. Bunty, you get in the back seat. Burt, you sit beside me and Frankie will sit on top of you. That okay?'

'Unless Burt thinks I'll squash him,' Frances said, laughing.
Pete avoided her eyes.

'No, it's all right,' he said, and climbed into the front seat.

Frances lowered herself on to his lap and put her arm round his shoulders. The feel of her soft young body and the smell of her faint perfume made his blood quicken. He sat motionless, his arm slackly round her, bemused. This was something that had never happened to him before; something that had happened only in his dreams.

Buster cranked the engine which started with a roar. Having made sure Bunty was settled in the back, he drove away from the garage and sent the car roaring towards the sea.

The noise of the engine prevented any conversation, and Pete was glad of the opportunity to savour this extraordinary experience of having a girl so close to him.

As the little car banged and bumped along at forty-five miles an hour, Frances had to cling to him and he to her to prevent her being thrown out. She was laughing, and once she screamed to Buster to drive more slowly, but he didn't appear to hear her.

Pete suddenly realized that the odd feeling he was experiencing was the nearest to excited happiness he had ever known, and he found himself smiling at Frances as she clung to him, and he felt a tingle run up his spine as she laughed back at him.

The car's off-wheel suddenly hit a pot-hole and jolted them violently together. Frances's skirts shot up to show the tops of her stockings and the smooth white flesh of her thighs. Pete hurriedly pulled down her skirt to save her from untwining her arms from around his neck.

'Oh, thank you,' she gasped, her mouth close to his ear. 'This is really awful. We must stop him.'

But Buster had already slowed down and was grinning at Pete and winking.

'I knew that would happen sooner or later,' he bawled. 'It never fails to work. I always provide a free show for my male friends.'

'Buster! You behave yourself or we'll go home!' Bunty screamed at him.

Frances removed one arm from around Pete's neck and anchored her skirts.

Long before they caught a glimpse of the sea, they heard the stupendous sound from the amusement park together with the shouting, screaming and laughing of the people like themselves who were stealing a day on the beach.

'I never know where all the people come from,' Frances cried above the noise of the car engine. 'It doesn't matter when you come here, it's always crowded.'

Pete was about to say something when he happened to glance in the little circular mirror on the off-wing of the car. In its reflection he saw the battered outlines of the Packard and caught a glimpse of Moe's sandy-coloured hair as he sat at the driving-wheel.

Pete felt himself turn hot, then cold. He realized, with a feeling of bewilderment mixed with fear, that for the past ten minutes he had completely forgotten Moe and had forgotten the orders Seigel had given him.

Buster drove into a packed parking lot, edged in between two cars and cut the engine. Cars were arriving at the rate of ten a minute, and as the four walked from the car towards the beach, they were immediately hemmed in by the noisy, jostling, perspiring crowd.

Frances held on to Pete's arm. He moved forward a step ahead of her, his shoulder turned slightly sideways to form a buffer against the swirling tide of people coming towards him. Buster led the way, cutting a path with his big shoulders for Bunty who walked immediately behind him, hanging on to his shirt tail.

They crawled past the low wooden buildings that housed fortune tellers, photographers with their comic animals and still more comic backgrounds, the freak shows and the hamburger stalls, being jostled, coming to a standstill, then moving on again.

From time to time Pete looked over his shoulder, but he couldn't see any sign of Moe, and he hoped feverishly that they had lost him in this crowd.

Finally they reached the rails at the outer edge of the sea front. Not far away was the snake-like structure of a roller coaster whose cars roared and clattered up and down the steep inclines, carrying a screaming, shouting cargo of people, determined to enjoy themselves and determined to scream or shout louder than his or her neighbour.

Outlined against the sky was the colossal Giant Wheel that slowly revolved, carrying little cars slowly up into the heavens; cars that spun and swayed ominously on what appeared to be thread-like anchors.

The four of them faced the beach, looking along the three-mile strip of sand at the seething mass of humanity that lay on the sand, played ball, deck tennis, leap-frog or rushed madly into the oncoming breakers and filled the air with noise.

'Phew! Half the town seems to be here,' Buster said, surveying the scene with his wide, india-rubber grin. 'Let's get at it. We'll have a swim first, then something to eat, then we'll go to the amusement park. How about it?'

'Did you bring a swim-suit?' Frances asked, turning to Pete. He shook his head.

'I'm afraid I don't swim.'

He saw Bunty pull a little face and lift her shoulders in a why-on-earth-did-you-come-then? gesture, and he felt the blood rise to his face, and that angered him, for he knew when he flushed the naevus on his skin turned livid and made him look repulsive. He saw Bunty turn away so she need not look at him.

65

But Frances was looking at him with no change of expression in her eyes.

'It doesn't matter,' she said quickly. 'We'll sit on the beach and watch the others swim. I don't feel like swimming myself.'

'No! Please; I want you to swim,' he said, trying to control his embarrassment.

'Burt will guard our clothes,' Buster said. 'We shan't be long. Come on, girls, let's get to it.'

They began to make their way cautiously through the sprawling crowd, until they finally came upon a small clearing in the sand and hurriedly staked out their claim.

Buster was wearing a pair of swimming-trunks under his clothes, and he was quickly stripped off. Pete eyed his muscles and his tanned body enviously.

Both the girls took off their shoes and stockings and slid out of their dresses. They both wore one-piece suits under their dresses, and Pete felt a little pang run through him when he looked at Frances. She had on an oyster-coloured swim-suit that moulded itself to her body. He thought she had the most beautiful figure he had ever seen.

As she adjusted her bathing cap, she went over to him.

'You're sure you don't mind being left? I'd just as soon stay.'

"No, it's all right. I'll wait for you.'

'Oh, come on, Frankie!' Bunty cried impatiently, and catching hold of Buster's hand she ran with him down to the breakers and plunged in.

Frances smiled at Pete. It was unbelievable, he thought, a lump coming into his throat, that a girl as lovely as she was could look at him and smile at him like this: just as if he were an ordinary human being like Buster.

'I'll be right back,' she said, and went after the other two.

Pete sat with his fingers laced around his knees, his shoulders hunched, and watched her long, slim legs, her straight boyish back as she ran with that slightly awkward movement most young girls have when they run.

He watched her plunge into the water and swim with powerful strokes after the other two.

'Wad the hell are yuh playin' at?' a voice snarled near him.

Pete stiffened and his heart skipped a beat. He looked quickly round.

Moe was sitting on his haunches, staring at Frances's bobbing head as she swam farther out to sea. He looked an incongruous figure in his black suit, his hand-painted tie and his pointed white shoes with black explosions, among the half-naked sun-bathers sprawling around him.

'The man came to the door,' Pete said, speaking rapidly and trying to keep his voice steady. 'Then the two girls came out. They mistook me for someone else. I hadn't a chance to get going, so I went with them, and I'm waiting now to get her alone.'

'That's wad happens when yuh don't case the joint,' Moe said, his small eyes bright with suspicion. 'I told that bum Louis.' He looked at his wrist-watch. 'The cops will be at her place by now. Yuh got to hit her quick, Pete.'

'Amongst this lot?' Pete said sarcastically.

Moe turned his head and looked at the Big Wheel as it carried the little cars far into the sky.

'Get her on the Big Wheel,' he said. 'Yuh can be nice an' private in one of those cars. Hit her when yuh get to the top and shove her under the seat. They won't spot her before yuh get away.'

Pete suddenly felt sick.

'Okay,' he said.

'Don't slip up on this,' Moe said, his voice suddenly harsh. 'Yuh don't make more than one mistake in this outfit. She's got to be hit. That's orders, and if yuh can't do it, I can.'

'I said okay,' Pete returned curtly.

'It'd better be okay.' Moe got to his feet. 'I'll be around, Pete. Yuh ain't got much time; use it or I will.'

Pete looked back over his shoulder and watched the broad-shouldered, squat figure walk across the sand, picking his way over recumbent bodies, by-passing children building castles in the sand, stepping past fat matrons in one-piece swim-suits, and their fatter husbands, lolling in deck-chairs.

Pete watched him until, melting into the crowded background, he lost sight of him. But he knew he wouldn't be far away, and he would be watching every move from now on.

Pete sat in the hot sun, sweat on his face and fear clutching at his heart. He faced up to the fact at last that he wasn't going to kill Frances. He realized he had made up his mind about that when he had first seen her. He knew Moe would have struck her down as she came out on to the landing, and would have got away. He could have done the same thing, but that friendly smiling look in her eyes had saved her. He had to face up to the fact now, and he knew what it would mean. He was deliberately throwing his own life away. No one in the organization ever disobeyed an order and survived. Several of them had kicked against the organization's discipline: three of them had actually got out of town before the organization had realized they had gone. One of them reached New York, another Miami, and the third one had got as far as Milan, Italy, before the long arm of the organization had struck.

But Pete wasn't thinking of himself. This girl was too young, too lovely and too kind to die, he thought, digging his fingers into the sand as he tried to think how to save her. If he delayed much longer, Moe might strike himself. He had the nerve to walk up to Frances, stab her on this crowded beach and then shoot his way out. Moe might do it, unless he was satisfied he was going ahead with the job.

The only safe thing he could do was to warn Frances, and then tackle Moe himself. If he killed Moe, Frances would have an hour or so to get out of town and hide herself somewhere before the organization realized she had slipped through their fingers.

He would have to be very careful how he tackled Moe. Already Moe was suspicious. Moe was very fast with a gun: faster than he ever could hope to be. He would have to lull his suspicions somehow, and then go for him at the right moment.

But first he had to warn Frances, and before he could do that he had to get her away from the other two. If he told her when they were there, Buster would probably call a cop and stop him fixing Moe.

Everything depended on Moe's death, Pete told himself. He looked towards the glittering sea. Frances's blue bathing cap was bobbing towards him: she was coming in.

He took a grip on his fluttering nerves and waited for her.

III

The black-and-white checkered police car swung into Lennox Avenue, slowed to a crawl while Conrad leaned out of the window to catch a glimpse of the numbers of the houses.

'Across the road, about ten yards up,' he said to Bardin, who was driving.

Bardin pulled across the road and stopped the car outside the four-storey house. Both men got out of the car and stood for a moment surveying the house.

Conrad's heart was beating unevenly. He was excited. When McCann had telephoned through to his office to tell him the girl, Frances Coleman, had been located at 35, Lennox Avenue, he could scarcely wait for Bardin to collect him in the police car.

'You'll be soon out of your misery,' Bardin said, grinning. 'What's the betting she didn't see anyone?'

'Come on, let's ask her,' Conrad said, pushing open the garden gate. As he walked up the path to the front door, he spotted a movement in the ground-floor window and caught sight of the shadow of a man, lurking behind the curtains. The shadow hurriedly ducked back out of sight as Conrad turned his head to look at the window.

Conrad paused to read the name-plates on the door, then dug his finger in the second bell, opened the front door and walked briskly across the hall and up the stairs, followed by Bardin.

They stopped outside the front door on the second-floor landing, and Conrad knocked. They waited a few moments, then as no one answered the door, Conrad knocked again.

'Looks as if no one's at home,' he said, frowning, after another minute's wait. 'Damn it! Now what are we going to do?'

'Come back later,' Bardin said philosophically. 'I would have been surprised if anyone was in on a morning like this.'

They walked down the stairs together.

'Maybe the guy at the window knows where she's gone,' Conrad said as he reached the hall. 'From the way he was peeping at us, he shouldn't miss much.'

'What's the excitement?' Bardin said. 'We'll come back this afternoon.'

Conrad was already knocking on the front door to the right of the main entrance. There was a longish delay, then the door opened and a tall, bent old man in a tight-fitting black suit regarded them with big, watery blue eyes.

'Good morning, gentlemen,' he said. 'Is there something I can do for you?'

'I'm Paul Conrad of the District Attorney's office, and this is Lieutenant Bardin, City Police,' Conrad said. 'We have business with the people in the second-floor apartment. They seem to be out. You wouldn't know when they will be back?'

The old man took out a big red silk handkerchief and polished his nose with it. Into his watery blue eyes came a look of intense excitement.

'You'd better come in, gentlemen,' he said, standing aside and opening the front door wide. 'I'm afraid you will find my quarters a little untidy, but I live alone.'

'Thank you,' Conrad said, and as they followed the bent old figure into the front room, he and Bardin exchanged resigned glances.

The room looked as if it hadn't been dusted or swept or tidied in months. On the old, well-polished sideboard stood an array of whisky bottles and about two dozen dirty glasses. Most of the bottles were empty, but the old man found an unopened one and began to pick off the tinfoil around the cap with unsteady fingers.

'Take a seat, gentlemen,' he said. 'You musn't think I'm used to living like this, but I lost my wife some years ago and I sadly miss her.' He managed to get the bottle open and looked vaguely at the dirty glasses. 'I should introduce myself. I am Colonel Neumann. I hope you gentlemen will join me in a drink?'

'No, thank you, Colonel,' Conrad said briskly. 'We're in a hurry. Did you happen to notice if Miss Coleman went out this morning?'

'Then if you really won't, I think I will,' the Colonel said, pouring a large shot of whisky into one of the glasses. 'I'm an old man now and a little whisky is good for me. Moderation at all times, Mr. Conrad, and there's then no harm in it.'

Conrad repeated his question in a louder voice.

'Oh, yes. They all went out,' the Colonel said, carrying the glass of whisky carefully to a chair and sitting down. 'You musn't think I pry on people, but I did notice them. Are they in trouble?' The hopeful, intent curiosity in his eyes irritated Conrad.

'No, but I'm anxious to talk to Miss Coleman. Do you know her?'

'The dark one?' The Colonel smiled. 'I've seen her: a pretty thing. What would the police want with her, Mr. Conrad?'

'Do you happen to know where they have gone?'

'They said something about the amusement park,' the Colonel said, frowning. 'I believe I heard one of them say something about going for a swim.'

Conrad grimaced. He knew it would be hopeless to try and find Frances Coleman if she had gone to the amusement park. The place was always packed. He lifted his shoulders, resigned.

'Thank you, Colonel. I guess I'll look back this afternoon.'

'You're sure nothing's wrong?' the Colonel asked, staring at Conrad. 'I didn't like the look of the man who followed them. He looked a rough character to me.'

Conrad stiffened to attention.

'What man, Colonel?'

The Colonel took a sip from his glass, put the glass down and wiped his mouth with his silk handkerchief.

'You mustn't get the impression that I'm always at the window, Mr. Conrad, but it did happen I looked out as they were walking down the street, and I saw this man in a car. He drove slowly after them: a yellow-headed man; a young man, but I didn't like the look of him at all.'

'Who was Miss Coleman with?' Conrad asked sharply.

'With her friends.' The Colonel showed his disapproval by a gentle snort. 'That fellow who wears his shirt outside his trousers: I wish I had had him in my regiment. I'd have taught him how to dress like a gentleman! Then there's that Boyd girl: a cheeky little piece if ever there was one. It's a damn funny thing how some girls don't mind what a fellow looks like. Different in my day, I can tell you. I shouldn't have thought Miss Coleman would have cared to be seen out with that fellow with the birth-mark. But she's a kind little thing: perhaps she took pity on him.'

Conrad and Bardin exchanged looks. Both of them knew Pete Weiner by sight, although he hadn't actually been through either of their hands, but they knew he had done some jobs for Maurer.

'What fellow with a birth-mark?' Bardin barked.

The Colonel blinked at him.

'I don't know who he is. I've never seen him before. He had a naevus – isn't that what they call it? – down the right side of his face.'

'Was he dark, slightly built, looked like a student?' Bardin demanded.

'Yes. I'd say he could be a student.'

'And this other fellow; the one in the car: was he driving a Packard? A short, square-shouldered guy with light blond hair and a white face?'

'That seems a very fair description of him: a vicious character.

I don't know about the car. I didn't notice it. Do you know him then?'

'You say this guy with the birth-mark went with these other three?' Bardin said, ignoring the Colonel's question.

'Oh, yes. I watched them go down the street. They picked up a little car at the garage you can see from here. The blond man in the car followed the little car.'

By now Conrad was alarmed. From the description the Colonel had given of these two men, he had no doubt they were Pete Weiner and Moe Gleb.

'Thanks,' he said, moving to the door. 'Sorry to have taken up so much of your time.'

'But you're not going so soon?' the Colonel said, getting to his feet and slopping what was left of his whisky in his anxiety to head Conrad off from the door. 'You're surely going to explain. . . .'

But by this time Conrad was half-way down the path with Bardin at his heels. They got into the police car.

'Well, how do you like it now?' Conrad asked grimly. 'We've got to get moving, Sam. We'll go to the garage first. They may have a description of the car. I'll go on to the amusement park and you organize some help. We'll need forty or fifty men in a hurry.'

'For crying out loud!' Bardin exclaimed blankly. 'What do we want with forty or fifty men? You and I can handle this.'

'Can we?' Conrad was pale and his eyes angry. 'That girl is in a crowd of about fifty thousand people. Right at her heels are two of Maurer's hoods. What do you imagine they are there for? Do you think I'm going to let them wipe her out the way Paretti wiped out all those other witnesses? We'll want all the help we can get. I'm going to save that girl if it's the last thing I do!'

IV

'Hey! Wait a minute,' Buster said, coming to a standstill. He was clutching in both arms an odd assortment of dolls, gaudy-looking vases, coconuts and two big boxes of candy. 'I've got to park this lot. I'm fed-up with humping them wherever we go.'

'You shouldn't have won them then,' Bunty said, laughing. 'Where are you going to park them?'

'Let's go back to the car; then we can all go on the Big Wheel.'

'We don't all want to go,' Bunty said. 'I'll come with you. You go on, Frankie, and we'll meet at the Big Wheel. I'm still not sure I'm going on it, but at least I can watch you three.'

Pete's heart skipped a beat. For the past hour he had tried desperately to get Frances to himself without success, and now the opportunity had made itself. He looked over his shoulder. Not far away, standing by one of the Bingo stalls, was Moe, his hard white face set in vicious lines.

'All right,' Frances said, 'We'll meet you at the entrance to the Big Wheel.'

Pete was sure Moe wasn't going to wait much longer. He had to get Frances somewhere away from the crowd and away from Moe. He looked right and left and his eyes alighted on a big neon sign that read:

THE GREAT MIRROR MAZE
Do You Want To Be Alone?
Come and get lost in the most baffling maze in the world

'You'll take at least twenty minutes to get to the car and back,' he said to Buster. 'We'll go and have a look at the maze over there. Suppose you meet us at the entrance?' He turned to Frances. 'Will you come with me? I've always wanted to see this thing. It could be fun.'

'For heaven's sake!' Bunty exclaimed. 'You'll only get lost, and you'll be in there for hours.'

'Oh, no,' Pete said quickly. 'It's really quite easy. All you have to do is to keep moving to the left and you come out in about ten minutes. Will you come?'

Frances nodded.

'All right.'

She wasn't particularly keen, but Pete had fallen in so readily with all her suggestions that she felt it was only fair to fall in with his now.

'Well, please yourself. If you're not out in half an hour we won't wait for you,' Bunty warned. 'Come on, Buster. Let's go.'

As the two pushed their way slowly through the endless stream of people, Pete again looked in Moe's direction. There was an intent expression on Moe's face as he watched Bunty and Buster disappear into the crowd.

Pete turned quickly to Frances.

'Shall we go?' he said. 'It'll be amusing, and we won't be long.'

She moved along with him, her hand on his arm towards the entrance to the maze.

'Do you know that man?' she asked suddenly.

Pete stiffened and looked sharply at her.

'What man?'

'The one you keep looking at. The one in the black suit. He's been following us all the morning.'

'Has he?' Pete tried to keep his voice steady. 'I – I think I've seen him somewhere before.'

By now they had reached the pay-box outside the maze, and Pete moved forward to buy the tickets. It seemed to be the only side-show where there was no queue, and the blonde, middle-aged woman seemed glad to sell him the tickets.

'Keep to your left as you go in,' she said as she gave him the change. 'If you get lost ring the bell. You'll find plenty of bell-pushes as you go through the maze. Someone will come and find you.'

Pete thanked her and joined Frances who was waiting at the entrance. He followed her down a long passage and at the last moment he looked back anxiously over his shoulder. He could see no sign of Moe.

'What do we do?' Frances asked as she walked just ahead of him. 'It's awfully stuffy in here, isn't it?'

'You won't find it stuffy once we get into the maze,' Pete assured her. 'It's in the open air.'

They walked a few yards and then they found themselves suddenly in the maze.

The maze was constructed of fifteen-foot-high walls, lined on either side by mirrors. The passage between the wall was six foot wide, just wide enough for two people to walk side by side. The mirrors were so angled that they reflected from one mirror to the other, and as Frances and Pete stepped into the first long passage they were immediately hemmed in and surrounded by their own reflections, multiplied thirty or forty times.

The effect was so startling and overpowering that Frances came to an abrupt standstill.

'I don't think I'm going to like this,' she said, turning to Pete. 'Do you think we'll ever find our way out?'

'It's all right,' he said, taking her arm. 'We just go straight ahead, and when we come to a cross section we turn to the left. If we keep turning to the left we'll be out in ten minutes or so.'

'Well, all right,' Frances said doubtfully. 'But I don't really like it.'

He took her arm and walked her forward. He wanted to get her into the centre of the maze in case Moe had seen them and was following them. For some minutes they walked along the mirror-lined paths, turning to the left when they came to the cross sections.

Above them as they walked they could see the blue sky and hear the strident noise of the amusement park. Each path that they came to was a replica of the one they had just left. Their reflections surrounded them. What appeared to be an endless path would suddenly terminate in a cul-de-sac so they had to retrace their way until they found a turning which they had passed without noticing it.

After they had walked for two or three minutes, Frances said suddenly, 'I think we should try to get out now. It's rather dull, isn't it?'

Pete stopped. He looked back down the path along which they had come. Twenty faces with twenty disfiguring birth-marks stared at him, making him feel a little sick.

Now he had come to the moment when he had to tell her the truth, he realized how difficult it was going to be. There was so little time. Any moment Moe might appear at the end of one of these paths.

'I brought you here to tell you something,' he began. 'I'm afraid it is going to be a shock to you.'

She looked quickly at him, and he saw her stiffen slightly.

'What do you mean?'

'I'm not Burt Stevens. My name is Pete Weiner. We haven't much time. Please listen to me and please don't be frightened.'

He saw alarm jump into her eyes, and he felt desperately sorry for her. To suddenly find herself in this complicated maze with someone who now turns out to be a complete stranger was an alarming experience, he thought, as he tried to smile at her.

'I don't understand,' she said steadily. 'Is this a joke?'

'I wish it was,' he said earnestly. 'Before I say anything more I want you to know I wouldn't harm you for anything in the world. You're safe with me. So please try not to be frightened.'

She moved a step away from him.

'What do you mean?'

'There's so little time,' he said, his mind groping for the right words. 'I don't know what it is all about myself. I was sent to hurt you. That man who has been following us came with me. He's dangerous. I know it sounds unbelievable, but he will kill you if he can get you alone. The only way to save you is for me to kill him while you escape. That's why I brought you here. You must do exactly what I tell you . . .' He broke off as he saw terror darken her eyes.

As she listened to the quiet, tense voice, she believed that she was listening to a madman. The newspapers were always mentioning horrible cases of lunatics who trapped girls in lonely places and murdered them. She backed away, staring at Pete, and she raised her hands in an imploring gesture for him to keep his distance.

Seeing her rising panic, Pete remained still. He had realized the danger of telling her the truth. He guessed she might jump to the conclusion that he was a lunatic, and with a sick feeling of despair he saw now that that was exactly what she was thinking.

'Please don't be frightened, Frankie,' he said. 'Please trust me. I'm not cracked, and I wouldn't hurt you. Can't you see that? Can't you see I only want to help you?'

'Please go away,' she said, white-faced but still calm. 'I can find my way out without your help. Just please go away and leave me.'

'I will go,' he said earnestly, 'but you must first listen to what I have to say. This man who is following us has been told to kill you. I don't know why, but he will do it unless I stop him. They sent me a photograph of you so I should know you. Look, I'll show it to you. Perhaps it will convince you I'm speaking the truth.'

Seeing her mounting panic, he hurriedly thrust his hand inside his coat for his billfold. He felt if he could only show her the

74

photograph she must realize the danger she was in.

He jerked out the billfold, and as he did so his wrist-watch became entangled with the handle of the ice-pick, and the pick slid out of its sheath and fell on the path at his feet.

Frances looked down and saw the ice-pick. She stared at the murderously sharp blade in horror. Then she looked up and met Pete's frightened, guilty eyes. A cold chill settled around her heart.

She didn't hesitate. She was sure now he was a dangerous lunatic who had tricked her into this labyrinth of mirrors to do her harm, and she knew if it came to a struggle she would stand no chance against him. So she spun around and ran.

'Frankie! Please!'

His agonized cry only acted as a spur, and her long legs carried her down the straight, narrow path as fast as she could drive them.

As she ran she kept the fingers of her left hand against the wall of mirrors. It was only by feel that she found a turning, down which she sped. She took another turning, this time to the right, and she ran frantically down yet another nightmare path, her dark hair streaming behind her, her face white, her breath coming in laboured gasps.

She had no idea how long she ran, how often she twisted and turned. It was like running on a treadmill; every step she took brought her to the same place, or what appeared to be the same place.

Finally she could run no more, and she leaned against the mirrored wall, her hands pressing her breasts, her eyes closed as she struggled to regain her breath.

After a few moments she opened her eyes and stared at her reflection in the mirror opposite her. She was shocked to see how frightened she looked, how big her eyes were and how wild and disordered her usually sleek, neat hair had become.

She had no idea where she was. She might still be only a few yards from Pete or she might be in the centre of the maze.

She wondered if she should shout for help, but suppose Pete was close by and got to her before outside help could reach her? She decided it would be safer to try and get out by herself.

She looked up and down the path that seemed in the reflection of the mirrors to have no ending and no beginning, and she felt a wave of panic sweep over her.

It was as if she were caught up in some ghastly nightmare. She wanted to sit on the ground and cry: to give up weakly, to hide her face in her hands and wait until someone found her.

But suppose Pete found her first? She fought back her tears and made an effort to pull herself together. If she continued down this path, she told herself, and at every intersection she turned left, surely it would bring her to the exit?

She started off, walking slowly, her ears strained to catch

the slightest suspicious sound that might come to her above the roar of the amusement park. She hadn't gone more than a few yards when she had an irresistible urge to look behind her.

She stopped and turned.

At the far end of the path she saw something move, and her heart stopped beating, then began to race madly. She half turned to run, but stopped when she saw the figure behind her make a similar movement. She realized with a little sob of hysteria that she was watching her own distant reflection.

She went on.

At the end of the path, seeing herself grow larger as she approached the mirror facing her, she realized she had come up another cul-de-sac and once again she had to fight against a rising panic.

She turned around to retrace her steps. Her eyes caught a movement at the far end of the path. She wasn't to be caught like that again, and she kept on. Then suddenly she felt a cold chill crawl up her spine. The figure ahead of her wasn't moving as she was moving.

She stopped and peered down the path.

A squat, square-shouldered man in a black suit stood watching her. In his hand glittered a nickle-plated automatic.

It was Moe.

CHAPTER FIVE

CONRAD spent a feverish twenty minutes searching for the three-seater sports car in the various car parks that surrounded the amusement park. He was still at it, but realizing the hopelessness of the task, when he heard a police siren, and saw Bardin with a car full of prowl boys swing into the avenue leading to the main entrance of the amusement park.

Conrad ran out to meet the car, waving his hands.

The car pulled up and Bardin, looking hot and irritable, scowled out of the window.

'How are you getting on?' he demanded. 'Found the car yet?'

'Shut that damned siren off!' Conrad snapped. 'Do you want to scare those two hoods into action?'

Bardin got out of the car as the sergeant driver flicked off the siren.

'Well, come on. Did you find the car?'

'There're about ten thousand blasted cars in here. Get your men spread out and searching. Any more coming?'

'A couple of wagons just behind. The Captain will raise hell when he hears I've pulled out the reserve.'

'If this girl gets killed, the D.A. will raise all the hell McCann will ever want! Get your men into action!'

'Hey! Wait a minute,' Bardin said, putting his hand on Conrad's arm. 'Look who's coming,' and he jerked his thumb towards a tall young fellow with a crew hair-cut, who was wearing a red-patterned shirt outside his trousers. In his arms he held a collection of dolls, vases and boxes of candy. By his side walked a blonde girl in a white sports frock. 'Think those are the two we're looking for?'

'There must be ten thousand punks who're wearing their shirts like that right in this park,' Conrad growled, 'but I'll ask him.' He strode up to Buster Walker. 'You just come from Lennox Avenue?' he demanded, and felt a little shrill crawl up his spine at Buster's look of blank astonishment.

'Why, sure,' Buster said. 'How did you know?'

Conrad looked at Bunty.

'You Miss Boyd?'

'Yes,' Bunty said blankly.

Conrad signalled to Bardin, who joined them.

'These are the two. You'd better handle it, Sam.'

Barkin flashed his buzzer.

'I'm Lieutenant Bardin, City Police. Where's Miss Coleman?'

'Frankie?' Buster gaped at him. 'What do you want her for?'

77

What's the idea?'

'Answer the question and snap it up!' Bardin barked. 'Where is she?'

'We left her in the amusement park.'

'Alone?'

'No, she's with Burt.'

'Burt – who?'

'Why, Burt Stevens, of course. What's all this about?'

Bardin glanced at Conrad, who asked, 'Has this Stevens guy got a birth-mark?'

'That's right. A port-wine stain down the right side of his face.'

'Are you sure his name is Stevens?'

'He said it was. Is there something wrong, then?'

'But you don't know for certain?'

'No, we don't,' Bunty broke in. 'I didn't like the look of him when he came to the house. You see, we were all going to the beach: Frankie, Buster, Terry Lancing and myself. Terry phoned to say he couldn't make it, and was sending his friend Burt to take his place. This boy turned up. He said he was Burt Stevens, but of course as I've never seen him before I don't know for certain if he really is Burt Stevens.'

'Where exactly did you leave Miss Coleman?'

'They were going into the maze,' Buster said.

'What maze?'

'The mirror maze. It's at the end of that avenue, next to the big tent. I wish you'd tell me what this is all about.'

'No time right now,' Conrad said curtly. 'Stay right here. We may need you again.' He turned to Bardin. 'Come on!' He didn't wait to see Bardin's reaction, but broke into a run, and began forcing his way through the crowds towards the big tent.

Bardin paused only long enough to give instructions to his sergeant.

'Get that maze surrounded. Don't let anyone out. You know who to look for. Watch out for Moe. He'll try to shoot his way out.'

He turned and ran after Conrad, leaving Buster and Bunty staring blankly after him.

II

The rays of the sun, striking obliquely into the maze, caught the nickel plate of the automatic and made the gun glitter in Moe's hand.

For a brief moment Frances stared at the pointing gun. Moe's appearance struck terror in her heart. His black suit, his hunched shoulders and his stillness sent a cold chill up her spine. She knew instinctively that he was a killer, and she realized he was about to shoot at her.

78

There was no retreat. She looked desperately along the row of mirrors and saw an opening about ten feet ahead of her. She braced herself and jumped forward. As she moved Moe shot at her.

The crash of gunfire, hemmed in by the confined space, sounded like a bomb exploding. Frances screamed wildly as a mirror right by her smashed into pieces. Fragments of glass flew like shrapnel. A splinter of glass sliced her frock missing her flesh by a hair's breadth.

She bolted down the turning, and ran as she had never run before. Ahead of her stretched an endless path of mirrors. Behind her she heard the soft pad-pad-pad of running feet, coming at a much faster speed than she was going. She flew over the ground, reached another turning and sped round it, cannoning into a mirror as she took the turning.

She tried desperately to regain her balance, then slid down on one knee. As she struggled up, the automatic cracked again and a bullet zipped past her face, smashed a mirror, ricocheted against another mirror and smashed that too.

The narrow path became full of flying fragments of glass. Covering her face with her arms, Frances blundered on down the path, running slower now, her breath coming in hard sobbing gasps.

Moe pulled up short as he reached the pile of broken glass. He knew time was running out. He had been told to kill this girl, and he knew if he failed his own life would be snuffed out. His small hard eyes looked along the path at the racing figure in the blue dress. He watched for a brief moment her slim flying legs and her black silky hair floating out behind her. He brought up the automatic and levelled the sight in the exact centre of her slim young shoulders. His finger curled around the trigger. He couldn't miss now. She was running as straight as a foot rule, and the sun made her pale blue frock a dazzling target.

Then he felt a violent blow against his shoulder, and gunfire crashed in his ears. His gun hand jerked up as his gun went off. He staggered back and looked up.

Standing on one of the walls was the figure of a man, gun in hand. Moe recognized him immediately: the Special Investigator to the District Attorney's office. He flung himself flat as Conrad shot at him again.

Blood was running down Moe's sleeve and down his fingers. He felt a dull burning pain in his right shoulder. He looked along the path, but the girl had now vanished, and he drew back his lips in a snarl of fury.

Conrad was about fifteen yards from where Moe crouched. Two paths divided him from the path in which Moe was. He couldn't see him now, but he knew he was still there. The wall was only six inches thick and it wasn't easy to stand on it, let alone jump the six feet to the next wall.

Already a dozen police were climbing up on to the top of the walls and were spreading out slowly to surround the maze.

'He's here,' Conrad shouted, and pointed to the path where Moe was crouching.

Moe straightened up and fired at Conrad, who felt the slug zip past his face. As he automatically ducked, he lost his balance and fell into one of the mirrored paths.

The police had called for planks and were crossing the paths by laying the planks across the tops of the walls, and then pulling the planks after them.

But by the time they reached the path where Moe had been, he had vanished, leaving only a smear of blood on one of the mirrors to show where he had been.

A police sergeant, squatting on the wall, looked down at Conrad.

'You all right, sir?'

'I'm okay,' Conrad said tersely. 'I'll stay here. See if you can spot him, then direct me on to him. If you see the girl, let me know at once. And watch out!'

The sergeant nodded and started off, bent double, along the narrow wall.

Moe in the next path watched him come, a savage gleam in his eyes. He lifted the automatic and shot the sergeant through the head.

The sergeant threw up his arms and fell heavily into the next path to the one Moe was in.

Gripping his wounded arm, Moe ran down the path, turned a corner and then paused to listen. He saw something blue reflected in one of the mirrors, and his lips came off his teeth in a grinning snarl.

The girl was standing at the next intersection, and as he watched her, he saw her edge into the path where he was, looking away from him.

Moe transferred his gun to his left hand. He lifted the gun and sighted it, aiming at the centre of her young full breasts. The gun sight wobbled as he fought against the increasing feeling of faintness, and he cursed under his breath.

Suddenly a voice sounded over a loudspeaker: a voice that rolled over the maze, amplified like the sound of thunder.

'Miss Coleman! Miss Coleman! Attention please! The police are looking for you. Will you shout so we can find you? Be on your guard. Keep looking to your right and your left. The gunman is still at large!'

Frances caught her breath in a gasp of relief and alarm. She hastily looked to her right, then her left, and her heart skipped a beat when she saw the black suited figure not more than thirty yards from her, the automatic pointing at her. She shut her eyes and screamed wildly. Gunfire crashed against her ear drums. She felt a scorching pain bite into her arm and she felt herself falling.

Moe watched her fall, his eyes alight with vicious triumph. He was aware of the sound of running feet, but he fired again at the still figure as it lay on the ground. The slug smashed the mirror an inch or two above Frances's prostrate body, bringing a shower of glass down on top of her.

The running feet sounded very close now, and Moe swung around.

Conrad pulled up as he reached the corner of the path. He caught a fleeting glimpse of Moe, crouching, with his gun pushed forward, and beyond Moe, the body of a girl in a blue frock. He ducked back as Moe fired at him, the slug throwing a spray of glass splinters dangerously near his face.

Dropping flat, Conrad edged around the corner. Moe spotted him as Conrad lifted his gun and they both fired simultaneously.

Moe's slug cut through the crown of Conrad's hat. Conrad's shot was more accurate. He saw Moe drop his gun, clutch his side and pitch forward on his face.

Two policemen arrived above Conrad and jumped down beside him.

'Watch him,' Conrad cautioned as he stepped into the path where Moe lay.

But Moe didn't move when they reached him. One of the police turned him over on his back.

Moe's white face was twisted into a snarl of pain and fear. His sightless eyes stared up at the blue sky. Blood soaked the front of his coat. Even as Conrad looked down at him, Moe's jaw dropped and the last of his breath came through his open mouth in a tired, hissing sigh.

III

Naked, her body still rose-pink from the vigorous towelling she had given it, Dolores sat on a stool in one of the luxurious shower rooms in the Paradise Club and carefully dried between her toes with a piece of cotton wool.

She had just come in from a swim, and following her usual practice, she had taken a shower to wash the salt water from her skin.

Her expression was thoughtful and her almond-shaped eyes had lost their usual alive gleam and were cloudy with angry anxiety.

An hour ago Jack Maurer had abruptly told her he was going on a fishing trip; destination unknown, and he would be away probably for three weeks to a month. Even now as she glanced out of the window that overlooked the ocean she could still see the yacht as a minute speck in the horizon.

She had guessed Maurer had gone on Abe's advice, and because of June Arnot.

She had known about June ever since the affair had started. She had watched the affair progress, and had felt her own power over Maurer weaken as the months passed. She knew her throne was tottering. It gave her no satisfaction that June was dead. If it wasn't June, then it would be someone else. She knew that Gloria Lyle, a second-rate movie actress with a bust like a pouter pigeon's and the morals of an alley cat, had gone aboard the yacht, ten minutes before Maurer had left the club for the harbour.

June's murder had shocked Dolores. To her it was the writing on the wall. When Maurer came back, she was sure that her reign would end. The odds were that he wouldn't bother to divorce her; he would get rid of her as brutally as he had got rid of June.

Dolores had no illusions about Maurer. She knew he thought no more of taking a life than he thought of drinking a Scotch and soda.

She had been his wife now for four years, and the wonder was she had lasted so long. It was only because she had never given him a chance to complain, never looked at any other man, that she had lasted. She knew he was growing impatient for his freedom. He wouldn't dare divorce her. She knew too much about his business affairs to risk her being free from his watchful influence. She was sure that before long, probably when he returned, he would tell one of his hoods what to do, and she would die. She would have a car smash or a shooting accident; she might get carried out to sea when she was bathing. There were many convenient ways in which she could die: convenient for Maurer, of course.

She reached out for a cigarette, lit it and released two thin trails of smoke down her finely shaped nostrils.

She wasn't alarmed, but she realized she would have to do something if she were going to survive. Already her quick wits and her shrewd razor-sharp mind had created a possible solution. Now Maurer was out of the way, she must make immediate use of her opportunities.

She stood up and walked over to the wall mirror and surveyed herself. She smoothed her hands down her long, sleek flanks as she studied her body with thoughtful narrowed eyes. She thought of Gloria Lyle with her short legs and ridiculous bust. What did Maurer see in her, she wondered. What could he see in her? He was no better than an alley cat himself in search of any new sensation with an animal urge for something fresh, no matter how ugly it was.

Shrugging her shoulders, she began to dress, her mind still occupied. Her position was dangerous. She had thought of taking her jewellery and the clothes he had once showered on her and trying to hide herself somewhere, but she knew there was nowhere safe from his long-reaching arm.

She snapped a garter into place, smoothed her dress over her solid hips and walked out of the shower room and along the passage to the cocktail bar.

Abe Gollowitz sat on a high stool, sipping a martini. His fat buttocks spread over the stool, making the stool look like a grotesque mushroom.

She stood in the doorway, looking at him. In him was her only hope, and she felt a little shiver of disgust run through her. Pot-bellied, oily old men were her only refuge, she thought: the only men who had the power and the money that were essential to her way of life. If only Abe were like that flash, hard-muscled Seigel. She had often wondered what Seigel would be like as a lover. Several times she had been tempted to experiment, but she knew the danger. Once she had made Seigel her lover, her life would be hanging on a thread.

She studied Gollowitz as he sipped his martini, unaware of her presence. She could do anything with him, and she had long known he lived for the day when he would take over Maurer's position. But would he be strong enough to protect her when the time came?

'Hello, Abe,' she said, coming up to him and smiling her brilliant, sensual smile. 'So Jack's gone.'

He hurriedly slid off the stool, his fat, dark face lighting up.

'Yes, he's gone,' he said, his eyes undressing her. 'How beautiful you look, Dolly. How do you manage it?'

She shrugged and climbed up on a stool next to his.

'Oh, I don't know. Jack doesn't notice it any longer, Abe.'

He scowled.

'Jack doesn't appreciate the best things in life.'

'You know he's got that Lyle woman on board?' Dolores said, taking the ice-cold martini the barman gave her.

Gollowitz stiffened.

'I had heard. It's no business of mine.'

'Abe, is Jack in trouble?'

'No, no, nothing like that. He suddenly decided . . .'

'Please, Abe, tell me. You're the only one I have now who I can trust. He is in trouble, isn't he?'

Gollowitz glanced over his shoulder to make sure no one was within earshot.

'He could be. We thought it wiser for him to be out of reach – for the time being.'

'It's because of June?'

Gollowitz hesitated, then nodded.

'How will the organization react, Abe? Could this be the end of Jack?'

'This is dangerous talk, Dolly, but since you ask me, I can only tell you I don't know. He's not paying much attention to the organization these past months. He has said something about making a clean break.'

This was news to Dolores, but she was careful not to let Gollowitz see her startled surprise.

'I know. He's said something about that to me. Isn't it unwise, Abe?'

'I think so.'

This time it was her turn to hesitate, but she knew if she didn't seize every opportunity it might be too late when Maurer returned.

Lowering her voice, she said, 'If anything happened to Jack, you would take over, wouldn't you?'

Gollowitz eyed her uneasily. He was on perilous ground, but he was also aware that Dolores's present position was still more perilous.

'It would depend on the organization. They may have someone else in mind.'

She shook her head.

'That's not likely.' She looked up suddenly, her green eyes an open invitation. 'If you did take over, Abe, would you have anything for me?'

She watched him trying to keep calm. She already knew the answer before he said, 'If I took over, Dolly, you would have nothing to worry about.'

She gave a pleased little smile.

'I have plenty to worry about now, Abe.'

Gollowitz nodded. He restrained himself from reaching for her hand. He was aware that several people in the bar were watching them.

'Yes, and so have I.'

The bell of the telephone standing on the bar rang sharply. The barman picked up the receiver, listened, said, 'Yes, sir,' and replaced the receiver. He turned to Gollowitz. 'Mr. Seigel's asking for you, sir. He's in your office. It's urgent.'

Gollowitz scowled. Couldn't Seigel hold down his job for ten minutes without bothering him? he thought as he got off his stool. He'd have to go. No sense in risking trouble at the beginning of his reign.

'That guy can't blow his own nose without me helping him,' he said, smiling at Dolores. 'Perhaps we might have lunch together in twenty minutes?'

She shook her head.

'Better not, Abe. Too many spies around,' She gave him a warning look. 'I'm going home now.' She slid off the stool. 'One of these days we'll have lunch together. I'm looking forward to the time, Abe, when there will be no restrictions between us.' Her look was full of meaning as she smiled a good-bye.

He watched her walk across the bar to the door, his eyes feasting on her, watching the slow rolling movement of her hips under the thin material of her frock as she walked, her broad, square shoulders and her long, tapering legs. He felt sick with desire for her.

Seigel was pacing up and down when Gollowitz entered his office. His face was pale and his breath stank of whisky as he approached Gollowitz.

'They've got the girl!' he said breathlessly.

Gollowitz stiffened.

'What do you mean? Who's got the girl?'

'Goddamn it! The police have got her! Those two blasted punks made a mess of it!'

Gollowitz felt a chill run up his fat spine. Failure! The moment his hand was on the helm, the ship floundered. What would the organization think of him? This might kill his chances of ever succeeding Maurer! Cold, vicious rage seized him.

'But Jack told you to wipe her out!' he cried shrilly. 'Do you mean to tell me she isn't wiped out?'

Seigel backed away. He had never seen Gollowitz look like this; he looked now as dangerous and as crazy as Maurer could look when things went wrong.

'They trapped her in a maze in the amusement park. The police must have been tipped. They arrived before they could find the little bitch. Moe was killed.'

'Are you telling me the police have got her after what Maurer told you?' Gollowitz screamed, his fat fists clenched and his face contorted with rage and fear. 'Didn't you hear what McCann said? Goddamn it! What's the matter with you?'

'I warned Mr. Maurer,' Seigel snarled. 'We had no time to case the joint. It blew up. She was surrounded by people. The boys couldn't get near her. I warned him!'

'Shut up!' Gollowitz cried. 'I don't want to listen to your weak, spineless excuses. Maurer said she was to be hit, and you've failed to carry out an order!'

'Gleb and Weiner failed to carry out the order,' Seigel said, his face chalk white.

'And you're responsible! What are you doing about it? What the hell are you doing here, making excuses? Get after her! Wipe her out! I don't care how you do it, but do it!'

'The D.A.'s got her,' Seigel said. 'We can't get at her. That's the one place we can't get into.'

Gollowitz struggled to control his rage and fear. He realized he wasn't behaving as the boss. Maurer wouldn't act this way; yelling, swearing and raving. He would have a plan ready to rectify the mistake. He pulled himself together with an effort and walked unsteadily to an arm-chair and sat down.

'If she saw Jack at that Arnot woman's house, we're finished,' he said, as if talking to himself. 'Everything will go. The organization will be wiped out. But did she see anything? Can we afford to gamble on what she saw or didn't see?'

'Of course we can't,' Seigel said. 'We've got to stop her talking. Maybe McCann can handle it for us.'

Gollowitz grimaced.

'McCann? He only thinks of himself. No. We've got to handle this ourselves. Where is she exactly, do you know?'

'They took her to the D.A.'s office. She's somewhere in the building.'

Gollowitz thought for a long moment. Then he looked up sharply.

'You said Gleb was killed. What happened to Weiner?'

Seigel shrugged.

'I don't know. He disappeared.'

Gollowitz felt the blood drain out of his face.

'You don't know?' he repeated, starting out of his chair.

Seigel stared at him.

'He'll turn up. I'll kick hell out of the punk when I do catch up with him!'

'You goddamn fool!' Gollowitz shouted, his face twitching. 'That girl will give a description of him. A blind man could find the punk with that stain on his face. The police will pick him up quick enough, and if he talks we are really sunk. Don't you see that? All the girl needs to hang the lot of us is corroboration, and to save his skin Weiner will corroborate till he is black in the face. He got his orders from you, didn't he? Well, they'll slap an attempted murder charge on you if Weiner talks! And he will talk, make no mistake about that!' He waved his fat fists in the air. 'Get after him! Find and silence him! Leave the girl to me! I'll handle her, but get after Weiner. Put every man you've got after him. Go yourself!'

Seigel stood rooted, gaping at the screaming, gesticulating figure, then he realized Gollowitz was talking sense.

'I'll get him!' he said, and snatched open a drawer in his desk. He took out a .45 automatic and shoved it in his hip pocket. 'I'll get him – I'll get him myself,' and he went out of the room at a run.

IV

Conrad had never seen the D.A. look so excited as he listened to Conrad's story of the killing of Moe and the finding of Frances Coleman.

'Where's the girl now?' Forest asked when Conrad had completed his tale.

'On the tenth floor, sir. Miss Fielding and a nurse are with her. Jackson and Norris are guarding the door. There are three police officers taking care of the elevator and the stairs. She's safe enough for the time being.'

'Was she hurt?'

'More scared than hurt. She had a nasty cut on her arm from flying glass, but otherwise, apart from shock she's all right.'

Forest rubbed his hands.

'When can you talk to her?'

'I'm waiting for the okay from Doc. Holmes. He said as soon as she has had a rest I can see her.'

'Fine. Now how about Weiner?'

'I don't know how he slipped through the cordon. There was so much excitement cornering Gleb he was unfortunately overlooked. No one seems to have noticed him. Every man on the force is hunting for him now.'

'We've got to find him before Maurer's mob does,' Forest said grimly. 'If he talks, Paul, we've got that bunch just where we want them, and they know it. His life's not worth a dime right now.'

Conrad nodded.

'We can't do more than we're doing now. It's a question of time. He can't get far with that birth-mark. The local radio station is broadcasting a description of him. They are interrupting programmes to ask for all information concerning him to be telephoned to us immediately.'

A buzzer sounded on Forest's desk. He picked up the inter-office phone, listened, raised his eyebrows, grunted and hung up.

'Seems we have started something,' he said with evident satisfaction. 'Maurer's skipped. His yacht left two hours ago. He's supposed to be on a fishing trip, destination unknown.'

'Putting himself out of our reach for the time being,' Conrad said. 'Well, if we get the evidence we want, we'll pick him up fast enough. Looks as if we're on the right track at last, doesn't it, sir?'

'If only this girl saw him!'

'We'll know before long.' Conrad was controlling his own impatience with an effort. 'Do you want to talk to her yourself?'

Forest shook his head.

'You handle it, Paul. You have a lighter touch than I have. I don't know why it is, but I seem to scare the pants off people when I talk to them.'

'Only if they happen to have a guilty conscience.' Conrad got to his feet. 'I'll have a written report for you by this afternoon. I may as well go upstairs and see what's happening.'

'Let me know as soon as they pick up Weiner.'

'I will, sir.'

Conrad took the elevator to the tenth floor. Jackson and Norris sat on straight-backed chairs either side of a door at the far end of the passage. Both of them nursed Thompson guns. Conrad was leaving nothing to chance. He realized Frances could be a vitally important witness, and Maurer's mob would stop at nothing to silence her.

'Any news yet?' he asked Jackson.

'Doc's just gone, sir. All quiet here.'

Conrad rapped on the door which was opened by Madge.

'I was just going to call you. Doc, says you can talk to her now.'

'How is she?'

'A bit jumpy. I don't wonder at it. She's had a bad time.'

'Yes.'

'She's in the far room,' Madge said. 'Do you want me?'

'Not right now. If she's ready to make a statement, I'll call you.'

As he was speaking the nurse came out of the inner room and nodded to him.

'Don't let her talk too much. She needs a good sleep.'

'I won't keep her long,' Conrad said, and aware his heart was beginning to beat unevenly, he walked into the inner room.

Frances lay on a couch with a rug thrown over her. She was very pale, and her big dark eyes looked at Conrad with uneasy anxiety.

He was aware of a sudden tightening of his throat as he looked down at her. Her face in the photograph had fascinated him, and he realized with a sense of shock that he could be in love with her. It was fantastic, of course, as he hadn't even spoken to her as yet, but the feeling was there, and for a moment he remained still, unable to collect his thoughts or to say anything.

She lay motionless, watching him, and he pulled himself together with an effort.

'I expect Miss Fielding told you I wanted to talk to you,' he said, and his voice was husky. 'I'm Paul Conrad, special investigator to the District Attorney's office. How are you feeling, Miss Coleman?'

' I – I'm all right, thank you,' she said in a small voice. 'I want to go home.'

'We'll fix all that in a little while,' he said soothingly. 'There are a few questions I want to ask you first.' He pulled up a chair and sat down near her. 'I'm not going to keep you long because the nurse said you should have some sleep.'

'I don't want to sleep. I just want to go home.'

'Have you any relations, Miss Coleman? Someone you would like me to get into touch with to let them know where you are?'

He saw a scared expression jump into her eyes, and she looked quickly away from him.

'I haven't any relations.'

'No one at all?'

'No.'

He suddenly realized that this interview might not be as straightforward as he had imagined.

'Miss Coleman, I believe you called on Miss Arnot on the 9th, around seven o'clock.'

Her dark eyes flickered uneasily over his face, then moved away.

'Yes, I did.'

88

'Did you see Miss Arnot?'

'Yes.'

Conrad was aware now that the palms of his hands were moist and his heart was beginning to bang against his ribs.

'May I ask why you wanted to see her?'

'I – I would rather not say.' A faint flush rose to her face and she looked anxiously around the room as if she were trying to find a way of escape.

'Well I won't press that question. You did see Miss Arnot?'

'Yes.'

'How long were you with her?'

'Oh, about five minutes. Not longer.'

'Do you know why I am asking these questions?' Conrad said gently, his eyes on her face.

'I – I suppose it's because of Miss Arnot's death.'

'That's right: because of her murder.'

He saw her flinch, and bite her under-lip.

'What did you do when you left Miss Arnot?'

'Why, I came away.'

'Did you walk down the drive?'

'Yes.'

Conrad took out his handkerchief and wiped his hands. The next question would decide Maurer's fate.

'While you were in the grounds of the estate, did you see anyone, apart from the guard or Miss Arnot?'

'I – I don't think so.'

She was looking down at the pattern of the rug that covered her, and Conrad stared at her, a feeling of sick disappointment coming over him.

'You're sure of that?'

'Yes.'

Why didn't she look at him? he wondered. Could she be lying?

'Miss Coleman, this is vitally important. I want you to think carefully before you answer my next question. You know Miss Arnot has been murdered. She was killed on the 9th, a few minutes after seven o'clock: at the time you were there. We had hoped you might have seen the killer. Are you absolutely sure you didn't see anyone except the guard and Miss Arnot?'

There was a long pause. He noticed she was trembling under the rug and her hands had turned into small white knuckled fists.

'Yes,' she said at last.

'You mean you didn't see anyone?'

'I didn't see anyone.'

He looked down at his hands, his mind busy. If she had looked him in the face when she said she hadn't seen anyone he would have instantly believed her, but the fact she couldn't meet his eyes made him doubt whether she were telling the truth.

He studied her. She was still staring down at the rug, her hands still clenched into small tight fists.

'Did you arrive at Miss Arnot's place by car?' he asked quietly.

She looked up, startled, and her eyes told him she was searching for a trap in the question.

'I – I walked.'

'It's a long walk. It must be three miles from the boulevard.' She flushed.

'I – I like walking.'

'Did you see anyone as you were coming from Dead End on the sea road? Anyone in a car, Miss Coleman?'

'No.'

'And yet that was the way the killer had to come,' he pointed out patiently. 'There is no other approach to Dead End except by that road. It's odd, isn't it, that you were within a quarter of an hour of Miss Arnot's murder and yet you didn't see anyone?'

She didn't say anything, but her face went whiter and she looked anxiously towards the door as if hoping someone would come in and stop his questioning.

In spite of the growing conviction that she wasn't telling the truth, Conrad felt sorry for her and he had to force himself to continue to badger her.

'When you talked with Miss Arnot, did she give you any idea that she was expecting someone?' he asked.

He could see the girl was growing tense, and her trembling increased.

'I don't know anything about it,' she said in a tight small voice. 'Please stop asking me questions. I – I'm not feeling well. I want to go home.'

'That's all right, Miss Coleman,' he said and smiled. 'I'm sorry to be a nuisance. You have some sleep. We'll talk about this tomorrow.'

'But I don't want to!' she cried fiercely. 'I want to be left alone. I don't want to go to sleep! I want to go home!'

'I'm afraid you will have to stay here until tomorrow,' Conrad said as gently as he could. 'One of the gunmen who tried to shoot you is still at large. We can't let you go until he is caught.'

'But he wouldn't hurt me,' she blurted out, sitting bolt upright. 'He said he wouldn't and I believe him. This is just an excuse to keep me here! I'm not going to stay! You can't keep me here! You've no right to keep me here!' Her voice was rising hysterically, and Conrad got to his feet, a little alarmed at the wild trapped look in her eyes.

The door opened and the nurse came in quickly.

'Perhaps you had better leave her to me,' she said, crossing the room.

Frances threw the rug off and struggled to her feet.

'I won't stay here! You can't make me stay!' she cried wildly, and took a few tottering steps to the door.

Conrad saw all trace of colour suddenly leave her face and her eyes rolled back. He jumped forward and caught her as she crumpled to the floor in a faint.

v

Sam's street saloon was an old-fashioned honky-tonk on the waterfront, frequented by dockers, sailors and prostitutes. Its long, low-ceilinged room had high-backed booths along one side where Sam's clients could talk and drink without being seen or disturbed. The other side of the room was given up to a long S-shaped bar that glittered with mirrors and lighted advertising signs.

Pete Weiner sat in the last booth at the far end of the room where he could watch the swing doors of the saloon. A bottle of Scotch and a glass stood before him and an ash-tray piled high with butts indicated the time he had been in the booth.

Pete felt cold, frightened and sick. Already he was regretting what he had done. In Frances's company he had been brave enough, but now he was on his own, a slow chill of terror was creeping over him.

He knew the word would have gone out by now, and the streets would be death traps. But what was he to do? He was short of money, and he thought longingly of the five hundred dollars he had in his room. He dared not go back there to collect the money. His room would be the first place they would go to, and one of them would be waiting for him at this very moment.

He pulled out a few crumpled bills from his trousers pocket and checked them. He had fifteen dollars and a few cents. He hadn't even a car. The railroad depot would be watched. If only he knew of some place where he could hole up for a few days! Without money he was helpless.

He shifted his mind away from his immediate troubles and thought of Frances. He had gone after her when she had run away from him, but he had quickly lost himself in the maze, and lost her, too. He had run on and on blindly until suddenly he had found himself at the exit. He had had no intention of getting out. He had wanted to kill Moe, but instead he had found himself out among a vast crowd that instantly hemmed him in as they gaped at the arriving police who swarmed up the walls of the maze and spread out, guns in hand.

Pete had heard the shooting, and had stood in the crowd, waiting, sure Moe had killed Frances. It wasn't until he had seen an ambulance arrive and watched Moe's dead body loaded on board and had seen Frances carried to a waiting police car that he had thought of his own safety.

He got away from the amusement park as quickly as he could, and knowing how quickly the mob swung into action, he had taken refuge in Sam's saloon.

The odds were he had only a few hours longer to live. The moment he showed himself on the streets he would be done for. He knew the technique well enough. A fast-moving car would pass him, and he would go down under a hail of bullets.

He lit a cigarette, drank a little of the whisky and wiped his sweating face with the back of his hand. He couldn't stay in the saloon all day. If only he could find somewhere to hide until darkness came! It was just possible, under the cloak of darkness, he might get out of town, but in broad daylight with this accursed birth-mark to give him away, he wouldn't last ten minutes before they were on to him.

A shadow fell across the table, and he felt his heart leap in his chest. His right hand remained as if paralysed on the table, although his mind was frantically willing it to flash to his gun. He looked up.

A young girl, corn-coloured hair piled high on top of her head, wearing a red sweater and a white skirt, smiled down at him.

'Hello, bright eyes,' she said, leaning forward, her hands on the table and her breasts heavy against the thin casing of her sweater. 'Want a little company?'

He stared at her, trying to recover from the shock. What was the matter with him? He hadn't even seen her approach. Suppose it had been Dutch or one of the mob? He would have been dead by now without even having a chance to hit back.

'I have a place just around the corner,' the girl went on. 'We could have fun.' She smiled, showing small white teeth, but her eyes were hard and calculating as she looked down at him.

Pete realized the advantages of going with her. Once in her place he could hold a gun on her and wait until darkness came. But dare he leave the saloon? What did she mean: *just round the corner*? It might be a few yards or it might be a few hundred yards. These girls said anything to get you to go with them.

'Where's your place?' he asked, trying to keep his voice steady.

'Just across the street, darling,' she said. 'Just at the corner. Will you come?'

'Well, all right,' he said, and stood up. He went over to the bar and paid for his drinks.

The barman gave him a long hard stare. There was something in the way the barman eyed him that frightened Pete. He walked quickly down the long room with the girl who held his arm.

'You seem nervous, honey,' the girl said, smiling at him. 'Don't tell me I'm your first?'

He didn't bother to answer as he stepped into the hot sunshine, feeling suddenly naked and horribly vulnerable on the bright, noisy waterfront.

'Where do we go?' he asked anxiously, his eyes searching the crowded scene, hunting for a familiar face.

'Just down here,' the girl said. She walked at his side with small mincing steps, balancing herself unsteadily on her three-inch heels. 'You'll like it. I've got a radio. If you make it worth my while I'll dance for you. Most of my friends like to watch me dance.'

She was leading him away from the waterfront towards a narrow dark street of tall sordid-looking houses.

He hurried her along, looking back from time to time over his shoulder, ready to break into a run at the slightest suspicious movement.

'Here we are,' the girl said, pausing outside a house at the corner of the street. 'I said it wasn't far, didn't I?'

She climbed the steps, opened her handbag and took out her latch key.

He followed her into a dimly lit, shabby hall, and as he shut the front door he drew in a tight gasping breath of relief. He had made it! He was at least safe now until dark. He had no qualms about handling the girl. She wouldn't start anything when he showed her his gun.

She began to climb the stairs, and he followed closely. When they reached the second-floor landing, she stopped outside a door facing the head of the stairs.

'This is it,' she said, and turned the handle of the door. 'Oh, damn! My fool maid has locked me out again. She's always doing it. Just wait here, darling, while I run down and get the spare key. I keep it in my mailbox.'

She patted his arm, giving him a bright, fixed smile, then she started down the stairs.

Pete took out his handkerchief and wiped his face and neck. He fumbled for a cigarette, lit it and flicked out the match. Then he moved over to the banister rail and looked down into the hall, two flights below.

The girl had just reached the hall. She paused and looked up. Their eyes met, and Pete felt a cold wave of fear sweep through him when he saw the scared look on the girl's face. Instinctively he realized he had walked into a trap.

What a mad fool he had been to have accepted her on her face value!

The mob wouldn't want to walk into Sam's bar and kill him in front of witnesses. They would fix it to get him somewhere alone, and through her they had got him alone!

His hand flew to the inside of his coat as he heard a key turn in the lock behind him. He spun round in time to see the door to the girl's apartment was opening slowly.

He didn't hesitate. Swinging up the gun, he fired, aiming to the right and just a little above the door handle. The slug smashed through the door, spraying wood splinters, and Pete heard a gasping groan, then the sound of a heavy fall behind the door.

He spun around and threw himself down the stairs, taking three stairs at a time. He ran blindly along the short passage to the head of the stairs leading to the hall. He took these in two jumps, arriving in the hall with a crash that shook the house.

The girl, her eyes wide with fright, crouched against the wall, her hands crossed over her breasts, her painted mouth wide open in a soundless scream.

He jumped to the front door, stopped as he saw through the glass panels, two men coming up the steps.

He recognized them: Goetz and Buzz Conforti, two of Maurer's expert killers. He sprang back, his heart contracting, then turned and retreated down the passage that ran to the right of the hall.

He reached the girl as she dived for the stairs, grabbed hold of her, turned her so her back was to him, and keeping her against him, his left arm round her waist so she was shielding his body, he continued to back down the passage.

'Scream or try to get away and I'll kill you,' he panted. 'Is there a way out at the back?'

'Let me go!' she gasped, digging her nails into his wrist.

He gave her a chopping blow on her shoulder with the gun barrel, making her squeal.

'Is there a way out at the back?'

'Yes.'

The front door burst open and Goetz jumped into the hall.

Pete took a hurried shot at him. The girl screamed wildly as she felt the heat of the gun-flash. Goetz dropped down on one knee, his dark, vicious face creased in a snarl.

'Don't shoot!' the girl screamed, waving her hands imploringly as Goetz swung up a .45.

Pete continued to back away, dragging the girl with him. He saw Goetz trying to get the sight of his gun on to him, but Pete kept his head down, hoisting the girl higher so she completely concealed him.

She kicked out wildly, her shoes flying off and her white skirt riding above her thighs.

Pete's back thudded against a door. He fired again at Goetz, a near miss this time, for Goetz's hat flew off.

Goetz's finger squeezed the trigger and the heavy gun went off. He fired three times. The bullets slammed into the girl's writhing body. Pete could feel the shock of them.

The girl stiffened so nearly jerked herself out of his grip, then she went limp; the sudden dead weight almost pulling him off balance.

He groped behind him, found a door handle, turned it and pulled the door open.

Conforti had crawled into the hall by now. As he lifted his gun, Pete fired at him. Not waiting to see the result of his shot, he threw the body of the girl from him, jumped back through the open doorway, slammed the door and ran madly down a small yard, heaved himself over a wooden fence and landed, sobbing for breath, in a twisting, narrow alley.

He sprinted down the alley, hearing the sound of foot-falls behind him. He ran for some hundred yards, following the twisting alley, keeping close to the wooden fence.

Ahead of him he could see the main street with its traffic and crowds. He somehow managed to increase his speed and reached the street just as Goetz turned the last bend in the alley.

Goetz half raised his gun as he caught sight of Pete, but lowered it as Pete vanished round the corner.

Pete dashed through the crowds that thronged the street, pushing people out of his way. He had concealed his gun in his coat pocket, but people stared after him, sensing something was wrong, startled by his sweating, frightened face.

He was out in the open now. Any second a car would overtake him, and he would be cut down. He paused at the edge of the kerb, his chest heaving, while he looked to right and left. He saw a taxi, and he waved frantically. The taxi swung, to the kerb and pulled up beside him.

'The park,' Pete gasped, and wrenched open the cab door.

Hands grabbed his arms from behind and he gave a cry of terror as he looked around. Two big patrolmen had hold of him.

'Take it easy,' one of them said. 'We want you, Weiner. Get his rod, Jack.'

The other cop expertly found Pete's gun and shoved it into his hip pocket.

'We'll take the cab,' the first cop said. 'Headquarters, bud, and snap it up.'

Out of the corner of his eye, Pete caught sight of a big black car bearing down on the taxi.

'Look out!' he yelled, and wrenched himself free from the cop who was holding him. He flung himself face down on the floor of the cab as the black car swept past.

Above the noise of the traffic came the violent hammering of a machine-gun.

The cab rocked crazily under the impact of the hail of bullets. One of the cops was caught across his face by a burst from the machine-gun. His head and face dissolved into a mess of blood and smashed bone.

The other cop threw himself down on top of Pete. The taxi driver was caught by the tail end of the burst. The shock of the bullets smashing into him lifted him out of the cab and flung him on the sidewalk.

The crowd on the street broke and ran in all directions, yelling and screaming. Several of them were caught by the burst and lay in huddled heaps on the sidewalk and the street.

The black car swept on and disappeared around the corner. The big cop covering Pete got unsteadily to his feet.

'The bastards!' he said through clenched teeth. 'The god-damn bastards!'

He dragged Pete out of the cab.

'Come on, you!' he snarled, and ran Pete across the sidewalk into the sheltering porch of a store. He wedged Pete into a corner between two plate-glass windows and stood in front of him, gun in hand.

'Get me inside!' Pete shouted excitedly. 'You goddamn fool! Do you imagine glass'll stop bullets?'

'Shut your trap!' the cop snarled. 'There ain't going to be no bullets.'

Even as he spoke the black car made its second run. The crowds on the street, seeing it coming, flattened on the sidewalks or dashed madly into the shops and stores for shelter.

Cars, swerving to avoid the black car that came straight down the middle of the street, mounted the kerbs. One car crashed through a plate-glass window.

'Look out!' Pete screamed, and shoving the cop with all his strength gained enough room to lie flat.

The cop, as brave and as stupid as a charging rhino, started firing at the car as it swept past. The answering burst of fire from the concealed machine-gun was devastating. The cop seemed to fly to pieces as the whip lash of bullets tore open his chest and flung him back on to Pete.

The car braked and pulled up. Goetz and Conforti spilled out of the car, their faces glistening with sweat, their mouths wide open with soundless yelling.

They had been told to get Pete at all costs, and they were carrying out orders.

Somewhere in the porch of the shop, under the dead cop and the heap of smashed glass, was Pete, and they knew it.

Conforti held the Thompson. Goetz had a gun in each hand.

Conforti started spraying the porch with bullets as he ran towards it.

Pete saw the line of bullets hammering into the sidewalk, spraying chips of concrete, and advancing like a carpet of death towards him.

He pulled the dead cop over him, held on to his belt, feeling the dead cop's blood dripping on his face, and he shut his eyes.

He felt the dead body kick and jerk as bullets smashed across the dead legs. Then a new sound started his heart beating again : the sound of police sirens and the sharp crisp crack of police automatics.

Goetz, swearing, spun around as three police cars screamed down the street towards him. He raised his gun, but the first car, accelerating, hit him like an express train and flung him high into the air. He dropped like a half-filled sack of corn on to the sidewalk.

Conforti didn't look back. He ran into the porch.

Pete caught a glimpse of Conforti's legs as he bent over the dead cop. He tried to squeeze himself into the ground, clinging with all his strength to the dead cop's belt.

Conforti spotted him and his teeth showed in a triumphant grinning snarl. He dragged the cop away with Pete still clinging to the cop's belt.

'Get away!' Pete screamed, trying to hide himself behind the cop's body. 'Don't do it!'

Conforti lifted the Thompson. The barrel swung up. Pete stared at the sight as it covered his face. His eyes started out of his head. He saw Conforti's finger whiten as Conforti took in the slack on the trigger.

Then guns cracked behind Conforti.

Pete saw the sudden look of agony come over the thin rat-like face. He saw the eyes go lifeless. The Thompson jerked up as the dying hand stiffened and began firing as the dying finger automatically tightened on the trigger.

Then Conforti dropped the gun, took one step and pitched forward on his face.

A moment later Pete was surrounded by grim-faced policemen.

CHAPTER SIX

THE fat desk sergeant shifted his bulk on his creaking chair and nodded his bullet-shaped head.

'The Lieutenant's questioning him now,' he said. 'He's expecting you, isn't he?'

'Yes, he's expecting me,' Conrad said. 'What's he doing – pushing Weiner around?'

A dreamy expression came over the sergeant's face.

'Well, he ain't exactly combing his hair,' he returned. 'Three of our best boys got killed through him.'

Conrad swung around, crossed the charge room in three strides and went quickly along the passage, down a short flight of stone steps, then to a door at the end of another passage. He turned the handle and pushed the door open.

Pete sat in a hard, bright circle of light. The small room was full of tobacco smoke and the smell of sweat and dust. It was also full of bull-necked, red-faced detectives. Bardin was standing in front of Pete, and as Conrad entered the room, Bardin drew back his arm and hit Pete across his face with the flat of his hand. The sound of the blow was like the bursting of a paper bag, and Pete's head jerked back and then forward.

Blood ran down to his chin from a cut lip. His dark eyes, narrowed and full of hate, looked up at Bardin without flinching.

'So you've never heard of Maurer,' Bardin sneered. 'Don't you read the newspapers?'

'Only the sports column,' Pete said through gritted teeth.

Bardin swung his arm again, but Conrad reached out and caught his wrist.

'Take it easy, Sam,' he said quietly.

Bardin swung around. There was a dull, cold expression in his eyes as he stared at Conrad.

'That's right,' he said with savage bitterness. 'Take it easy. Never mind the guys who got killed. Never mind about their widows or their kids. Take it easy. What do you expect me to do? Put my arms around this little rat and suckle him?'

Conrad released Bardin's wrist.

'Sorry to break up the session, but I want this guy.' He pulled out a sheet of paper and tossed it on to the desk. 'This will cover you, Sam. Want me to sign for him?'

Bardin's face grew dark with congested blood. He picked up the paper, glanced at it and tossed it back on the desk.

'What are you going to do with him?' he asked in a hard, rasping voice. 'Tuck him up in bed with a radio and four good meals a day?'

Conrad looked at Bardin steadily and didn't say anything. Bardin gave a heavy snort, walked around to his desk, took out a receipt book, wrote savagely, spluttering ink and shoved it across to Conrad.

'Okay, take the little rat. He's not talking. He knows nothing. He's never heard of Maurer. He wasn't within a mile of the amusement park. If you think you'll get anywhere with him without beating the guts out of him, you've got another think coming.'

'I want him in a wagon and escort,' Conrad said. 'Fix it for me, will you, Sam?'

Bardin got up, nodded to one of the detectives who went out. Then he walked over to Pete and glared down at him. 'You'll be back, Weiner. Don't imagine you're going to have it nice and easy just because the D.A.'s interested in you. You'll be back, and we'll cook up something for you.' He swung his hand and caught Pete a smashing backhanded blow that knocked him over backwards, taking the chair with him.

Pete sprawled on the floor, his eyes dazed, his hand holding his puffy right cheek.

Conrad turned away. He didn't approve of these methods, but he didn't blame Bardin. To lose three good policemen in saving the life of a worthless young gangster was something to make any Lieutenant bitter.

Pete got unsteadily to his feet and slumped against the wall.

No one said anything. No one moved. Minutes dragged by, then the door opened and the detective came back.

'Okay. At the side entrance, sir.'

'Take him,' Bardin said to Conrad with a gesture of disgust. 'And don't forget, when you're through with him, we want him back.'

'You'll get him,' Conrad said. He looked at Pete. 'Come on, Weiner.'

Pete crossed the room. He felt as if he were walking through a forest of menacing giants as he weaved his way around the big detectives who made no attempt to move out of his way and who watched him with hot, intent eyes.

A heavy steel-walled wagon stood at the side entrance in a big enclosed yard. Police stood around with riot guns at the ready. Six speed cops sat astride their motor-cycles, their engines ticking over, their hard, sun-burned faces watchful.

Pete climbed into the wagon and Conrad followed him. The steel door slammed shut and Conrad pushed home two massive bolts.

'Sit down,' he said curtly.

Pete sat down. He heard the motor-cycle engines roar, and then the wagon jogged into life and began its guarded run to the City Hall.

Conrad took out a pack of cigarettes, shook out two, handed

one to Pete, lit it and then lit his own.

'What are you going to do when a bondsman posts bail for you, Weiner?' he asked quietly.

Pete looked up sharply.

'You're charging me with murder, aren't you? That's a non-bailable offence.'

Conrad looked at him thoughtfully.

'Maybe I won't charge you with murder. Suppose I charge you with consorting with known criminals? You'll be out on bail within a couple of hours.'

He saw Pete change colour.

'I don't want to go out on bail.'

'Why not?'

Pete didn't say anything. He stared down at the handcuffs around his wrists, feeling sweat start out on his face.

'You're not scared to be out on bail, are you?'

'I'm not talking,' Pete said.

'You'll change your mind. Think it over. Once you're out of my hands, Weiner, I wouldn't give a dime for your life. I'm not protecting you unless you're going to do some talking.'

'I don't know anything about anything,' Pete said sullenly, and shifted around so his back was half turned to Conrad.

'You stupid fool!' Conrad said. 'The girl will identify you. Do you think you can get out of this? You were sent to kill her weren't you? You acted on Maurer's orders.'

Pete didn't say anything.

'You'll have to talk sooner or later,' Conrad said quietly. 'You can't spend the rest of your days suspended in space. You've got to come down on one side of the fence. You either talk and we'll protect you or you'll keep your mouth shut and we'll turn you loose. There's no other out for you.'

Still Pete didn't say anything.

'We're not interested in you,' Conrad went on. 'We're after Maurer. Play with us and we'll take care of you.'

Pete twisted around.

'Take care of me? That's a laugh! Do you imagine you can protect me? So long as I keep my mouth shut I stand a chance: not much of one, but a chance. If I talk I'm as good as dead. Neither you nor the whole goddamn police force could keep me alive!'

'Don't be a fool!' Conrad snapped. 'Of course we can protect you. I'll guarantee it.'

Pete stared at him for a long moment, then leaned forward and spat on the floor.

II

Van Roche was waiting as Conrad entered his office.

'Did you get him?' Van Roche asked.

'I've got him,' Conrad said, and walked over to his desk and sat down. 'He's up on the tenth floor with a couple of guards taking care of him. What are you looking so excited about?'

'Abe Gollowitz is talking to the D.A. He's got a writ for Miss Coleman's release.'

Conrad stiffened.

'You kidding?'

Van Roche shook his head.

'He blew in about ten minutes ago. The D.A.'s stalling him until you got back. He's demanding to see Miss Coleman.'

Conrad got to his feet.

'I'd better see the D.A.'

He walked along the passage to the D.A.'s office, tapped and pushed open the door.

Forest sat behind his desk, his hands folded on his blotter. He looked up as Conrad came in, lifted his shoulders in a resigned shrug and waved a hand towards Gollowitz who was sitting by the desk, his round swarthy face bland.

'I was just telling the D.A. that I want to see Miss Coleman,' Gollowitz said as Conrad shut the door and came across to the desk.

'Why?' Conrad asked curtly.

'She is being unlawfully detained here, and I happen to be her legal representative: that's why.'

'Well, well, that's news,' Conrad said. 'Does she know of her extraordinary good fortune? After all, I should have thought you had more important work to do than to bother about a penniless movie extra.'

Gollowitz chuckled.

'As the legal representative of the Norgate Union I take under my care any of its members, and Miss Coleman happens to be a member.'

'Yeah, I should have thought of that,' Conrad said, and glanced over at Forest.

'He wants to see her right now,' Forest said.

'And no one can stop me seeing her,' Gollowitz said smoothly. 'I don't have to tell you that.' He got up and leaning forward tapped a paper lying on Forest's desk. 'You're satisfied with this, aren't you?'

'I guess so,' Forest said, shrugging. He looked over at Conrad. 'You'd better ask Miss Coleman if she wants to see Mr. Gollowitz. We'll wait.'

Conrad nodded and went out of the office. He was sure Frances would want to see Gollowitz, and he stood for a moment thinking. He could warn her, but was she in the mood to listen to warnings? Did she realize the danger she was in? Once Gollowitz got her away from the D.A.'s office, she would disappear. He was sure of that.

He returned to his office.

'Get me six photographs of any of our customers,' he said to Van Roche, 'and include in the six a picture of Maurer.'

Van Roche went to the files, and after a minute or so handed Conrad six half-plate prints.

'I want you to come up with me,' Conrad said. 'When I give you the tip, bring Weiner into Miss Coleman's room. Okay?'

Van Roche looked startled.

'What's the idea?'

'You'll see. We haven't much time. Come on, let's get upstairs.'

They rode up in the elevator to the tenth floor.

'Stick with Weiner until I send for you,' Conrad said, and walked quickly down the passage to Frances's door.

Jackson and Norris, still at their posts outside the door, gave him bored nods as he rapped. The door was opened by Madge. There was an exasperated expression on her face.

'Is she being difficult?' Conrad asked, keeping his voice down.

'I'll say she is.'

Conrad nodded and walked into the inner room. He was aware of a feeling of suppressed excitement to see Frances again, even after only a few hours.

She was looking out of the window. The nurse got to her feet and went out silently when she saw Conrad.

'I hope you're feeling better now, Miss Coleman,' Conrad said.

She turned quickly. Her eyes were angry and she came across the room to face Conrad.

'I want to go home!' she said fiercely. 'You have no right to keep me here!'

'I know,' Conrad said mildly. He thought how animated she looked in her anger. Not like Janey's anger. There was nothing spiteful about this girl, 'And I'm sorry about it, Miss Coleman. We don't think it's safe for you to leave just yet.'

'I'm the judge of that!'

'Are you?' He smiled at her, hoping to win a smile from her, but she remained straight-faced and angry, staring at him. 'Look, sit down, won't you? If after what I'm going to tell you you still want to go home, then I'll have to let you go. I can't hold you here against your will.'

Her anger began to fade, but her eyes were suspicious.

'I don't want to listen. I just want to go right now.'

'I wish you would try to be reasonable. We're only thinking of your own safety. Why do you imagine that gunman tried to kill you? Have you thought of that?'

He saw uncertainty chase suspicion out of her eyes.

'He – he must have been mad.'

'Do you really think so?' Conrad sat down. 'Sit down for a moment. I won't keep you long.'

She hesitated, then sat down, her fists tight clenched on her knees.

'You're still quite sure you didn't see anyone when you were at Miss Arnot's place?' Conrad asked, taking the six photographs from his pocket.

He saw her face tighten.

'I've already said I didn't see anyone. If you're going to start all that over again . . .'

'Please be patient with me. Would you look at these photographs and tell me if you recognize any of the faces?'

He handed her the photographs and she took them reluctantly. She shuffled through them, and when she came to Maurer's photograph he saw her stiffen. She dropped the photographs as if they had become red hot and jumped to her feet.

'I'm not going to have any more of this!' she cried, her face pale. 'I insist on going home!'

Conrad bent down and picked up the photographs. He didn't let her see his excitement. He was sure now she had seen Maurer at Dead End. Why else should she have reacted like this?

He held Maurer's photograph out to her.

'Do you know who this is?'

She didn't look at the photograph.

'I don't know any of them.'

'Have you ever heard of Jack Maurer?'

'Of course; he's a racketeer,' Frances said, turning away. 'I'm not interested in him, and I'm not interested in any of the others.'

'I want to tell you about Maurer,' Conrad said, studying the photograph. 'He's quite a character. I'd say he was the most powerful man in the State right now. When he was fifteen he became a bodyguard to Jake Moritti. Before he was sixteen he had been arrested three times for homicide, but each time he made sure no witness lived to give evidence against him. When Moritti ceased to be a power, Maurer joined Zetti. Over a period of ten years he was responsible for thirty murders; mainly gang slayings. When Zetti went to jail, Maurer teamed up with Big Joe Bernstien. A little later he became one of the head men of the Crime Syndicate. You've heard about the Syndicate, haven't you? Their organization spreads over the whole of the country. It is divided into territories and Maurer got California. He has been the racket boss of California now for ten years, and it is remarkable what he has done in that time. He has taken over all the main labour groups. Every member of these unions pays him dues for which he gives them nothing in return, and they're too blind and stupid to realize it. He has taken over the Shylocking business. Do you know what that is? It's one of the greatest profit-making rackets in the country. For every five dollars borrowed, the borrower has to pay back six dollars, and the period is for one week. It works out at 120 per cent in forty-two days. If the borrower fails to pay up on time, two of

Maurer's men call on him, and they give him a schlammin. If you don't know what that is, I'll tell you. A schlammin is a beating, given with a lead pipe wrapped in newspaper. If the borrower still can't pay after a schlammin, then the debt's written off and the borrower gets a bullet in the back.'

Conrad paused to look at Frances, but she had turned her back on him and was looking out of the window.

'Maurer has also taken over the wire service,' he went on, 'without which no bookmaker dare operate, and for the privilege of using this service every bookmaker in the State has to kick in with a weekly payment or else. He has now control of the gambling concessions in the district, and that alone brings him in fifty-five thousand dollars a month.'

Frances turned suddenly.

'Why are you telling me all this? I'm not interested, and I don't want to hear any more!'

'Since Maurer's reign began here, there have been over three hundred murders,' Conrad continued, as if she hadn't spoken. 'We have had only ten convictions, and in each case the convicted men were known to be working for Maurer. Maurer himself is known to have murdered thirty-three people, but that was before he became the boss. Now he gives orders from a safe distance. We have never been able to slap a murder charge on him. But on the 9th of this month he slipped up. For the first time in fifteen years he killed with his own hands. It was he who killed June Arnot who was his mistress and who was cheating him. We have no proof as yet that he did kill her, but we have very strong circumstantial evidence that he did do it. We have only to place him on the scene of the murder and at the time of the murder to convict him and rid California of the most dangerous, murderous, powerful gangster of this or any other century.' He leaned forward and pointed at her. 'I believe you saw him leave or arrive at Dead End. With your evidence I can successfuly prosecute him. It's your duty, Miss Coleman, to give evidence against him, and I'm asking you to do it!'

Frances backed away. Her face was now as white as a fresh fall of snow, and her big eyes looked like holes in a sheet.

'I didn't see him! I keep telling you! And I'm not going to give evidence!'

Conrad stared at her for a long moment, then he shrugged.

'Is that your last word?'

'Yes! Now I'm going home!'

'Well, I can't stop you. I've told you the kind of man Maurer is. He thinks as I do that you saw him. He knows a word from you will wreck a kingdom worth several millions of dollars a year. Do you imagine he'll take the risk that you didn't see him? Do you imagine a man like that will let you live for five minutes if he can get at you? Two of his men have already tried to wipe you out, and you're lucky they failed. They won't fail next time if you leave our protection!'

'I don't believe you. You're trying to frighten me! I didn't see anything, and I'm going home!'

Conrad restrained his temper with difficulty.

'Miss Coleman, I beg you to think about this. We can protect you. There's nothing to be frightened about. Are you frightened of Maurer? Tell me why you don't want to stay here for a few days?'

'I have no intention of staying and I don't want your protection,' she said angrily. 'I think you're just saying these things to frighten me into giving evidence, and I'm not going to do it!'

Conrad went to the door.

'Madge, will you phone down to the D.A. and tell him Gollowitz can come up?'

Madge stared at him, her eyes alarmed.

'Gollowitz? You're not letting . . .?'

'Will you please do as I tell you!' Conrad snapped. He turned back to Frances. 'There's a lawyer downstairs asking for you. He has a writ for your release. We can't hold you against the writ, but if you refuse to go with him, he can't make you. It's up to you.'

Frances met his eyes defiantly.

'I shall certainly go with him!'

Conrad walked up to her.

'Listen, you little fool! Why do you imagine a lawyer should go to the trouble of taking out a writ for you? He's Maurer's lawyer! That's why.'

'How do I know Bunty Boyd hasn't sent him?' she demanded. 'You want me to stay here, don't you? I don't believe anything you're saying!'

A tap came on the door and Madge looked in.

'Mr. Gollowitz.'

Gollowitz came in, a smooth smile on his dark face.

'Miss Coleman?'

Frances faced him, her eyes searching his face.

'Yes.'

'I'm a lawyer, and I represent the Norgate Union. The secretary of the union called me and told me you were detained here. The District Attorney tells me he has no reason to hold you any longer. Are you willing to come with me?'

Frances hesitated for a moment. There was something about Gollowitz that made her nervous.

'I don't want to go with you, thank you,' she said. 'I just want to go home.'

Gollowitz chuckled.

'Of course. I simply meant that I would escort you as far as the entrance. If you would communicate with the secretary of your union and tell him I have arranged for your release I should be obliged.'

Conrad moved quietly to the door and beckoned to Madge.

'Tell Van to bring Weiner in here,' he whispered.

As he turned back he heard Frances say, 'Can I leave here at once?'

'Of course,' Gollowitz said.

'Just a moment,' Conrad broke in. 'While you're here, Mr. Gollowitz, you might be interested to go bail for another of our customers. Come in, Weiner.'

Van Roche threw open the door and gave Pete a hard shove so he entered the room with an unbalanced rush. When he saw Gollowitz, he jumped back as if he had seen a snake.

Gollowitz had been too busy getting the writ for Frances's release to find out what had happened to Pete. Seigel had assured him he would get Pete, and seeing Pete so unexpectedly completely threw him off balance. His fat face turned livid, and he took a step towards Pete, his lips drawn off his teeth in a snarl of fury.

'Leave me alone!' Pete exclaimed, and backed away.

Too late, Gollowitz realized he had given himself away. He twisted his face into a forced bland smile, but he saw the look of horror on Frances's face.

'Don't you want to take Weiner along with you as well as Miss Coleman?' Conrad asked quietly. 'I doubt if he'll come, but at least you can ask him.'

His eyes glittering with rage, Gollowitz turned to Frances.

'Come along, Miss Coleman. I'll get you a cab.'

'Don't go with him!' Pete shouted. 'He belongs to the organization. Stay here where you are safe! Don't go with him!'

Gollowitz put out his hand and laid it gently on Frances's arm.

'I don't know who this fellow is, but he sounds crazy to me,' he said. 'Let's go, Miss Coleman.'

Frances shuddered and jumped back.

'No! I'm going to stay here. I don't want to go with you. I won't go with you!'

'I'm afraid you are being rather a foolish young woman, Miss Coleman,' Gollowitz said. The silent threat in those black eyes turned Frances cold. 'Are you coming with me or aren't you?'

'Oh, tell him to go!' Frances cried, and sat down on the couch, hiding her face in her hands. 'Please tell him to go!'

Gollowitz looked at Pete, then he walked quietly from the room.

No one moved as he crossed the outer room. They watched him open the door, step into the passage and close the door behind him.

He left behind him an atmosphere charged with threatening danger.

'Janey!'

Conrad stood in the small hall and waited for her reply. She wasn't in any of the downstairs rooms, and he had an idea she might be out. Two or three times lately she had been out when he had returned from the office. During the past three days their relationship had worsened. She didn't tell him where she went and he didn't ask.

'Is that you?' Janey called from upstairs.

A little surprised to find her in, Conrad ran up the stairs and pushed open the bedroom door.

Janey was sitting in front of her dressing-table. Clad only in a brassière and a pair of frilly panties, she was engaged in rolling up one slim leg a black nylon stocking.

'You're early, aren't you?' she asked, without looking up. 'It isn't half-past six yet.'

He pushed the door shut and wandered over to the window. It no longer gave him any pleasure as it used to do to see her like this.

'I have to go away for a few days, Janey. I'm leaving right now.'

Janey gave his broad back a sharp glance as she fixed the suspender grip to the top of her stocking.

'Oh. I suppose I'm not included. Where are you going?'

She reached for the other stocking, her mind suddenly busy. A few days. What exactly did that mean? A week – ten days? She felt a sudden hot flush sweep over her body. Would it be safe to ask Louis to come here? she wondered.

'I have charge of two important witnesses,' Conrad said, turning to look at her. 'They have to be kept under cover until the trial. The D.A. wants me to look after them.'

She adjusted the seams of her stockings and stood up.

'What on earth for? Since when have you become a nurse-maid to witnesses?'

'It just happens they are important and in danger,' Conrad said shortly. 'I'll be away until Thursday. I'm sorry, Janey, but there it is.'

She went over to the wardrobe and took out a wrap.

'All right, if you've got to go, you've got to go,' she said in-differently. 'It won't make much difference to me. It's not as if I see all that much of you. Where are you going?'

'I'll write the address down,' Conrad said, taking out his bill-fold and finding an old envelope. 'It's out near Butcher's Wood. And listen, Janey, this is important, no one but you may know where I've gone. Don't tell anyone, do you understand?'

'Who am I going to tell, do you imagine?' Janey said scorn-fully, slipping into her wrap. 'You talk as if I'm surrounded by people instead of being left alone night after night in this dreary house.'

'There's no need to talk nonsense,' Conrad said curtly. 'You have dozens of friends, and you know it. It's just that you're not interested to entertain people at home. You prefer to be taken out.'

'Who the hell wants to cook and wash up when one can go out?' Janey snapped.

Conrad put the envelope in a small drawer in the dressing-table.

'I'd better throw some things in a bag,' he said, side-tracking the way to an inevitable row.

'And who are these precious witnesses you have to take care of?' Janey asked, sitting down before the dressing-table again. 'A woman – I bet.'

'Never mind who they are,' Conrad said shortly. He began hurriedly to pack a bag. 'I'd better leave you some money.' He put a few bills on the mantelpiece. 'That should hold you until Thursday.'

It would be too risky to ask Louis to come here, Janey decided as she made up her lips. Too many prying neighbours, but she could go to his place. Again she felt a hot flush run over her. He had been like an animal, she thought. His love-making had been brutal, selfish and insatiable. He had left her bruised and gasping, but with an overwhelming desire to be caught up again in his hard, muscular arms.

'I must get along,' Conrad said, shutting the bag. 'Why don't you get Beth to spend a few days with you? I don't like leaving you entirely alone here.'

Janey smiled mysteriously.

'Your remorse is very touching, darling. Considering you leave me here alone fifteen hours a day, a few more hours won't hurt me.'

'For goodness sake, Janey! Don't go on and on. You know I have to work late hours,' Conrad said impatiently.

'Then it will be a nice change for you to sit beside some woman and hold her hand in Butcher's Wood, won't it?'

Conrad looked at her in disgust.

'Well, so long, Janey.'

'So long,' she said, and turned back to the mirror.

She didn't move until she heard the front door slam, then she jumped to her feet and ran over to the window. She watched Conrad drive away, then she stood for a long minute, her arms across her breasts and her eyes closed, savouring a sense of freedom.

She had four days and three nights alone! She didn't intend to waste such a gift.

She ran across the room, down the stairs to the telephone. As she dialled the number of the Paradise Club she was aware that her heart was beating wildly and her breath was coming in quick, uneven gasps. She reached for a cigarette, lit it and tried to control her breathing.

'Mr. Seigel, please?' she said, as a woman's voice came over the line.

'Who's calling?'

'Mr. Seigel is expecting me. Put me through, please!' Janey said sharply. She had no intention of advertising her name to a receptionist.

'Hold a moment.'

After a long pause Seigel snapped, 'Who is it?'

He sounded curt and angry.

'Louis? Janey here.'

'Oh – hello: what do you want?'

The casual indifference in his voice sent a stab into Janey's heart.

'You don't sound very pleased to hear my voice,' she said plaintively.

'I'm busy. What's on your mind?'

'He's gone away for two or three days,' Janey said. 'I'm on my own. I thought you would be interested.'

There was a long pause. She could almost hear Seigel thinking.

'That's fine,' he said suddenly, but his voice still remained curt. 'Well, come on over.'

'You mean to the club?'

'Sure. Come on over. I'll buy you a dinner.'

'I don't know if I should come to the club. Couldn't I go to your place, Louis?'

'Come to the club,' he said irritably. 'See you around nine. I can't get free before nine. So long for now,' and he hung up.

Janey slowly replaced the receiver. He wasn't treating her as she had hoped he would treat her, but she didn't care. She didn't even care that he must know she was throwing herself at him. His brutal rudeness fascinated her. All she wanted was to be caught up in his arms, to be treated like a woman of the streets, to be bruised and to be left gasping. That was an experience she had never known before: an experience she must have.

IV

Seigel walked along the passage to his office, a heavy scowl on his face. For the past three days, he had been waiting for McCann to warn him a warrant had been sworn out for his arrest. The fact McCann hadn't telephoned made him jittery and bad-tempered. He was worried, too, that Gollowitz had taken the whole affair out of his hands. It was not as if Gollowitz had anything to brag about. He said he would take care of the girl – and what had happened? Nothing! Not a damn thing!

The D.A. had the girl and he had Weiner. Those two must be talking their heads off by now. If he had his way he would be in New York by now, but Gollowitz had told him to stay where he was.

'There's nothing to worry about yet,' Gollowitz had said. 'McCann is covering you at his end. When Forest decides to make a move, then it'll be time for you to skip, and not before.'

Seigel turned the handle of his office door and pushed the door open. He came to an abrupt standstill when he saw Gollowitz sitting behind his desk.

'What are you doing here?' Seigel demanded, coming in and shutting the door.

'I'm waiting,' Gollowitz said quietly.

The past three days had left their mark on him. His fat face sagged and there were grey-blue bags under his eyes. He had realized the danger the organization was in, and his shrewd brain had worked ceaselessly for a legal way out, but there was no legal way out. There was only one way to stop those two from giving evidence that would upset his future kingdom. They must be silenced, and silenced for good.

Too late, he realized that Seigel was a broken reed, that Seigel's thugs were brainless killers who would never get near those two now Forest was alerted. He had finally taken a decision that hurt his pride and weakened his position. He had reported to the Syndicate, admitted he couldn't handle the situation and had asked for help.

'Waiting?' Seigel snarled, coming over to sit in an armchair. 'Waiting for what?'

Gollowitz glanced at his wrist-watch.

'I'm waiting for Ferrari. He should be here any minute.'

Seigel scowled.

'Ferrari? Who's Ferrari?'

'Vito Ferrari,' Gollowitz said.

Seigel stiffened. His big hands closed over the arms of his chair until his knuckles stood out white and bony. His tanned face went blotchy, turning red, then white, and he half started out of his chair.

'Vito Ferrari? He's not coming here, is he?'

'Yes.'

'But why? What's the idea? What the hell is he coming here for?'

Gollowitz stared at Seigel, his small black eyes like glass beads.

'I asked him to come.'

Seigel got slowly to his feet.

'Are you crazy? You asked Ferrari to come here? Why?'

'Who else do you imagine can handle this mess?' Gollowitz asked, spreading his fat hands palms up on the blotter. 'You? Do you imagine you can handle it?'

'But Ferrari . . .'

'If those two go into the witness-box we're all finished,' Gollowitz said quietly. 'They must be silenced. You have had your
chance. I have had mine. We both failed. We can't afford to
fail. I asked the Syndicate to send Ferrari. They said I had done
the right thing.'

'What will Maurer say?' Seigel asked, licking his dry lips.
'You know he wouldn't have a Syndicate man on his territory.'

'He's not here. If he had stayed, maybe we shouldn't have
had to ask for Ferrari, but he didn't stay. I've got to save the
organization. There's only one man who can do it for me –
Ferrari!'

The name Vito Ferrari struck a chill into Seigel's heart the
way the name Inquisitor must have struck a chill into the heart
of a heretic in the Middle Ages.

Vito Ferrari was the Syndicate's executioner. Fantastic and
unbelievable tales had been told of his cruelty, his ruthlessness,
his crimes and his lust for blood. He had become a legendary
figure in the underworlds of the world.

Seigel knew that if he ever stepped out of turn, it would be
Ferrari who would be sent by the Syndicate to kill him. To have
asked Ferrari to come to Pacific City was like asking for Death
itself to pay a visit, and Seigel stared at Gollowitz with horrified
eyes.

'You must be crazy!' he said.

Gollowitz again spread out his fat hands.

'It is either he or the organization. I didn't want to have him
here. If you had shown you could handle this thing, do you
imagine I would have sent for him?'

Seigel started to say something when a knock came on the
door.

Seigel started, then spun around to face the door, his eyes
sick and frightened.

'Come in,' Gollowitz said.

Dutch pushed open the door. There was a blank, stupid expression on his face, like the face of a man who comes out into
the sunshine after sitting through a two-feature programme.

'There's a guy asking for you,' he said to Gollowitz. 'He says
you're expecting him.'

Gollowitz went a shade paler. He nodded his head slowly.

'That's right. Let him in.'

Dutch looked at Seigel questioningly, but Seigel turned away.
Dutch plodded across the room and opened the door that led
into the outer office.

'Come in,' Seigel heard him say.

Seigel stood waiting, his heart thudding against his ribs.
Although he had heard Ferrari's name many times during his
career of crime, he had never seen him, nor had he seen a photograph of him. He had, however, conjured up in his mind a
picture of him. He had imagined him to be a great ox of a man,

coarse, powerful, brutal and ferocious. With the reputation such as Ferrari had, no other picture would satisfy Seigel. It came as a considerable shock to him when Vito Ferrari came quietly into the room.

Ferrari was an inch or so under five feet; almost a dwarf, and there was nothing of him except skin and bone. His black lounge suit hung on him as if draped over a tailor's dummy made of wire.

Seigel was immediately struck by Ferrari's extraordinary walk. He appeared to glide over the parquet floor, as silently and as smoothly as a phantom, as if his feet were treading on space, and when Seigel looked at his face, he was again reminded of a phantom.

Ferrari's face was wedge shaped. He had a broad forehead that tapered down to a narrow square chin. His nose was hooked and over-large, his mouth was a thin line as near lipless as made no difference. His yellowish skin was stretched so tightly it revealed the bone structure of his head and face to give him the appearance of a death's head.

His small eyes were sunk so deeply into dark-ringed sockets as to be almost invisible, but when Seigel looked closer it seemed to him he was looking into the fixed, unnatural eyes of a wax effigy.

Both Gollowitz and Seigel were so startled by Ferrari's unexpected appearance that they remained staring at him, unable to utter a word.

Ferrari took off his black hat. His thick mass of dark hair was turning a little grey at the temples. He put the hat on the desk and then sat down in the chair Seigel had occupied.

'A woman and man, that's right, isn't it?' he said. He had a queer husky voice that sent a chill up Seigel's spine. It was the kind of voice you might hear come from the mouth of a medium at a seance.

Gollowitz hastily collected himself.

'I am very glad to have you here,' he said, and was aware that he was gushing without being able to help himself. 'It was very good of Big Joe . . .'

'Where are they?' Ferrari interrupted, his sunken eyes on Gollowitz's face.

Gollowitz gulped, stuttered and looked helplessly at Seigel.

'You mean these two you've come to take care of?' Seigel asked, his voice off-key.

'Who else?' Ferrari said impatiently. 'Where are they? Don't you know?'

'They are in a hunting lodge in Butcher's Wood,' Gollowitz told him hurriedly. He had received detailed information from McCann only this morning. 'I have a map here.' He opened a drawer in the desk, took out a neatly prepared plan and pushed it across the desk.

Ferrari picked it up, folded it into four and put it in his pocket without looking at it.

'How do you want me to kill them?' he asked.

'I'll leave that to you,' Gollowitz said. 'But it is essential that both of them should appear to die accidentally.'

Ferrari pursed his thin lips.

'When are they to die?' he asked, sitting down.

'Wouldn't it be better to discuss the means of getting at them?' Gollowitz suggested, stung by Ferrari's arrogant tone. 'If it were all that easy I wouldn't have sent for you. They are guarded night and day. No one can get near the lodge without being seen. There are police dogs, searchlights and a small regiment of police guarding the only approach to the lodge. There are six picked detectives, all expert shots, who take it in turns to guard these two. Two women detectives never leave the Coleman girl for a moment, even when she's asleep. Two detectives guard Weiner in the same way. It's not a matter of when they are to die, but how we're going to get at them.'

Ferrari ran a bony finger down the length of his nose while he regarded Gollowitz the way a scientist would regard an unknown microbe.

'I asked you when they are to die,' he said.

Gollowitz looked over at Seigel and shrugged his fat shoulders.

'As soon as possible, of course,' he said curtly.

'Very well. When I have studied the map and have looked the the place over, I will give you a date,' Ferrari said, speaking in slow, precise English with a noticeable Italian accent. 'It will probably be in two days' time.'

'You mean you will kill them in two days' time?' Seigel exclaimed. 'It's not possible!'

'It won't be possible for both of them to die in two days' time,' Ferrari said, 'but certainly one of them will die in this time. Both of them could go within two days if you didn't insist their deaths should appear accidental. Two people to die so quickly would be too much of a coincidence.' He looked across at Gollowitz. 'You are quite sure you want them to die accidentally?'

'It is essential,' Gollowitz said, secretly pleased to make Ferrari's task even more difficult. 'If the newspapers suspect they have been murdered they will raise such a stink there may be an inquiry, and we can't afford that.'

'Yes.' Ferrari ran his claw-like hand over his hair. 'Very well, one of them will go in two or three days' time. We'll have to consider what to do with the other when the first job has been taken care of.'

'You'll forgive me for being sceptical,' Gollowitz said dryly, 'but we have discussed ways and means of getting at these two, and we have failed completely to find a solution. You talk as if the job's already done, and yet you haven't even had the opportunity to study the ground.'

Ferrari again ran his finger down his nose. It seemed to be an unconscious habit of his.

'But then I am an expert,' he said quietly. 'You are an amateur. You have approached this job in the wrong frame of mind. You have looked for difficulties. You have told yourself that it is impossible. You have defeated yourself; the situation hasn't defeated you.' He leaned back in his chair and interlaced his bony fingers, resting them on his crossed knee. He looked like something not of this world, Seigel thought, watching him in a kind of sick fascination. When Ferrari crossed his spindly legs, both feet swung free of the ground. 'I approach a job with confidence. I have never failed, and I don't intend to fail. I have had much tougher jobs to handle than this one.'

'This is a damned tough job,' Seigel said, trying to meet the sunken fixed eyes that felt as if they were boring holes in his brain. 'You'll be damned lucky to get one of them, let alone both of them.'

Ferrari leaned forward and smiled. His teeth were big, yellow and decayed. He reminded Seigel of a vicious horse, reaching forward to snap at him.

'Luck doesn't come into it,' Ferrari said. 'If I relied on luck I would never get anywhere. This I tell you: they will both die. I guarantee it. I don't expect you to believe me. Wait and see. Only don't forget I've told you already: when I go after anyone, I get him! I've never failed and I never will fail!'

Listening to him, Gollowitz felt the sick tension that had gripped him ever since he had heard the girl and Weiner were in the D.A.'s hands begin to lessen. He had a sudden premonition that this dreadful little man wasn't bluffing. Asking Ferrari to help him had been the smartest thing he had ever done. He felt certain now Ferrari would save his kingdom.

CHAPTER SEVEN

'COME in, Paul,' Forest said, pushing aside some papers he was studying. 'Sit down. What's the news?'

Conrad sat down, and as he shook a cigarette out of a pack he said, 'The treatment's worked at last. Weiner's talking.'

Forest nodded.

'I thought he would. It was a gamble, and we'd have looked pretty silly if he had accepted bail, but somehow I didn't think he would have the nerve to go out in the cold hard world. How about the girl?'

Conrad pulled a face.

'No. She still swears she didn't see anyone at Dead End, but at least she isn't asking to go home any more. I think she realizes she'll have to stay hidden until things cool off a little.'

'We'll come back to her in a moment,' Forest said, reaching for a cigar. As he removed the band, he went on, 'What's Weiner got to say?'

'He's admitted going after Miss Coleman. He says he was told to kill her by Seigel, but I can't get much more out of him.'

'In other words, he's given you enough to hold him and to keep him out of danger, but no more.'

'That's about right. He says he doesn't know anything about Maurer. He makes out he is Seigel's man, that he doesn't even know Seigel works for Maurer. He's lying, of course, and I'm hoping to persuade him to change his story. There's no point in going after Seigel. We want Maurer, and if we arrest Seigel we'll only be side-tracking ourselves.'

Forest nodded.

'We've got to hook Seigel to Maurer if Weiner's evidence is going to be of any use.'

Conrad frowned. He flicked ash into the glass bowl on Forest's desk.

'I just can't make Weiner believe he is safe with us,' he said irritably. 'He's completely convinced that sooner or later the organization will reach him. If I could convince him they can't get at him, then I think he would open up.'

'Is he safe, Paul?' Forest asked quietly.

Conrad nodded.

'Yes. I've taken every precaution. It's impossible for anyone to get near the lodge. That's why I picked the place. There is only one road to the lodge. It is cut through country that doesn't offer a scrap of cover. The only other way is up a two-hundred-foot precipice that a fly couldn't climb. I have men patrolling the top just in case someone attempts to get up with ropes and climbing tackle. Miss Coleman and Weiner are never left for a moment. So long as they stay at the lodge they're safe enough.'

'And yet Weiner still imagines he'll get wiped out?'

'The trouble there is he knows none of the mob have ever talked and survived. It's become the accepted thing to believe Maurer's arm will reach anywhere. Once I can break down that idea, I think he'll give us all the information we want, but at the moment nothing seems to convince him.'

'Frankly, I don't blame him,' Forest said seriously. 'Maurer has an unpleasant habit of silencing people who talk. Have you considered the human element, Paul?'

'Of course that comes into it,' Conrad admitted, 'but I've taken the precaution to pick men with good records. I've also taken the precaution to make certain no guard works alone. He has with him a companion at all times. Sergeant O'Brien, whom you know, is in charge of them. O'Brien is as safe as I am.'

'Sure,' Forest said. 'I've known O'Brien for years. He's my idea of a first-class policeman. How about leave? Isn't there a danger that these men can be got at when they take a day off?'

'They're not having any days off,' Conrad returned. 'I've told them this is a full-time job until it is over. The only three who are allowed to leave the lodge are Van Roche, O'Brien and myself. If I can't trust those two then I can't trust anyone.'

'Well, you've certainly got the situation in hand. I'll come out over the week-end and see for myself.'

'I wish you would. Any other ideas will be welcomed. If only I could convince Weiner he was safe.'

'Maybe he'll come around. We have a little time. Keep after him, Paul.' Forest shifted his chair back so he could cross his legs. 'Now tell me about the girl.'

'She's a bit of an enigma,' Conrad said, rubbing his chin. 'I'm damned if I know what to make of her.'

Forest, who missed nothing, was surprised at Conrad's despondent tone. He glanced quickly at the lean, strong face and wondered at the unhappy frown. He looked away, alert now. Why the sudden change of tone in Conrad's voice when the girl was mentioned? he wondered. From long experience in court he had learned to suspect any relation between man and woman. Was there something developing here?

'In what way, Paul?' he asked mildly.

Conrad lifted his shoulders.

'I'm as certain as I sit here she saw Maurer at Dead End. Why doesn't she admit it? After all, by keeping silent, she's making herself an accessory after the fact.'

'Have you reminded her of that?'

Conrad looked up. His eyes shifted away from Forest's inquiring gaze.

'Not yet. I thought it would sound as if I were threatening her. She's not the type to be threatened.'

'But she must be told. If we get other evidence that she saw Maurer she could be prosecuted.'

'I know, but I'll hold off a little longer if you agree,' Conrad said. 'I still think I can persuade her to talk. Since Gollowitz scared her, she's much more amenable.'

'Is she? In what way?'

'Well, she's more friendly. She's lost the chip on her shoulder. I – I think she's coming round.'

Forest moved a glass paper-weight aimlessly, his face was expressionless. The despondent look on Conrad's face began to worry him.

'We can't keep her for ever,' Forest said. 'You realize that?'

'I know. It's a hell of a problem. The only way in which she can ever be really safe now is for her to admit she saw Maurer so we can deal with him. So long as Maurer is at liberty she won't be safe unless she remains under our protection.'

'And she realizes that?'

Conrad shrugged.

'I suppose so. I've told her often enough.' He reached forward to stub out his cigarette. For a long moment he stared frowning down at the carpet while Forest watched him without appearing to do so. Then Conrad said. 'There is another problem I don't know how to handle. Maybe you can make up my mind for me.'

'Go ahead. What is it?'

'I think these two have taken a liking to each other. I'll go further than that: I think they've fallen in love with each other.'

'What two?' Forest asked sharply.

Conrad shifted restlessly; the despondent expression deepened.

'Miss Coleman and Weiner.'

'Fallen in love with each other?' Forest repeated, startled. 'How did they fall in love with each other?'

Conrad looked up then.

'How do people fall in love with each other?' he asked quietly. 'It's one of those damned odd things that can't be explained. Two people meet and then something happens. It's like two pieces of a jig-saw puzzle that have been floating about for years. Then suddenly through no known reason they come together and fit. It can happen as easily as that.'

'Are you sure about this?'

'I'm pretty sure. Miss Coleman asked me yesterday if she could talk to Weiner. Up to now we have kept them apart, but Miss Fielding, who is looking after Miss Coleman, tells me she remains at the window watching Weiner as he exercises in the grounds, and I hear he watches her when she is in the grounds.'

'But that doesn't mean they're in love with each other,' Forest said a little impatiently.

Conrad shrugged.

'You have only to see them when they talk about each other to know how they feel.' He got up abruptly and began to pace up and down. 'How the hell a nice girl like that could fall in love with a little rat like Weiner beats me. There's nothing to him. He's got that hideous birthmark. He's been a crook all his life. I just don't know how she could have any feeling for a man like that. It beats me.'

Forest raised his eyebrows. Surely Paul couldn't have fallen for this girl, he asked himself. He was certainly behaving like a rejected suitor. But surely not. Forest had met Janey and had been very impressed by her beauty. He had thought Conrad was a lucky devil to have married such a lively, glamorous girl.

'Maybe it's because of his background and his birthmark,' Forest said quietly. 'Girls can be damned funny animals.'

'I guess so.'

'But what's the problem, Paul? It's not our business if they have fallen in love with each other, is it?'

'No, but am I to let them meet? Miss Coleman asked if she could share Weiner's exercise time; a couple of hours a day.'

'I should say not. What do you think?'

Conrad continued to pace up and down.

'It's not as easy as that,' he said slowly. 'We mustn't lose sight of our objective. We want to persuade this girl to give evidence against Maurer. If she were allowed to talk to Weiner there is a good chance he'll talk about himself. It's possible he might even talk to her about Maurer. She's bound to want to know why he accepted the order to murder her. To justify himself in her eyes he may let her into the secrets of the organization. Coming from him it may have a startling effect. Up to now, she doesn't believe a word I say. She imagines I'm only interested in getting her to give evidence, and that I'm deliberately colouring the background to influence her. Coming from Weiner it might make her realize where her duty lies. I don't know. It's a problem, but I'm inclined to let them meet and talk.'

'Hmm, yes; there's something in that. But suppose he puts her off still more? He may throw a scare into her that'll keep her permanently quiet. Thought of that?'

'Then he won't be practising what he'll be preaching. At least, he's talked himself, and she knows he has admitted he was ordered to kill her. I've told her.'

'Well, all right. We've got to try something. We can't hold her much longer. Let them meet, but they are to be under constant surveillance. They are not to be allowed to go off together. Instruct the guards to keep out of earshot, but not to lose sight of them.'

'All right,' Conrad said. 'Well, I guess that's all. I'd better be getting back.'

'There's one thing we haven't decided,' Forest said, 'and that's why this girl, if she did see Maurer, won't admit it. That's something we've got to find out, Paul.'

'The obvious reason is she's scared of Maurer.'

Forest shook his head.

'I doubt that. A girl of her type wouldn't know much about Maurer, only what she's read in the press. I admit his reputation is damned bad, but people who learn about gangster's reputations from newspapers aren't really convinced they are as dangerous as the papers make them out to be. There's something more important than that that's keeping her quiet. Ever thought she might have a record and she's scared Maurer's counsel might bring it up at the trial?'

'That's a little far-fetched, isn't it?' Conrad said sharply.

Forest gently touched off the ash from his cigar.

'Yes, it's far-fetched, but we don't know. It might be something else. She might have run away from home or she may have a husband who's looking for her. What I'm getting at is this: if she does give evidence against Maurer her photograph and her name are going to be splashed on the front pages of every newspaper in the country. It may be she wants to avoid this publicity for a personal reason, and that's why she's keeping quiet. I think we should dig around and see if we can turn up this personal reason, always supposing it exists.'

'Yes, I think we should do that,' Conrad said in a flat voice.

Forest was now almost sure the girl had made a big impression on Conrad, and the discovery startled him. Could Conrad have fallen in love with her, he asked himself.

'All right, then let's dig a little,' he said. 'Would you like to handle it? Do you want to remain at the lodge out of circulation or would you rather come back here and see what you can find out about the girl's background?'

Conrad didn't hesitate.

'I'll stay on at the lodge. The important thing is to keep her safe. I've accepted the responsibility and I want to see it through. I'll send Van back. He can do the digging.'

It was then that Forest became sure Conrad had fallen in love with Frances Coleman.

He spread his hands on the blotter and his hard eyes searched Conrad's face.

'What do you think of this girl, Paul? I mean how does she strike you as a man regarding a woman?'

Conrad looked at Forest.

'Does that come into it? Does it matter what I think of her?'

Disconcerted by Conrad's straight look, Forest lifted his heavy shoulders.

'No, you're quite right.' He stubbed out his cigar. 'I shouldn't have asked that. Well, I guess I've got to get on with my work. Let me know how things develop.'

'I will,' Conrad said, and made for the door.

When he had gone, Forest stared gloomily down at his blotter.

He sat thinking for a few moments, his face worried, then with a sudden shrug of his shoulders, he reached for the pile of papers that were waiting his attention.

II

Sergeant Tom O'Brien stood at the foot of the bed and looked down at his son. O'Brien's usually granite-hard face had softened, making him look younger, and there was a twinkle in his eyes never seen by either his colleagues or by his customers.

'Go to sleep,' he said, 'or you and me will run into trouble when your mother comes home.'

His son, a freckle-faced youngster within reaching distance of a seventh birthday, gave his father a wide, disarming smile.

'How's about telling me how you cornered Little Caesar and the fight you had with him?' he inquired hopefully. 'It won't take long, and we needn't tell mummy.'

O'Brien pretended to be shocked. His son's hero-worship was the biggest thing in his life. For a moment he wrestled with the temptation to tell the old favourite again, but it was already past nine o'clock and he had promised his wife he would have the kid in bed and asleep by eight.

'Can't do it, son,' he said gravely. 'We've got to keep a bargain. You said you'd be satisfied if I told you about Lingle, and we're late as it is. I'll tell you about Little Caesar when next I get some time off.'

'Is that a promise?' his son asked gravely.

'Yes, it's a promise. Now go to sleep. If you want anything give me a call, but no false alarms.'

'Okay, pop,' his son said, accepting the inevitable. He had long learned it was useless to argue with his father. 'See you in the morning.'

'God bless, son.'

'God bless, pop.'

O'Brien turned off the light and went down the stairs to the hall. The little house was very quiet. His wife had gone to the movies with her mother. She wouldn't be back for another hour. O'Brien wondered if he should wash up the supper dishes or take a look at the fights on the television. The fights won after a minor wrestle with his conscience.

He pushed open the sitting-room door, then paused, frowning. He hadn't remembered leaving the standard lamp on. He was usually pretty good about turning the lights off. He entered the room and shut the door. He had scarcely taken three steps towards the television set when he came to an abrupt standstill, his senses suddenly alert.

O'Brien was a tough, hard cop, with nerves like steel, but in spite of his toughness he felt his heart skip a beat when he saw a small figure in black sitting in an armchair.

The figure was in the shadows, and at first glance O'Brien thought it was a child, but then he noticed the small feet in black suède shoes that hung a few inches from the floor and the spindly legs and bone thin ankles. They had a matured look about them, and couldn't belong to a child.

He had a sudden creepy feeling that he was looking at a ghost, and he felt the hairs on the nape of his neck stiffen. Then he pulled himself together and took a step forward.

'What the hell . . .?' he growled, and came to an abrupt stand-still as the glittering barrel of a .38 automatic appeared in the light and pointed at him.

'Hello, sergeant,' a husky voice said. 'Sorry to have startled you. Don't do anything brave. At this range I couldn't miss you.'

O'Brien felt sweat start out on his face. There could be only one owner to that husky, menacing voice. Years ago, when he had been on the New York force as a patrolman, O'Brien had once run into Vito Ferrari. It had been an experience he had often thought about, and there were times when he had gone to bed after a heavy dinner that he had even dreamed about it.

He peered down at the chair, and Ferrari looked up so the light touched his face. The two men stared at each other.

'I see you remember me, sergeant,' Ferrari said.

'What are you doing here?' O'Brien demanded, not moving a muscle. He knew how deadly dangerous Ferrari was, and his immediate thought was Ferrari had come to kill him. Why, he had no idea, but the Syndicate's executioner never made social calls. He only paid business visits.

'Sit down, sergeant,' Ferrari said, waving to an armchair opposite. 'I want to talk to you.'

O'Brien sat down. He was glad to; his legs felt shaky. He thought of his sleeping son upstairs and his wife due back in an hour. For the first time in his career he was aware that his work was putting his own family in danger, and the thought made him feel sick.

'What are you doing in Pacific City?' he asked, determined that Ferrari shouldn't know his fears. 'It's off your beat, isn't it?'

Ferrari put the automatic in a shoulder holster under his coat. This move gave O'Brien no hope. He knew Ferrari could get the gun out and kill him before he could lift himself a few inches out of his chair.

'Yes, it's off my beat, but I'm here on business. I've come for Weiner,' Ferrari said mildly. He crossed his spindly legs and swung one tiny foot backwards and forwards.

O'Brien stiffened, and for a moment he felt relieved. He should have thought of Weiner the moment he had seen Ferrari.

'Then you're unlucky,' he said. 'Weiner's inaccessible.'

'No one's inaccessible,' Ferrari returned. 'People just think they are. I want you to tell me how I can get at him.'

O'Brien was well aware of Ferrari's reputation. He knew Ferrari would never make a statement unless he was sure he could back it up.

'What makes you think I'm going to tell you?' he asked in a voice that was far from steady.

'What makes you think you're not going to tell me?'

O'Brien stared at him. He felt himself change colour, and his great hands closed into fists.

'How's your little boy, sergeant?' Ferrari went on. 'I saw him this morning. A fine boy.'

O'Brien didn't say anything. He had a sick feeling of being trapped. He could see what was coming.

'Shall we talk about Weiner?' Ferrari asked, after a long pause. 'You don't want me to draw you a map, do you, sergeant?'

'You won't get away with it this time,' O'Brien said hoarsely. 'And you'll be crazy to try.'

Ferrari lifted his emaciated shoulders.

'Let's skip talking crap,' he said curtly. 'What time does Weiner take a tub at night?'

'Ten o'clock,' O'Brien said. 'How the hell do you know he takes a tub at night?'

'I always study the background of my clients. It's little things like a bath-a-night habit that makes my work easy. Is he alone when he takes the tub or does a guard stay with him?'

O'Brien hesitated, but not for long. He was being threatened with something much worse than his own death.

'He's alone.'

'Describe the bathroom, please.'

'It's like any other bathroom. It's on the second floor. There's one very small window with a bar. There's a shower, a cupboard, a tub and a toilet.'

'Has the shower curtains?'

'You're wasting your time, Ferrari. Don't kid yourself. You couldn't get into the bathroom. A mouse couldn't get in without being seen. We've really got this set-up organized.'

Ferrari wrinkled his upper lip into a sneer.

'I can get in. I've cased the joint already. There's nothing to it. I walked around the joint this morning.'

'You're lying!' O'Brien said, shaken.

'Think so? Okay, I'm lying.' Ferrari ran his bony finger down the length of his nose. 'Before Weiner takes a tub is the bathroom searched?'

'Of course it is.'

'Who searches it?'

'Whoever's in charge for the night.'

'When are you in charge, sergeant?'

O'Brien drew in a deep breath.

'Tomorrow night.'

'I was hoping you'd say that. Now listen carefully: here's what you do. When Weiner's ready for his tub, carry out the search in the usual way, but be damned careful how you look in the shower cabinet. That's where I'll be. Understand?'

O'Brien wiped the sweat off his face with his handkerchief.

'You don't know what you're saying. You can't get into the bathroom. I don't believe you've been up there! The road's guarded so tight a cat couldn't get through without being seen.'

'I didn't go by the road,' Ferrari returned. 'I went up the cliff.'

'You're lying! No one could get up that cliff without ropes and tackle!'

Ferrari smiled.

'You're forgetting I have a certain talent for climbing.'

O'Brien remembered then he had heard that Ferrari's parents had been circus acrobats, and Ferrari had been trained for the circus. Years ago he had earned a lot of money as 'The Human Fly', giving exhibitions of fantastically difficult and dangerous climbs. He had once stopped the traffic on Broadway when he had climbed the face of the Empire State Building for a publicity stunt.

'I shall be there, sergeant,' Ferrari went on. 'Make no mistake about it. Can I rely on you?'

O'Brien started to say something, then stopped.

'Some hesitation?' Ferrari said mildly. 'I'm surprised. After all, who is Weiner? A cheap, treacherous little crook. You're not going to risk the life of your nice little son, are you, for a punk like Weiner?'

'We'll leave my son out of it,' O'Brien said hoarsely.

'I wish we could, but I have to be certain I can rely on you. You know I never bluff, don't you, sergeant? It's his life or Weiner's. Please yourself.'

O'Brien stared helplessly at the dreadful little man, watching him. If Ferrari said it was his son's life or Weiner's, he meant exactly that. O'Brien knew there was nothing he could do to prevent Ferrari either killing his son or killing Weiner. He knew that Ferrari wouldn't give him a chance to kill him: he was far too cunning and quick for O'Brien. Ferrari had never failed to make good a threat. There was no reason to suppose he would fail this time.

'And let's get this straight,' Ferrari went on. 'Don't try to set a trap for me. Maybe it'll come off, but I promise you your son won't live five minutes after you've betrayed me. From now on every move he makes will be watched. If anything happens to me, he will be killed. I don't want to sound dramatic, but that's the exact situation. You play straight with me, and I'll play straight with you. Can I rely on you?'

O'Brien knew it was a straightforward, simple situation; he had to make a decision on his son's life or Weiner's.

'Yes,' he said in a voice that had suddenly hardened. 'You can rely on me.'

III

Conrad had not been entirely correct when he had told Forest that Frances and Pete had fallen in love with each other.

Pete had certainly fallen in love with Frances. Love was something he had never before experienced, and it reacted on him with a tremendous impact.

But he realized the experience could be but short-lived, and could never come to fruition. He had no illusions about Maurer's power. He had been safe now for eight days, and this he considered to be a major miracle. He knew there could not be many days left for him to live: the margin, as the hours passed, was whittling away. Before very long Maurer would strike, and the combined vigilance of the police guards, Conrad's careful planning and the supposed inaccessibility of the hunting lodge would then be proved to be as flimsy a protection as a thin veil held up to ward off the scorching flame of a blow lamp.

Pete's discovery of love came to him with an added poignancy because he knew it would be so short-lived, and he realized the experience would only be a kind of waking dream in which his imagination would play the major role.

Whenever he caught sight of Frances when she sat in the walled-in garden and he stood at the window of his room, he conjured up vivid scenes in his mind of what they could have done together, how they might have lived, the house they might have owned, the children they might have shared if there had been no such man as Maurer to make such mind images impossible.

He was quite stunned then when Conrad told him that he could talk to Frances if he wished.

'She seems to think you saved her life,' Conrad said, moving about the big room where Pete slept. 'She wants to talk to you. Well, I have no objection – have you?'

Looking at the thin, narrow-shouldered young fellow with his serious eyes and the livid birth-mark across the right side of his face, Conrad suddenly realized that perhaps a girl like Frances could fall in love with such a man.

During the week Conrad had been staying at the lodge, seeing Frances every day, he had come to love her more each time he saw her. She seemed to him, especially now she was no longer angry with him, to be the exact antithesis of Janey. Her voice, her movements, her eyes, even the way she moved her hands, expressed a kindness and an understanding for which Conrad had unconsciously been groping all his life.

Janey had bitterly disappointed him. She took everything and gave nothing in return, but even then he might have been content to have an outlet for his affection had she not demanded more and more attention as if she were determined to find out the exact depth of his love.

The depth was deep enough, but it revolted against Janey's unreasonableness and her selfish and constant demands.

Frances wouldn't be like that, Conrad told himself. Experience had opened his eyes. He wished he had his time over again, and he cursed himself for being such a fool to have persuaded Janey to marry him.

His love for Frances had the same poignancy as Pete's, for he believed, like Pete believed, that his love would never come to fruition. Instead of Maurer standing in the way as in Pete's case, it was Janey.

Conrad had made the mistake that Frances's interest in Pete was founded on love when in fact it was founded on compassion.

Frances wasn't in love with Pete, but she was sorry for him, and in a girl of her sensibility, pity was as strong, if not stronger, than love.

She knew he had had the chance to kill her. He had had the weapon and the opportunity. He had been ordered to kill her, and he had risked his own life by staying his hand. That act made a great impression on her, and the fact that the crude naevus that disfigured his face must have embittered and soured his life made her want very much to try to make up in kindness for the years of bitterness he must have suffered.

When they met in the garden on the afternoon of the day Conrad had talked to Forest, Frances was very kind and sweet to Pete. They talked as other young people will talk to each other for the first time. They were shy and hesitant, groping for common ground.

It wasn't an easy meeting. They were sharply aware of the guards who patrolled the garden and who watched Pete with stony hard eyes.

Pete was painfully conscious of his birth-mark; he sat on Frances's right, and he kept his face turned so she shouldn't see the birth-mark. When he did turn to look at her, his hand went instinctively to cover the mark.

Frances felt that this embarrassment was a slight on her own feelings, and after they had talked for a little while, she said suddenly, 'That mark on your face is called a naevus, isn't it?'

He flinched and blood rushed to his face, and his eyes suddenly angry and hurt, searched for the slightest hint that she was about to bait him.

But he couldn't mistake the kindness he saw in her eyes nor the sudden friendly smile she gave him.

'I want to talk about it,' she said quietly. 'Because it so embarrasses you, and it shouldn't. I believe you think it shocks me, but it doesn't. Don't you realize when I'm talking to you I look beyond that, and I don't really see it?'

Pete stared at her, and he was convinced at once that she was speaking sincerely. He realized she had said something he had longed to hear said by someone – anyone – but had never believed he would hear it. He was so moved he had to turn his head while he struggled to control his feelings.

He felt her hand on his arm.

'I didn't mean to upset you, but isn't there something that could be done about it? I've read, I'm sure, that people can be cured. Haven't you thought about it?'

'I guess so,' he said, not looking at her. 'It means an operation, and I've got some blood condition that makes an operation unsafe.' He swung around to face her. 'But never mind about me. I want to talk about you. I've never met a girl like you before. You're real and kind and decent.' He looked down at her hand, still on his arm. 'You don't mind touching me. What a fool I've been! If I'd met you before I wouldn't have done what I've done. It was because the way people treated me, the way they looked at me, that I hooked up with the gang.' He moved closer to her. 'But never mind that either. I've got to tell you something. This guy Conrad wants you to give evidence against Maurer. You've got to realize what I'm saying is right. I know. Don't listen to Conrad or any of these coppers. They don't know; they only think they do. They think you saw Maurer at Dead End. Now listen, I don't want to know if you saw him or if you didn't see him. The thing that matters is you must never admit having seen him; not to me, nor Conrad, nor anyone; not even to your mother or your father. You must never admit you saw him; not even to yourself! You stand a slight chance of keeping alive so long as you say nothing. It's not much of a chance, but it is a chance. But understand this: if you let Conrad persuade you to tell him what you know – if you know anything – then no power on earth can save you!'

Frances was a little shaken by his tense fierceness, but she wasn't frightened. Conrad had explained the impossibility of anyone reaching her, and she had been impressed by the precautions he had taken.

'I know I can't stay here for ever,' she said, 'but so long as I'm here, I'm safe, and so are you.'

Pete stared at her blankly.

'Safe? Here? Of course we're not safe! Do you imagine Maurer couldn't reach either of us if he wanted to? How many guards are there here? Twenty? If there were a hundred, they wouldn't stop Maurer. No one has ever survived when he has given the word for him to die. No one! You don't know that guy. The moment he failed to make good a threat, the Syndicate would wipe him out. It's his life or ours, and it won't be his.'

'Aren't you letting your imagination run away with you?' Frances asked. 'Of course we're safe here. Mr. Conrad has shown me the precautions he has taken. No one could get near us.'

Pete clenched his fists and beat them on his knees.

'Maurer can go through those guards like a hot knife through butter. I didn't want to tell you this, but I'm going to, because you've got to realize what you're up against. When I warned you about Moe I disobeyed an order, and Maurer can't afford to let me live. If he lets me get away with it, some of the others will start disobeying his orders. That's why I talked to Conrad. I was buying a little time. I didn't tell him much, but enough for him to hold me. But in a while Maurer will get me. My time's running out. I'm not kidding myself. I haven't much longer to live; maybe an hour, maybe three or four days, but not longer.'

Frances suddenly felt sick. Although Pete spoke calmly, she could see the terror in his eyes. It was this terror that convinced her he believed what he was telling her.

'But they can't get at you,' she said, gripping his arm. 'You mustn't be frightened. How can they get at you?'

'Of course they can, and they will. When they're ready to take me, they'll take me.'

'But how?' Frances asked. 'With all these policemen watching you ...'

Pete threw out his hands in despair.

'Do you think I trust any of them? If Maurer offered them enough money one of them would sell me out. Maurer could buy them all if he wanted to. When the time comes for him to take me, he'll pay them to look the other way. It's been done before, and it will be done again.'

'But he can't get at them!' Frances pointed out. 'Mr. Conrad assured me these policemen are incorruptible.'

'Yeah, he assured me that too. I don't even trust him. He might be the one to sell me out for all I know.'

'Oh, that's nonsense,' Frances said sharply. 'I don't believe that for a moment. You are letting your imagination run away with you.'

'When I am dead,' Pete said quietly, 'please remember what I've told you. And please remember your only chance to survive is to say nothing. If Conrad persuades you to tell him what he wants to know, no one, no power on earth, can save you. Please remember that. No one, do you understand? The organization will never let you reach the witness-box. So say nothing, admit nothing, and there may be a chance that Maurer will believe you do know nothing and you'll survive. It's your only chance. Please, please, remember this.'

'Yes, of course,' Francis said soothingly. 'But you're not going to die. You mustn't think that.'

Pete stood up abruptly.

'You'll see,' he said. 'Time's running out. There's one other thing I want to say: you're the only girl who's ever been kind to me – ever, and I love you for it. You've given me more happiness in the short while we've been together than I've ever had in my life.'

While he was speaking, Conrad came across the lawn towards them, and Pete abruptly turned away and walked quickly to the house. Three of his guards went after him. By the time he had reached the entrance to the hunting lodge, they were close on his heels.

Frances sat staring after Pete, her face a little pale, and her eyes troubled. She didn't look up as Conrad joined her.

'What's wrong, Miss Coleman?' he asked. 'You look worried.'

She looked up then.

'He doesn't believe he is safe.'

'I know.' Conrad sat down beside her and lit a cigarette. 'He's a neurotic type. After he's been here a few weeks, he'll begin to realize just how safe he is. It's an extraordinary thing what suggestion will do. He's so convinced Maurer is all-powerful that no amount of persuasion can make him think otherwise. But don't worry about him. He'll be all right.'

She looked at him gratefully. His quiet voice gave her confidence.

'Will I be all right too?'

Conrad smiled.

'Of course, but with you I have a special problem. I can't keep you here much longer. I shall soon have to think what I'm going to do with you.' He looked down at his hands, frowning. 'The solution to your problem, and to Weiner's for that matter, would be the arrest of Maurer. Once I have got him behind bars, there would be little danger to you both. I could then hold you both as material witnesses and protect you until after the trial. When Maurer's convicted, I could arrange for you to go to Europe until all the fuss has died down. You could then come back and start your life over again and in perfect safety. But I can't get a conviction against Maurer unless you'll give evidence against him.'

He saw her immediately stiffen.

'I have a hunch you did see Maurer at Dead End,' he went on before she could speak. 'I believe you have a very personal reason for avoiding the inevitable publicity of the trial. Isn't this something we can discuss? Couldn't you trust me and let me help you?'

Frances didn't say anything. She had gone a shade paler and her hands began to tremble.

'Now look,' he went on quietly, 'we're alone together. No one can hear what we're saying. There are no witnesses. Won't you take me into your confidence? Forget I'm a police officer. Let's talk as private individuals. Put your cards on the table and let me advise you. I give you my word I won't use anything you tell me unless you say so. I can't be fairer than that, can I?'

He saw her hesitate, and for a brief moment he began to hope he was at last going to succeed.

But Frances was thinking of what Pete had said: *The thing that matters is you must never admit having seen him: not to me; nor to Conrad, nor anyone; not even to your mother or your father. You must never admit you saw him; not even to yourself! You stand a slight chance of keeping alive so long as you say nothing. But understand this: if you let Conrad persuade you to tell him what you know — if you know anything — then no power on earth can save you!*

She stood up.

'I have nothing to tell you. If you don't mind I'll go in now. I'm finding the sun rather hot.'

She turned and walked back towards the house, leaving Conrad staring after her.

CHAPTER EIGHT

Dolores felt Gollowitz's mind was wandering. He didn't appear to be as pleased to see her as she thought he should. She selected a low-slung armchair and sat down, taking a deliberate moment before adjusting her skirt. She saw his eyes go quickly to her knees, and she allowed him a moment to look at them before she hid them from his sight with a sweep of her hand.

'Then you haven't heard from Jack?' she asked.

Gollowitz shook his head.

'Not a word.' He rubbed his fat chin and wondered if it would be safe to go over and kiss her. But he didn't know where Seigel was, and he was afraid Seigel might come in at any moment. He regretfully decided to remain where he was. 'I wish he would let me know where he is. I don't like being out of touch like this.'

'But you're doing very well, aren't you, Abe?' she asked, watching him thoughtfully. 'You're not worried?'

'Of course I'm worried,' Gollowitz said sharply. 'Who wouldn't be? Even Jack would be worried if he had to handle this set-up. If we can't get at this girl . . .'

Dolores quickly decided she didn't want to hear about the girl nor Gollowitz's plans. The less she knew the safer she'd be if Gollowitz made a bad mistake.

'Well, never mind,' she said. 'I'm sure you will manage, darling.' She crossed her shapely legs. 'I only looked in to see if there was any news of Jack.' She opened her handbag, glanced in it and frowned. 'I seem to be getting short of money. Did Jack tell you to look after me?'

Gollowitz shook his head.

'No, he didn't tell me. I guess he forgot, but that's all right, Dolly; what do you want?'

'It will be your money?' She looked at him with her wide exciting eyes. 'I don't think I could let you . . .'

'No, Dolly, don't let's be silly about this.' He took out his bill-fold and put a sheaf of bills on the desk. 'Will five hundred hold you?'

'Of course.' She got up and came over to the desk. 'Abe, darling, you're very sweet to me. I don't know what I should do without you.'

He smelt the subtle perfume she was wearing, and he felt his mouth turn dry with desire for her. As she leaned forward he saw her breasts swing against the soft fabric of her dress.

He half started to his feet, his fat face congested and his eyes glittering when the door opened and Seigel and Ferrari came in.

Dolores picked up the bills and put them in her bag. She didn't look round. Her face was calm and her eyes a little amused as she watched Gollowitz struggle to control his emotion.

'Sorry,' Seigel said. 'I didn't know you were busy.'

'I'm just going,' Dolores said, turning to smile at him. Her eyes encountered Ferrari's sunken, gleaming orbs, and her smile stiffened. 'I – I was just getting some money.' She had never been confused before in her life, but this ghastly looking dwarf who stared at her with eyes that seemed to undress her frightened her.

'Come in, come in.' Gollowitz said, trying to sound hearty. 'Okay, Dolly. If there's any little thing I can do while Jack's away . . .'

Dolores nodded and walked to the door. She had to pass Ferrari, and she instinctively walked around him in a semicircle rather than get too near him.

Ferrari eyed her over, stared at her long legs, then ran his bony finger down his nose.

When she had closed the door behind her, he said, 'Who's the twist?'

'That's Mrs. Maurer,' Seigel told him. 'Didn't you know?'

Ferrari lifted his eyebrows and came over to an armchair near the desk and sat down. He wriggled himself into the chair until his feet hung a few inches from the ground.

'Looks like Maurer takes care of his nights as well as his days,' he said, and his thin mouth curled into a leering smile.

'What's the news?' Gollowitz asked abruptly, his face flushing.

'The news?' Ferrari repeated, staring at him. 'Well, it's okay. Weiner goes tonight.' He folded his claw-like hands in his lap. 'At ten sharp.'

Both Seigel and Gollowitz stared at him.

'You wouldn't be kidding?' Seigel asked blankly.

Ferrari ignored him.

'It'll be a nice smooth job,' he said, evidently very pleased with himself. 'One of my best jobs.'

'How is it to be done?' Gollowitz asked in a hushed voice.

'I had to have inside help,' Ferrari explained. 'That was essential. I have persuaded Sergeant O'Brien to help me.'

'O'Brien?' Gollowitz exclaimed, leaning forward. 'But you can't trust him. We've never got anywhere with him.'

Ferrari smiled.

'Maybe you didn't find out his particular weakness. Everyone has a weakness. O'Brien has a son. He happens to be very fond of him. I have a son too, and I have learned that sons are precious to fathers: more precious sometimes than wives. A man likes to think that when he dies his name will be carried on. O'Brien is no exception. So he has agreed to help.'

'Well I'll be damned!' Seigel exclaimed admiringly. 'I didn't even know he had a son.'

'It'll be accidental?' Gollowitz asked anxiously.

'Certainly. Weiner will come over faint in his bath. He will slip under the water and unfortunately drown. Will that suit you?'

Ferrari's face and voice were so cold-blooded and casual that both Gollowitz and Seigel exchanged uneasy glances.

'That's fine,' Gollowitz said. 'Then tonight for certain?'

'At ten. Weiner takes a tub at night. It's a habit.'

'But how will you get into the bathroom?' Seigel asked. 'I thought the place was sewn up tight.'

Ferrari shrugged.

'Getting into the bathroom won't be difficult. The window is small, but then so am I. The only snag was that before Weiner went into the bathroom it was searched. That was why I had to get O'Brien to co-operate. He will do the searching tonight.'

'Well, okay: I hand it to you,' Seigel said. 'You really think you'll succeed?'

'I've never failed.'

Gollowitz said huskily, 'And what about the girl? What are you going to do about her?'

'Don't let us be impatient. First things first,' Ferrari said. 'I shall have to make a very special plan for her. She'll be more closely guarded after Weiner's gone. It should be an interesting problem.' His sunken eyes studied Gollowitz. 'But she'll go too. I promise you that. It may take a little time: it will take a lot of thought, but she'll go.' He slid out of his chair. 'I think I'll take a nap. I don't expect I shall get much sleep tonight. You'll be here around half-past eleven? I shall then have news for you.'

Gollowitz nodded.

Ferrari walked to the door, opened it, turned to look first at Gollowitz and then at Seigel; then he went out closing the door behind him.

II

The night was hot and close, without a breath of air, and heavy, black clouds hung in the sky. All day there had been a brooding, still atmosphere that had been getting hotter and more electric as the hours passed.

Conrad stood on the stoop of the hunting lodge and stared up at the sky.

'I'll be glad when the storm breaks,' he said to Madge Fielding. 'This is making me feel like a wet rag.'

Madge, who had spent the entire day with Frances, had come out on the verandah for a change of air. In spite of the close atmosphere, it was at least a little cooler outside than in the lodge.

'I'm just off to check the guards,' Conrad said. 'Want to come?'

'I'll come,' Madge said. 'I don't think the storm will burst before we get back, do you?'

'I don't think so. There's no wind yet. Anyway, I'm going in the car as far as the road.'

As Madge got into the car, she said, 'You know I feel I've been here for months instead of a week. How long do you think we'll have to remain here?'

'I don't know. I wish I did. The D.A.'s coming down on Saturday. He's going to talk to Miss Coleman. It's up to him now. She's defeated me. If he can't persuade her to talk, we'll have to think what to do with her. We just can't keep her here much longer. But if she decides to talk, then we'll stay here until the trial: probably for three months.'

'What do you think of her, Paul?' Madge asked as Conrad drove down the mile-long drive.

'She's a nice girl,' Conrad said cautiously. 'What do you think?'

'I like her, and I feel sorry for her. I think she's in some kind of mess.'

'Has she said anything?'

'Oh, no. But I've watched her. She's having quite a time, trying to make up her mind about something. She broods an awful lot. I think she is wavering, Paul. A little more persuasion might bring her down on our side. She's very worried about Weiner. She keeps asking me if I think he's safe.'

'Oh, he's safe enough,' Conrad said impatiently. 'It'll be when I take him to the court-house that the trouble will start. They are certain to have a go at him between here and the court-house. It's their only chance.'

He slowed down as the massive gates came into his headlights.

Five policemen, each armed with a riot gun, were standing by the gates. One of them came up to the car as Conrad pulled up.

'All okay?' he asked through the open window.

'Yes, sir. Nothing to report.'

'There's a storm coming up. Keep your eyes open tonight. Have you all got slickers?'

'Yes, sir.'

'Stay out here even if it rains stair-rods,' Conrad said. 'Two of you will be enough. The other three can keep under cover, but I want two of you out here all night.'

'Yes, sir.'

'Okay. I'm going down to the road-block now.'

The policeman saluted and walked over to open the gates.

Conrad drove down the long narrow road until they came to the road-block. He spoke to the guards, warned them to keep on the alert, satisfied himself the search-light was working and there were no absentees, then he swung the car on to a dirt track that led to the cliff head.

Half-way up the track, he came to another guard post, and leaving the car, he walked with Madge up the steep path that brought them to the top of the perpendicular cliff.

There were three sentry-box huts on the cliff top, about a hundred yards apart. Guards were patrolling the cliff, and one of them came over when he caught sight of Conrad in the failing light.

Leaving Madge, Conrad walked the length of the cliff head with the guard.

'Watch out tonight,' he cautioned. 'It's going to be bad, and it'll be on a night like this they might try to reach the lodge, if they're going to try.'

'They won't come this way, sir,' the guard said. 'I've done a bit of mountain climbing myself. No one could climb up here. I've looked it over pretty thoroughly. It's impossible to climb.'

'All the same, keep your eyes skinned. Your lights all right?'

'All checked and correct, sir.'

As Conrad joined Madge, he felt a little puff of hot wind against his face.

'Did you feel that? The storm can't be far off now.' He looked up at the dark sky. The great black clouds were piling up and beginning to move. 'Let's get back. We don't want to get wet.'

'They must be safe,' Madge said, speaking her thoughts aloud as they drove back to the hunting lodge. 'No one could get through to them, could they, Paul?'

'Don't worry,' he returned. 'I'm satisfied it's all right. I don't think an attempt will be made so long as they remain here. Maurer will try to get them when they come into the open. That's the time we shall really have to be on our guard.'

Thunder was rumbling in the distance as Conrad put the car into the garage, and walked with Madge back to the lodge. Every now and then he caught a glimpse of one of the guards, a police dog at his heels, moving through the trees.

'It's still some way off,' he said, as they mounted the steps to the verandah. 'I'd better grab a slicker before they all go.'

'You won't be going out again tonight, will you?'

'It's the only way I can be sure the guards keep on their toes. If they thought I wasn't going to show up, they'd take cover as soon as it started to rain.'

Conrad saw a dim, shadowy figure sitting on the verandah. 'Is that you, Tom?' he asked.

'Yeah,' O'Brien said.

'I think I'll turn in,' Madge said. 'Miss Coleman's gone up. There's a light in her room. Good night, Paul. Good night, sergeant.'

Conrad wandered over to where O'Brien was sitting and flopped into a chair beside him.

'Phew! It's close.'

'Going to be a storm,' O'Brien said. There was a flat, uneasy note in his voice that made Conrad prick up his ears.

'It won't reach us for another hour yet. What's the time, Tom?'

'Quarter to ten. It's coming up a damn sight faster than you imagine. I bet you it'll be right over the house in ten minutes. Hark at that,' he went on as thunder crashed suddenly. 'Coming up fast.'

'All okay your end, Tom?'

'I guess so.'

The flat, uneasy voice had a disquieting effect on Conrad.

'Are you all right, Tom?' he asked, trying to see O'Brien in the darkness.

'Of course I'm all right,' O'Brien snapped, and heaved himself out of his chair. 'I guess that punk wants his bath now. It's coming up for ten o'clock.'

'I'll come with you,' Conrad said, still a little worried by O'Brien's apparent edginess. 'I want to make the rounds before I turn in.'

'Are you going out again?'

'Yes, about three, I guess.'

A flash of lightning lit up the verandah, and Conrad was startled to see how pale O'Brien looked.

'Are you sure you're all right, Tom?'

'Hell, yes! Maybe the storm's given me a headache, but there's nothing the matter with me,' O'Brien said, and wiped his glistening face with his handkerchief. 'I never did like thunderstorms.'

The crash of thunder that came while he was speaking shook the hunting lodge.

'Phew! It sounds overhead already,' Conrad said.

O'Brien walked into the hall where a guard sat nursing a riot gun.

Conrad joined him and together they walked up the stairs.

'Hot enough to fry eggs,' Conrad said, taking out his handkerchief to mop his face.

O'Brien didn't say anything. He was wondering if Ferrari had got inside the bathroom yet. His mouth felt dry, and he was aware the muscles in his legs were fluttering and his heart was pounding.

They walked along the lighted passage where another guard sat facing the head of the stairs.

'Hark at that: rain,' Conrad said. 'Well, you were right. There must be quite a gale blowing.'

They could hear the rain hammering on the roof. Conrad paused a moment to peer out of the window on the landing. A solid sheet of water streamed down the window pane, sending a white mist of spray as it cascaded down the sloping roof. Jagged flashes of lightning lit up the rain-soaked trees and lawn.

Thunder rolled and crashed in a deafening crescendo.

O'Brien opened Pete's bedroom door.

Pete was in his dressing-gown, a towel over his arm. He stood by the window, looking out.

Two of his guards were playing gin rummy at a table away from the window. The third guard nursed a riot gun and watched Pete's back with bored indifference.

At the sound of the door opening, Pete looked around. The two guards at the table stiffened, their hands moving to their hip pockets. The guard with the riot gun got to his feet.

'Okay, relax,' Conrad said, coming in. He was pleased to see how alert everyone was. 'Some night, huh?'

'I'll say,' the guard with the riot gun returned.

Conrad noticed Pete was looking past him at O'Brien, and there was an alert, quizzing look in Pete's eyes. Conrad looked quickly at O'Brien. He was surprised to see how white and hard O'Brien's face was, and there was a savage gleam in his eyes Conrad had never seen before.

'Well, come on,' O'Brien said, and he seemed to be speaking through clenched teeth. He walked out of the room and Pete followed him.

The two guards resumed their card game. The guard holding the riot gun groped for a cigarette.

Conrad stood hesitating, then he went after Pete.

Pete was walking just behind O'Brien, along the passage to the bathroom, which was down a few stairs and round a bend in the passage. They had to pass Frances's room which was a few feet from the bathroom.

Conrad caught up with Pete as O'Brien turned the bathroom door handle and pushed the door open.

'Stay here,' O'Brien growled to Pete, and turning on the light he walked into the bathroom.

Conrad moved around Pete and stood in the doorway, watching O'Brien, who glanced over his shoulder and saw Conrad. It was only with a tremendous effort that O'Brien managed to keep his face expressionless.

O'Brien opened the big cupboard door and glanced inside, then he crossed over to the shower curtains. His heart was beating so violently he could scarcely breathe.

He turned his broad back towards the door and partially blotted out the shower curtains from Conrad's view. Then he parted the curtains and glanced inside.

Even though he was expecting to see Ferrari behind the curtains, the shock of looking into those deep-sunken murderous eyes made his heart turn a somersault.

Ferrari, as still as a statue, held an automatic in his right hand which pointed at O'Brien's stomach.

For a split second the two men looked at each other, then O'Brien dropped the curtain and still keeping his face turned from Conrad's watching eyes, he went over to the toilet basin and began to rinse his hands.

Thunder crashed overhead, and lightning coming through the small window filled the bathroom with a dazzling flash of light.

Conrad came into the bathroom.

'I'll have a wash too,' he said. 'Phew! It's running off me.'

O'Brien stepped back, and without appearing to do so, forced Conrad away from the shower curtains.

'Think it's going on all night?' he asked as he began to dry his hands on a towel. He tried very hard to speak casually, but Conrad again caught the overtones of uneasiness in O'Brien's voice.

'I shouldn't be surprised.' He took the towel from O'Brien. Glancing up, his eyes took in the bathroom window. 'I've been wondering if I should put a second bar up there.'

O'Brien had to make an effort to keep his eyes from straying towards the shower curtains.

'Think anyone could squeeze through that?' he said, trying to sound scornful. 'Why, it's impossible.'

Conrad wandered to the door.

'I guess that's right.' He moved out into the passage. 'Okay, Weiner. Go ahead.'

Pete entered the bathroom.

As O'Brien pushed past him, their eyes met and Pete received a shock. What was the matter with the guy? he wondered. He looked like he had seen a ghost.

Then suddenly he felt a cold wave of fear wash over him. It was just as if a bodiless voice had whispered a warning in his ear. He became transfixed, more frightened than he had ever been before in his life.

O'Brien had reached the door.

'Wait . . .' Pete managed to stammer. 'I – I don't think . . .'

A crash of thunder drowned what he was trying to say, but O'Brien saw the livid fear on his face. He realized Pete was about to say he had changed his mind and he wasn't going to take a bath.

'Get on with it!' he barked as he stepped into the passage. 'I'm not going to stay up all night for you!'

He slammed the door as Pete started to speak again.

'These goddamn punks think they own the earth as soon as you treat them like humans,' O'Brien went on to Conrad, keeping his voice raised. 'A bath every night! Who the hell thought up that gag?' While he spoke he leaned his back against the door; his hand holding the door knob. He felt the door knob turn, and by the sudden pressure of the door he knew Pete was trying to open it.

'Hadn't you better go along and see if the girl's all right?' he said to Conrad. 'The storm may be upsetting her.'

He managed to keep the door closed by exerting his great strength. Pete was pulling at the door handle violently.

'Madge's there,' Conrad said, busy lighting a cigarette. He didn't notice O'Brien's strained, white face. 'I'll go along in a little while.'

Another crash of thunder rolled over the house, and faintly O'Brien heard Pete yell through the door panel.

'What was that?' Conrad asked, looking up.

'Thunder,' O'Brien said. 'What did you think it was?'

As he spoke he felt the pressure on the door suddenly cease; then the door handle twisted sharply.

'I thought I heard someone call out,' Conrad said, and moved along the passage. He paused outside Frances's door and listened.

O'Brien stood still, his heart beating unevenly.

Thunder crashed and rolled overhead. The hiss of rain against the windows and the gurgling of water in the gutters blotted out all other sounds.

Then he heard a faint groan come from behind the bathroom door. It was a sound that made the hairs on the nape of his neck stand up stiffly.

He stepped away from the door, took out his handkerchief and wiped his face.

III

Conrad came back along the passage.

'They're all right: talking like a couple of magpies,' he said, then catching sight of O'Brien's white, strained face, he went on, 'You're looking pretty sick, Tom. Why don't you get off to bed? I'll wait here for Weiner.'

'There's nothing the matter with me,' O'Brien snapped. 'For the love of mike, lay off, will you? I'm going to bed, anyway, as soon as this punk's finished.'

Conrad offered his pack of cigarettes, but O'Brien shook his head.

For a long moment the two men stood listening to the violence of the storm, then Conrad asked, 'How's your boy, Tom?'

'He's all right,' O'Brien returned, giving Conrad a quick, startled look.

'Ever thought how damned lucky you are?'

'What do you mean?'

'Just that. I've always wanted a son, but Janey won't hear of it. She says it'd spoil her figure.'

'It could at that,' O'Brien said, scarcely knowing what he was saying. 'A girl like your wife doesn't want to mess around with kids.'

Conrad shrugged his shoulders.

'Oh, well, what's the good of talking? All the same I would

like to have a son, and a daughter, too, for that matter.'

O'Brien wiped his face with his handkerchief.

'Why don't you turn in?' he asked, wondering how much longer Conrad was going to stay outside the bathroom door. 'If you're going out again at three you'll need some sleep.'

'I couldn't sleep in this storm. How long is he going to be in there?'

'Twenty minutes or so. Hark at that thunder.'

'I wish that Coleman girl would make up her mind to talk,' Conrad said after the rolling crash of thunder had died away. 'I'm positive she saw Maurer.'

'Doesn't look as if she'll talk now. What are you going to do with her?'

'The D.A. will have to decide that.'

The sound of water splashing behind the bathroom door made O'Brien's heart skip a beat.

'You know Weiner puzzles me,' Conrad said. 'I'm inclined to think his birth-mark drove him off the rails. There's no real vice in him: not like the rest of them. What's his record amount to? We have no evidence he ever committed violence. As far as I know he specializes in stealing cars for the gang. I've talked to him, and I think he could be put back on to the rails again.'

'The hell with him!' O'Brien said savagely. 'I've got no time for these hoods: and that's what he is. Just because a guy happens to have a birth-mark doesn't give him the right to steal cars.'

'Isn't it time he came out?' Conrad said, looking at his strap watch. 'He's been over twenty minutes.'

'Aw, he doesn't hurry himself.'

Conrad rapped on the door.

'Snap it up, Weiner!' he called.

O'Brien inwardly cursed Conrad. He wondered if Ferrari had gone. With an unsteady hand he lit a cigarette.

The noise of the storm was slowly receding. Every now and then thunder crashed, but it was now more distant. The rain continued to hammer down on the roof and hiss in the gutters.

O'Brien saw Conrad turn the bathroom door handle, then frown.

'He's locked himself in! There shouldn't be a lock on this door, Tom.'

'So what?' O'Brien growled.

Conrad rapped again.

'Are you ready, Weiner?'

The silence that greeted him alarmed him.

'Hey, Weiner!'

'What are you getting so heated about?' O'Brien asked. 'Why doesn't he answer?'

'Maybe he's sulking. I'll kick his tail off for him when he comes out.'

'Hey, Weiner!'

Conrad banged on the door with his fist. When there was no answer, he stepped back, his face hardening.

'Come on, Tom! Let's get this door open!'

'Take it easy,' O'Brien said. 'Let me have a go at the punk.'

'We're wasting time.'

Conrad set himself and drove the flat of his foot against the door lock. The door creaked but held.

'Let me get at it,' O'Brien said, sure now Ferrari must have gone.

He stepped back, then charged the door, turning his shoulder as he crashed against the door panel.

The door burst open and O'Brien staggered into the bathroom.

'Hell!' Conrad exploded, crowding in behind O'Brien. 'Quick, Tom! Help me get him out!'

Pete lay stretched out in the bath. The small room was full of steam. Pete's head was under the water, and around his head and shoulders the water was a pinkish colour.

O'Brien reached forward and pulled the waste plug out. He caught hold of Pete's hair and lifted his face clear of the water.

'He must have been crazy to have got into a bath this hot,' he muttered, his hand going down on Pete's chest. He felt for a heartbeat, then shook his head. 'He's gone, Paul.'

'Move over!' Conrad snapped. 'Let me get hold of his legs. Come on! Get him out and let's work on him.'

Together they lifted Pete out of the bath.

'Bring him into the passage. There's no room to work in here,' Conrad said.

They carried Pete into the passage and laid him face down on the floor. Conrad knelt astride him and began giving him artificial respiration.

Pete's personal guards had come out of Pete's bedroom and were standing, watching.

O'Brien leaned against the wall. The strength had gone out of his legs, and it was as much as he could do to stand upright.

Conrad worked steadily.

No one moved or spoke. Thunder continued to roll and rumble in the distance. The rain was falling less heavily now.

At the end of a quarter of an hour, Conrad sat back on his heels. His finger touched the artery in Pete's neck. He shook his head.

'I'm afraid he's gone. Here, Wilson, you take over. Keep at it. You other two relieve him.'

The guard came over and knelt astride Pete's lifeless body. He continued the rhythmic pressure on Pete's back.

Conrad went into the bathroom. O'Brien came to the door and watched him.

Conrad began a systematic search of the bathroom.

'There's blood on the taps,' he said. 'He must have slipped

and caught his head, lost consciousness and went under.'

'Yeah,' O'Brien said. 'The water was too hot.'

Conrad straightened and stared up at the window. The puzzled, searching expression in his eyes sent a chill up O'Brien's spine.

'What are you looking at?' he demanded.

'I was wondering if he did faint in his bath. He might have been got at.'

'For Pete's sake! How?'

'Yes – how?' Conrad said, and ran his fingers through his hair. 'There was no one hiding in here. If someone tried to get through the window Weiner would have had time to yell.' He turned quickly and stared at O'Brien. 'I did think I heard him call out.'

'I didn't; besides, no one could get through the window. It's too small. Even a dwarf would have to struggle, and Weiner would have had time to come out.'

'Yes, I guess that's right,' Conrad said after a moment's thought. He went out into the passage again. 'Any sign of life?' he asked Wilson, who shook his head.

'He's gone, sir. The hot water in his lungs would have finished him quicker than anything.'

One of the guards brought a blanket and spread it over Pete's body.

'Well, that's that,' Conrad said in disgust. 'After all the trouble we've taken to keep him safe from Maurer, he has to die accidentally.'

He heard a sound behind him and looked over his shoulder.

Frances's door was open and she was standing in the doorway looking down at Pete.

'Is he dead?' she asked as Conrad went quickly to her.

'Yes, he's dead. Go back to your room, please. There's nothing you can do.'

There was an expression of stricken horror in her eyes that frightened Conrad. Every scrap of colour had left her face.

'How did it happen?'

'He fainted in his bath. The water was too hot.'

'Fainted in his bath?' she repeated slowly. 'Are you trying to tell me it was an accident?'

'It was an accident all right. Now please go into your room.'

Madge came to the door and put her hand on Frances's arm, but Frances stepped away from her. She continued to look at Conrad, her eyes glittering.

'That man murdered him! Pete said he would do it, and he's done it! Pete knew he was going to die. He said one of you would sell him out! That's how they got at him! He knew it was going to happen! He knew it!' She began to cry, tears running down her white face. 'He said even you could sell him out!'

'You mustn't talk like that!' Conrad said sharply. 'It was an accident. No one could have got at him. Sergeant O'Brien and I were outside the door the whole time. No one could get in through the window. The water was too hot, he fainted and hit his head on the taps.'

She stared at him, her lips trembling.

'Do you really believe that?'

'That's how it happened.'

'But it didn't! He was murdered! You're not going to let this man get away with it, are you? You can't let him get away with it!'

'What man are you talking about?' Conrad said, a creepy sensation going up his spine.

'Maurer! Maurer did this! Pete said he was going to do it, and he's done it!'

'Maurer didn't kill Weiner,' Conrad said patiently. 'You're just guessing. It was an accident.'

'But he did do it!'

'Now look, please go and lie down. You're upset, and I understand that. You must leave this to us to handle. No one could possibly have got at Weiner. I'm sure of that.'

Frances stood for a long moment staring at Conrad, her fists clenched, and as he watched her, she seemed to grow older before his eyes, and her face hardened until he scarcely recognized her.

'I'm going to tell you something,' she said in a quiet fierce voice. 'Maurer must pay for this. I don't care now what happens to me. I'll give the evidence you want. I did see Maurer at Dead End! He did murder June Arnot! I saw him do it!'

IV

Charles Forest and Captain McCann got out of the police car and ran up the steps to the verandah of the hunting lodge, their shoulders hunched against the rain.

Conrad came out to meet them.

The three men walked into the big lounge, and as McCann pulled off his raincoat, Conrad said. 'She's going to talk! We've got Maurer where we want him at last! She actually saw him do the job!'

McCann paused, his arm half in and half out of his coat, and he glared at Conrad. His fleshy face turned purple and his small eyes gleamed redly.

'Then why the hell hasn't she talked before?' he snarled.

'It's quite a story,' Conrad returned. 'Before we go up, you'd better hear it.'

McCann threw his coat into an armchair and walked with a slow heavy tread to the fireplace. If this was true, he thought, then Maurer was finished. McCann didn't kid himself that

Maurer would go to the chair without blowing the lid off the organization, nor would he keep quiet about the money he had paid McCann in the past.

McCann was alarmed, and he had difficulty not to show it.

'Are you sure she isn't lying?' he said, clenching his fists behind his back.

'Yes, I'm sure of that,' Conrad returned, 'but you can judge for yourself when you hear what she has to say.'

Forest sat down and took out his cigar-case.

'Tell me about Weiner first,' he said.

'There's not much to tell,' Conrad said. 'It was damned bad luck. He had a bath tonight. O'Brien and I took him to the bathroom, and O'Brien thoroughly searched the room before Weiner went in. We waited outside. After twenty minutes I called Weiner to come out, but he didn't answer. We found the door locked. We broke it down and found him drowned in the bath. The Doc said he had a superficial injury at the back of his head. He thinks Weiner got into the bath, came over faint, tipped back and banged his head on the taps.'

'People usually face the taps when they take a bath,' Forest pointed out.

'Yes, but apparently Weiner didn't. Anyway, he was dead by the time we got him out, and there was nothing we could do for him.'

'Are you quite sure no one could have got at him, Paul? It seems odd to me that the door was locked.'

'It seems odd to me, too, but I'm certain no one could have got into the bathroom while he was in it. The window is much too small. It would take a dwarf a good ten minutes to wriggle through, and in that time Weiner could have raised the alarm. No, I'm positive it was an accident.'

'Hmm, this has shot a big hole in our case,' Forest said. 'We needed corroboration, and Weiner could have given it to us.'

'Wait until you hear what Miss Coleman has to say. I think you'll agree with me her evidence will stand up without corroboration.'

'Well, what are we waiting for?' McCann growled.

'You wanted to tell me something, Paul?' Forest asked, ignoring McCann.

'Yes.' Conrad lit a cigarette, went on, 'You remember you suggested she was keeping quiet for a personal reason? You were right. She had a very personal reason for not admitting she saw Maurer, and now I've heard her story, I can't say I entirely blame her for keeping quiet. She wanted to avoid the publicity. Her name's not Coleman. She has a name known all over the world. Her father was David Taleteller.'

Both Forest and McCann stared at Conrad.

'You mean the Boston vampire?' Forest said, and Conrad could see how shocked he was.

'Yes, that's the man. I don't suppose there is anyone who has read the papers who doesn't know about Taleteller, and hasn't been revolted by his ghastly child murders. You will remember he was finally caught in the act and lynched by an infuriated mob who wrecked his house, killed his wife and very nearly laid hands on his daughter. And that daughter is Frances Coleman. Now do you understand why she had a horror of being dragged into the limelight? She has successfully hidden her real identity and has started a new life for herself. For the past six years she has been living as Frances Coleman, and up to the time she called on June Arnot she believed she had hidden her real identity for good. Then June Arnot was murdered, and Frances actually saw the murder committed. She realized that if she gave evidence the press would quickly find out who she was, and once more she would be faced by the horrible stigma of being the daughter of the most revolting killer of the century. She couldn't face up to it, so she refused to admit she had seen Maurer, and I can't blame her, can you?'

'Well, no,' Forest said slowly. 'This is, of course, a very special case. But why has she changed her mind? You say she is now willing to give evidence?'

'Oh, yes, she'll give evidence. She thinks Maurer killed Weiner and she doesn't want him to get away with it.'

'And yet she was willing to let Maurer get away with June Arnot's killing?' McCann snapped. 'That doesn't add up, does it?'

'June Arnot meant nothing to her, while Weiner did. Weiner saved her life, and his death shocked her. Personally I think she has been wavering for some days, and his death clinched it. It's a psychological reaction.'

'Why does she imagine Maurer killed Weiner?' Forest asked sharply.

Conrad shrugged.

'I don't know. Weiner told her Maurer would get him, and I guess she believes him. Nothing I can say will change her mind on that. She doesn't pretend to know how Maurer got at Weiner, but she is absolutely certain he did get at him.'

'You're quite sure he didn't, Paul?' Forest asked quietly.

'I can't be positive,' Conrad said irritably. 'But I'll be damned if I can see how he did it, if he did do it.'

'You're both making Maurer a bogey man,' McCann snarled. 'When are you going to see this girl?'

Conrad swung around, stung by McCann's bullying tone.

'See here, Captain. I'll have you remember she is a material witness, and as such is under the court's protection. I'm not going to tolerate any police methods when we question her. You have been asked here as an interested party, but that gives you no right to get as tough as I imagine you think you're going to get! So watch it!'

McCann's eyes snapped and his face became swollen with pent-up fury.

'You can't talk to me that way ...' he began, when Forest interrupted.

'Yes, we can, Captain,' he said. 'I support what Conrad's just said. This girl's an important witness, and I'm going to see she gets treated right.'

'She's an accessory after the fact!' McCann said, controlling his temper with an effort. 'And there's nothing either of you can say that'll make her anything else!'

'Oh, skip it,' Conrad said impatiently. 'Let's go up and talk to her. We want Maurer, and this girl can give us Maurer. That's all there is to it. So get off your high horse and calm down.'

For a moment he thought McCann was going to take a swing at him, but McCann managed to control himself.

'Okay,' he said, biting off each word. 'Let's get at her!'

The three men went up the stairs to Frances's room.

They found Frances, white-faced with dark shadows under her eyes, standing by the window. Madge Fielding was with her.

'Miss Coleman, this is the District Attorney,' Conrad said, 'and this is Police-Captain McCann. They have come to hear your story. Gentlemen, this is Miss Coleman.'

Forest came over and smiled at Frances.

'Sit down, Miss Coleman,' he said. 'I'm glad you're going to help us. I want you to know I fully understand why you have hesitated to give us a statement before now, and I want you to know we shall do our best to protect you against publicity or any unpleasant consequences that may follow a trial.'

Frances didn't meet his eyes.

'Thank you,' she said, and sat down.

'You have no objection if your statement is taken down in writing?' Forest went on.

'Oh, no. I – I want it in writing.'

Conrad made a sign to Madge, who went over to the table, sat down, and opened a notebook she had ready.

'Go ahead,' Forest said to Conrad. 'You handle it.'

Conrad came over to Frances.

'Just to get the record straight, Miss Coleman. You are Frances Coleman, and you have no fixed address at the moment, is that right?'

Frances looked up at him.

'Yes.'

'On the 9th of this month you went to see June Arnot?'

'Yes.'

'Why did you go and see her?'

'I was out of work,' Frances said, twisting her hands in her lap. 'I hadn't any money. I once worked with Miss Arnot. I had a small part in one of her films. She was about to make

145

another picture so I went to ask her if she could find a part for me.'

'And did she see you?'

'Yes.'

'What time did you arrive at Dead End?'

'It was a little before seven: about ten minutes to seven.'

'The guard sent you up to the house?'

'No. He phoned through to the house and they told him Miss Arnot was in the swimming-pool. He phoned through there, and Miss Arnot said I was to join her at the pool.'

'And did you?'

'Yes. It was a long walk from the gates, and it was a very hot evening. Miss Arnot saw how hot I was and she told me to have a swim first. She was in the pool, and she swam to the edge when she saw me. She said I'd find a costume in the changing room and I was to come into the pool.'

'And did you?'

'I – I didn't have time to get to the pool. I went to the changing room and began to undress, then I heard Miss Arnot call out as if she were greeting someone.'

'What did you do?'

'I was undressed by this time. I didn't do anything. I stayed in the dressing room, trying to find the costume Miss Arnot said was in one of the cupboards.'

'While you were looking for the costume, did you hear anything?'

Frances gave a little shiver.

'Yes. I heard a shot; it sounded some way off. Then after a minute or so, five or six more shots.'

'What did you do?'

'I stood listening, then I heard Miss Arnot scream out. It was a horrible sound. I grabbed up my dress and holding it to me I ran to the door of the changing room.'

'And did you see anything?'

Frances nodded. Her face was now white and strained.

'What did you see?'

'Miss Arnot was lying on the ground, near the pool, and a short, thick-set man in a black suit was bending over her. He wrenched off her swim-suit. In his right hand he was holding a knife: it was a broad-bladed thing, and it glittered in the sunshine. Miss Arnot seemed partially stunned. She was feebly trying to push his hand away. Before I could do anything, he – he stabbed her.'

'Did you cry out? Did you let him know you were there?'

Frances shook her head.

'Oh, no. I knew he had killed her. No one could have lived after the awful wound he gave her. It was horrible!' She looked away, her lips trembling. 'I was paralysed with fear. I couldn't move or make a sound. He straightened up and kicked her as

146

she lay dying on the ground. I saw his face. I'll never forget it. He looked like a wild beast.'

Conrad took a packet of photographs from his pocket.

'Will you look through these and see if you can recognize the man who killed Miss Arnot?'

Her hands shaking, Frances took the photographs. She had only to turn two over before she found the picture of Maurer. She handed it to Conrad.

'This man.'

'All right,' Conrad put the photographs down. 'What happened next, Miss Coleman?'

'Another man joined him, and they both stood over Miss Arnot. I was terrified. I hid in a shower cabinet.'

'I would like to establish this other man's identity,' Conrad said. 'Would you look at those photographs again and see if you can recognize him?'

Frances went through the photographs. When she came to Toni Paretti's photograph, she studied it for a brief moment, and then handed it to Conrad.

'That's the man.'

'Well, fine,' Conrad said. 'What happened when you were in the shower cabinet?'

'The two men remained outside the changing room for several minutes, then I heard a splash as if they had thrown Miss Arnot's body into the pool. Then the short thick-set man came into the changing room. His hands were covered with blood. I could see him through a gap in the curtain. He washed his hands, and all the time he hummed under his breath.' She suppressed a shiver. 'It was the most cold-blooded sound I have ever heard.'

McCann couldn't restrain himself any longer. Inwardly raging as he listened, realizing the deadliness of this girl's story, he burst out, 'That's a fine piece of imagination! Do you know what I think of it? I think the whole story's a damned lie! I don't believe you saw Maurer!' He leaned forward, his bull neck swelling with rage. 'You've got a thing about Weiner, haven't you? You fell for him, didn't you? Just because he's got a face that'd haunt a house you went soft on him. You've got a nutty idea Maurer killed Weiner. Okay, you want to take it out on Maurer, so you cooked up this yarn. That's the way it goes, isn't it?'

Conrad, his face flushing and his eyes snapping, started to say something, but stopped as Forest gave him a sign. Forest was looking at Frances, and Conrad looked at her too.

Far from being cowed by McCann's shouting voice, she faced him angrily.

'I'm telling the truth!' she said fiercely.

'Yeah? Then why the hell didn't you come out with this story before? You don't kid me, and you wouldn't kid a jury!

You've got hot pants for Weiner, and you're trying to get even with Maurer!'

Again Conrad started in to take Frances's part, but again Forest stopped him.

'How dare you speak to me like that!' Frances flared. 'You sound very anxious to protect Maurer! Pete said there were policemen who'd sell him out. Were you the one who sold him out?'

If she had struck him across the face, McCann couldn't have reacted more violently.

'By God!' he shouted, his face going blotchy. 'You can't talk to me like that, you little bitch!'

'That's enough!' Forest snapped. 'Watch your language, Captain! I'm sure Miss Coleman didn't mean what she said.'

McCann clenched his fists, words refusing to come. He was badly rattled. This girl had got unpleasantly near the truth, and he realized he was to blame for trying to take Maurer's part.

'I can prove what I'm saying,' Frances went on, turning to Forest. 'I can prove every word!'

'How can you do that, Miss Coleman?'

'Maurer took a handkerchief from his breast pocket and wiped his face with it,' Frances said quietly. 'As he did so, he flicked out a gold pencil. It fell on his shoe, and then rolled across the floor and went down a drain in one of the shower cabinets. Maurer tried to get it up, but he couldn't reach it. This other man said they had to go, but Maurer said the pencil had his initials on it, and he had to get it. The other man said no one would ever see it down there, and there was no way of recovering it. Maurer finally agreed to leave it.' She turned to look at McCann who was standing stiff and motionless. 'There was blood on Maurer's shoe,' she went on, 'and some of the blood got on to the pencil. You have only to get the pencil, prove the blood belongs to Miss Arnot, and then perhaps you'll believe I'm telling the truth!'

Conrad looked at Forest.

'Well, is that the corroboration you want?' He swung around and grinned at McCann. 'She thought that one up entirely on her own. She's quite a detective, isn't she, Captain?'

FERRARI pushed open the door and came into Seigel's office. He walked over to the desk, sat down in the armchair and wriggled himself into it.

'Is he dead?' Gollowitz asked in a strangled voice.

Ferrari stared at him.

'Does the sun shine? Is the grass green? Why do you waste time on the obvious? Of course he's dead. When I say I'll do a thing, I do it.'

Gollowitz sank back in his chair. He took out his handkerchief and wiped his face.

'And they'll think it's an accident?'

'Yes, they will think it's an accident,' Ferrari said. 'It went just as it was planned.' He folded his claw-like hands across his flat stomach, and looked at Gollowitz with eyes that were as lifeless and as still as the eyes of a doll. 'If you make a proper plan, you must succeed. He is dead, and now we must think about the girl.'

'I'm glad I sent for you,' Gollowitz said, and at the moment he meant what he said. 'I wouldn't have thought it possible to have done the job so easily.'

'It was only easy because I have had years of experience,' Ferrari said. 'With no experience and no plan, it wouldn't have been possible.'

'Now about the girl,' Seigel put in. 'How are you going to take care of her?'

'Another accident?' Ferrari asked, looking at Gollowitz.

'Yes; that's essential. We may have to wait a week. If she died immediately after Weiner it would look bad, wouldn't it?'

'If we have the time, a week would be better,' Ferrari agreed.

At this moment the telephone bell rang, and Seigel picked up the receiver. He listened for a moment, then the other two saw his face tighten. He handed the receiver to Gollowitz.

'McCann,' he said. 'Sounds as if he's blowing his top.'

Gollowitz said into the mouthpiece, 'Yes, captain?'

'Why the hell didn't you tell me you were going to take Weiner?' McCann snarled, his voice blurred on the humming line. 'You've really started something this time. Listen, that girl's talked!'

Gollowitz raised his eyebrows. With Ferrari sitting close by, he felt comfortably safe.

'Let her talk, Captain,' he said. 'I don't care. Why should you?'

There was a slight pause, then McCann said viciously, 'You

crazy? I tell you she's talked! She actually saw Maurer kill that woman. She's ready to go on the stand and swear to it!'

'Let her go on the stand. It's her word against Maurer's. She's got no corroboration. Why should we worry?'

'She doesn't need corroboration,' McCann snarled. 'She's got proof!'

Gollowitz stiffened.

'What do you mean?'

'I tell you she's got proof! She says Maurer pulled out a handkerchief after he had killed June Arnot. A gold pencil fell out of his pocket and dropped on his bloodstained shoe. Then it rolled across the floor and went down a drain. Maurer tried to retrieve it, but he couldn't reach it. The crazy bastard left it there! The girl saw it happen! The D.A.'s only got to get the pencil and Maurer's sunk. It has his initials on it and his finger-prints and June Arnot's blood. There was no blood in the chang-ing room, so the blood must have come from him. It's proof a jury would love. Do you still want me to stop worrying?'

Gollowitz's face suddenly turned a greenish hue.

'Is this true?'

'How the hell do I know? It's what she's just told Forest. They'll soon find out it it's true or not!'

Gollowitz's brain was working fast. If this was true then Maurer was as good as in the chair.

'Where is this drain?' he asked.

'In the changing room at Dead End: the changing room to the swimming-pool.'

'What's the D.A. doing about it?'

'Conrad and O'Brien with a photographer are going out there now.'

'Are they on their way?'

'They will be in five minutes.'

'Thanks, Captain. I'll take care of it,' Gollowitz said, and hung up. He looked at Seigel. 'Maurer dropped a gold pencil down a drain in the changing room of the swimming-pool at June Arnot's place. It might tie him into Arnot's murder if it is found. Three cops are going out there to get it. I want that pencil. Go and get it!'

This was something Seigel could understand. He had been worried by his failure to kill Weiner, and still more worried that Gollowitz had called in Ferrari. He felt now that he could reinstate himself by succeeding in this job.

'I'll fix it,' he said, and went quickly from the room.

Ferrari wriggled out of the armchair and stretched his thin, short arms.

'I think I'll go to bed,' he said. 'I think better in bed.' He paused to run his finger down his bony nose. 'Did Maurer kill this woman?'

Gollowitz shrugged.

'I wouldn't know. It's not my business anyway.'

Ferrari moved about the room, his hands clasped behind his back.

'The Syndicate doesn't like private killings.'

Gollowitz didn't say anything.

'The Syndicate isn't too pleased with Maurer anyway,' Ferrari said softly. 'He's getting a little too independent.'

Gollowitz felt a cold chill run up his spine, but he still didn't say anything.

'Well, never mind,' Ferrari went on. 'All that can be taken care of.' He looked sharply at Gollowitz. 'Is Seigel a good man to have in this outfit?'

'He's all right,' Gollowitz said carefully. 'He slipped up on Weiner, but I've never had any trouble with him before.'

Ferrari nodded.

'One slip would ruin even a very good man where I come from,' he said, and walked slowly over to the door. 'Still, it's your affair.'

He went out and along the passage to the bar. He felt like a drink. He seldom drank, but after a successful killing he usually allowed himself one small whisky.

As he entered the bar he saw Dolores come in through the opposite entrance. He paused for a moment, his sunken eyes taking in her lithe, sensual beauty, then he crossed over and joined her.

She was leaning against the bar, waiting for the bartender, and she didn't notice Ferrari as he came up behind her. But his presence was like the presence of a snake, and she sensed him, as one senses danger, and she looked quickly round.

As she looked into the still, lifeless eyes, a chill of fear went through her.

'What are you drinking?' Ferrari asked, his head just appearing over the top of the bar. 'Let me join you. Beautiful women should never be alone.'

She not only sensed the danger in him, but she also sensed his power. With any other man of his appearance she would have crushed him, but she knew at once this man couldn't be crushed.

'I want a martini,' she said, looking away from him. 'You are a stranger here, aren't you?'

'I am Vito Ferrari.'

He watched her lose colour, and he smiled, pleased to see that she knew who he was.

'You have heard of me?'

'Yes, I have heard of you,' she returned, knowing now why she was frightened of him.

'Good.' He rapped on the bar, and the bartender, turning to glare at him quickly changed his expression and jumped forward to give service.

Ferrari climbed up on a stool, and Dolores didn't feel quite so ridiculous now the little man was perched up so that at least his shoulders were above the bar.

Ferrari waved his glass in her direction and sipped, then he set down the glass, took out a cigarette-case and offered it to her.

She reached for the cigarette, then her hand paused as she stared down at the case. She had never seen anything like it before, and its ornate beauty fascinated her.

It was solid gold. The inside of the case was one mass of glittering diamonds, slightly larger than a pin's head and set so closely together they formed a white mosaic of fire. Seeing her look at the case, he closed it and handed it to her. In the centre of the case was a big ruby the size of her thumb nail, and on the back of the case were his initials in emeralds.

'You like it?' he asked, watching her face, seeing her amazed expression.

'I think it's the most beautiful thing I have ever seen.'

'It was given me by a Rajah for a little job I once did for him,' Ferrari said carelessly. He took the case from her, rubbed it on his sleeve and regarded it with smug satisfaction. 'I have many things like this. Are you interested in diamonds?'

'Who isn't?' she returned, looking at him with new respect. Neither Maurer nor Gollowitz for all their money had anything to touch that case. This little horror might be a dwarf, but he had power and money. It might be interesting to find out if his power were greater than Gollowitz's.

'I have a diamond collar that would interest you,' Ferrari said. 'You must see it.' He sipped his whisky while he studied her. 'You are friendly with Gollowitz?'

Dolores stiffened; startled by the unexpected question.

'He's Jack's friend,' she returned, her voice cold. 'Jack's friends are my friends.'

'That's very nice.' He leaned forward so his death's-head face was close to hers. 'But you shouldn't rely on him too much.'

'I don't rely on him at all,' Dolores said sharply.

Ferrari smiled.

'Then perhaps he is relying on you. I had the impression that one of you or both of you were relying on each other, and my impressions are never wrong.'

Dolores felt frightened. Had she and Gollowitz been so obvious? Was Seigel suspicious of them too?

'I really don't know what you're talking about,' she said, and looked away.

'And yet you strike me as an exceptionally smart woman,' Ferrari returned. 'Well, never mind. So long as you don't pin your faith on Gollowitz you won't come to any harm.'

She felt a chill run through her. Was he warning her?

'I don't like riddles,' she said, swinging round to face him. 'Suppose I do pin my faith on Gollowitz as you put it — and I most certainly don't — but suppose I do, what then?'

'You will be disappointed, that's all.' He finished his whisky. 'Can you keep a secret?'

She felt then he wasn't talking idly. He had a reason for asking.

'Yes,' she returned. 'I can keep a secret.'

'Gollowitz thinks he will take over this organization if anything should happen to your husband. I see no reason why anything should happen to your husband, but one never knows. Gollowitz will be disappointed. He is a good lawyer, but a bad leader. So don't pin your faith on a fading star.'

Dolores stared at him. So he had guessed she was preparing a back door. But this information he had just given her was so valuable that she forgot to feel frightened.

'You would know, of course?'

Ferrari smiled.

'I would know.'

'You would know, too, who will take over the organization?'

Ferrari nodded.

'I *should* know.' He patted himself on his chest, looked at her and smiled. 'I don't say anything will happen to your husband, but if something did happen, would you mind very much?'

She realized this wasn't the time to conceal her cards.

She shook her head.

'Not very much.'

Ferrari nodded.

'It's time I had someone to take care of my leisure moments,' he said. 'I've been looking around. There are plenty of good-looking women in this town, but I only want the best, and I'm in no immediate hurry. I can wait.' He slid off the stool. 'Would you be interested to see the diamond collar? I have it in my room upstairs. You might like to try it on. One of these days you might even own it.'

She sat motionless, staring at him. She knew there would be more to it than trying on a diamond collar.

'And at the same time I could satisfy myself that what I'm now looking at is gold and not brass,' Ferrari went on, confirming her suspicions. 'You don't have to come up unless you want to. You are following what I'm saying, or do I still speak in riddles?'

Dolores struggled with a sense of revulsion. To let a little horror like this touch her, and yet was he any worse than fat, oily Gollowitz?

She didn't struggle for long.

'I wasn't born yesterday,' she said, and gave him a long stare from her big exciting eyes. 'You won't be disappointed. Where's your room? I still have to be careful. I'll come up in a few minutes.'

II

Conrad pushed open the door of the changing room and groped

for the light switch. He could hear O'Brien's heavy breathing just behind him.

'Where the hell's the switch?' he asked, still groping.

O'Brien turned on a flash-light and swung the big beam around the room.

'Bit more to your left.'

Conrad turned on the lights and walked into the luxuriously furnished room. Facing him were the shower cabinets, each equipped with a fitted wardrobe, a chair and a shower. In one of these cabinets, he thought, Frances had hidden and had watched Maurer wash his blood-stained hands.

Mallory, a police photographer, came in and set up his camera. He looked inquiringly at O'Brien who was examining the floor.

'This must be it, Paul,' O'Brien said, and pointed to a brass grill that covered a six-inch-square hole in the floor.

Conrad joined him, and O'Brien directed the beam of his flash-light down into the drain. The light picked out a mass of dry leaves that lay at the bottom of the drain.

'I wonder where they came from?' Conrad said. 'Must have been washed in from an outside vent. Doesn't look as if any water's passed through the drain for some time. If the pencil is down there, it should be dry, and the blood won't have been washed off.'

O'Brien examined the grill covering the drain.

'Cemented in. No wonder Maurer couldn't retrieve his pencil. Did you bring the tools, Mallory?'

'I dumped them just outside. I'll get them.'

Conrad sat back on his heels and lit a cigarette.

'If the pencil's down there, we've got him,' he said quietly. 'I can't believe it. I've been after that thug for years.'

'You haven't got him yet,' O'Brien reminded him. 'Don't be too hopeful.'

'Sergeant . . .!'

The sharp note in Mallory's voice made both men straighten up.

'There's someone outside.'

Mallory was standing in the doorway of the changing room, silhouetted against the light. Even as he spoke there came a crash of gunfire and he staggered back, holding his arm.

With a muttered oath O'Brien jumped forward and flicked up the light switch, plunging the changing room into darkness.

'You hurt?' he asked, pulling Mallory away from the door.

'Got it in the arm,' Mallory said, and sat down abruptly on the floor.

Conrad had gone over to the door, and keeping well back, he peered into the darkness. He couldn't see anything.

O'Brien joined him.

'Maurer's mob,' Conrad said, and groped in his hip pocket

for his gun. 'There's a telephone somewhere around, Tom. Better get some boys up here.'

O'Brien grunted and closed the door.

'Watch out how you use the light,' Conrad went on. 'I think I spotted the telephone standing on a table to your left.'

O'Brien snapped on his flash-light and located the telephone. Out in the darkness a riot gun started up. The black of the night was split by yellow flashes. Lead smashed a window and scattered a shower of glass that whizzed over Conrad's and O'Brien's ducking heads. Plaster came down from the opposite wall, filling the room with dust.

'Hell!' O'Brien muttered, flattened out and began a slow crawl across the room to the telephone.

Conrad aimed at where the flashes had come from and fired a probing shot into the darkness.

Automatics cracked; pencil points of flame appeared in a semi-circle, bullets hummed through the smashed window and thudded into the opposite walls.

'There's quite a bunch of them out there,' Conrad said. 'Get moving, Tom!'

O'Brien had got the telephone down on the floor. Conrad could hear him dialling.

'It'll take them the best part of a quarter of an hour to get out here unless there's a prowl car near by. If these punks rush us. . . .'

Conrad crawled over to where Mallory was sitting.

'You bleeding?'

'A little. It's okay. Just nicked me. I wish I had a gun.'

Conrad caught a movement at the window. He swivelled round, his arm coming up. He fired as a shadowy figure moved away. He heard the *thunk* of lead against bone, and then the sound of a body slumping to the ground.

'Well, that's one of them,' he said grimly.

The still night was made hideous by machine-gun fire. Plaster came down on top of him as he hurriedly flattened out on the ground. Slugs sprayed against the opposite wall: glass and wood splinters joined company with ricochetting bullets.

'Like Tunisia all over again,' Mallory muttered as he flattened out beside Conrad. He never let a chance go by of reminding anyone of his war service.

'Got headquarters yet?' Conrad called over to O'Brien.

'Just about. The goddamn phone's gone dead, but I got through in time.'

'Let's get over to the door. We've got to stop them rushing us.'

Conrad crawled to the splintered door and peered cautiously into the darkness. On the far side of the pool he caught sight of a man running along the tiled walk. O'Brien took a snap shot at him, and the man disappeared into the shadows with a yelp of pain.

'We're not bad, are we?' Conrad said, and grinned. 'That's two in the bag.'

'I'm going to make a grab for the tools,' O'Brien said. 'We've got to get that pencil.'

'Watch it,' Conrad cautioned. 'Better wait.'

O'Brien crawled forward, ignoring Conrad's warning. He got his head and shoulders beyond the doorposts and his hand had hold of the tool-case when a burst of automatic rifle fire made him duck down. Bullets whizzed over his head. He began to move back cautiously.

'I've got it.' He looked back into the darkness. 'Here, Mallory, see if you can get the drain cover off.'

More machine-gun fire started up and for a long moment the three men lay pressing themselves into the floor as a hail of lead tore down more plaster and pulverized the walls.

'Look out!' Conrad snapped as he raised his head. He had seen two men come running along the tiled walk, guns in hand. Both O'Brien and Conrad fired at them. One of them swerved and fell into the pool. The other tossed his gun high into the air, took two staggering steps and fell flat on his face.

'That's three up,' Conrad said. 'I've only four more slugs left. What have you got?'

'I've a couple of spare clips,' O'Brien said. 'You hold your fire and let me take care of this.'

He crawled nearer to the door.

Mallory said 'I've got it! The sonofabitch didn't want to come, but it's come.'

'See if you can find the pencil. Careful how you handle it,' Conrad said, watching O'Brien. 'Don't let them see you, Tom.'

O'Brien fired out into the darkness, cursed under his breath and fired again.

Two machine-guns opened up on him. In the brilliant flashes Conrad saw him suddenly lifted off the ground and swept backwards as if riding a giant wave.

'Get his gun and guard the door,' Conrad said and crawled over to O'Brien. He bent over him trying to see in the darkness. 'Tom! Are you hurt?' He knew it was a stupid question. O'Brien had caught the full blast of the machine-guns.

Conrad pulled out his flash-light and shielding it with his coat, he turned it on.

O'Brien looked up at him in the dim light, his face, the colour of putty, was twisted in agony.

'It wasn't an accident, Paul,' he gasped, struggled to say something else and then choked blood.

Conrad lifted his head.

'Take it easy, Tom. Don't try and talk.'

O'Brien struggled, clutching hold of Conrad's arm.

'Ferrari . . . my kid . . .' He managed to get out, then his eyes rolled back and he slumped against Conrad.

Conrad touched the artery in his neck, shook his head and lowered him to the floor. He turned quickly as Mallory started firing.

He was in time to see three men coming along the tiled walk, bent double and running. Mallory hit one. The other two opened up with riot guns.

Conrad fired over Mallory's ducking head and saw the second man pitch into the pool. The remaining man rushed forward, spraying lead in front of him, sending a creeping carpet of death towards the open doorway.

Conrad wriggled back, dragging Mallory with him. For a long moment of time, they huddled against the wall while slugs sang around the room.

Then more guns started up on the far side of the pool: sharp reports of revolvers, and then the yammering sound of a Thompson.

The man firing into the changing room stopped firing. Conrad was in time to see him bolt back the way he had come.

Gunfire raved and crashed outside.

'Sounds like our boys have arrived,' Conrad said shakily. He went cautiously to the door. As he looked out into the darkness the gunfire suddenly ceased and a silence fell over the pool that could almost be felt.

Out of the darkness came the burly figure of Sam Bardin.

'Paul?'

'Right here.' Conrad came out into the open. 'Phew! That was quite a battle.'

'Got the pencil?'

'I haven't had time to ask. Poor Tom bought it.'

'He did? That's tough.' Bardin turned on his flashlight and swung the beam around the ruined changing room. 'They certainly made a hash of this. There're five of Maurer's mob outside, deader than mackerel. Two others got away.'

'Find that pencil?' Conrad asked Mallory.

'Sure,' Mallory said. 'I've got the sonofabitch,' and he waved the gold pencil above his head.

III

A black Cadillac swung into the narrow lane that ran alongside the east wall of the Paradise Club and drove fast down the lane to the gates that guarded the rear entrance to the club.

The driver slowed down, flicked his lights off and on: twice fast, twice slow, and then sent the car forward as the guard opened the gates.

The guard stepped up to the car and peered at the driver. He caught his breath in a gasp of surprise, stiffened to attention and saluted.

The Cadillac moved on up the circular road and pulled up

outside the rear entrance to the club.

A short, thick-set man got out of the car, looked uneasily to right and left, then walked up the steps and rapped on the door.

The guard who opened the door gaped, and his florid face changed colour.

'Why, Mr. Maurer . . .' he gasped.

'Shut your goddamn trap!' Maurer snarled. 'Where's Gollo-witz?'

'In Mr. Seigel's office,' the guard said, stepping back hurriedly.

Maurer's swarthy face was tight with rage, and there was a bleak murderous expression in his eyes.

He walked down the passage, paused for a moment outside Seigel's office, his head bent to listen. A murmur of voices came through the door panel, and Maurer's face tightened. He turned the handle and pushed the door open.

The office was full of tobacco smoke. Seated near the desk in a semi-circle were Seigel, McCann and Ferrari. Gollowitz sat behind the desk, a cigar in his fat white fingers.

The four men looked around sharply as Maurer came in. The only one who didn't react to his sudden appearance was Ferrari. The other three stared at him as if they were seeing a ghost.

'Why, Jack . . .' Gollowitz gasped, his face going white. 'For God's sake, Jack . . . !'

Maurer came in and shut the door. His right hand was buried deep in his bulging coat pocket. He stood looking at the four men, his little eyes insane with rage.

'What's he doing here?' he snarled, pointing at Ferrari.

'Jack! You – you can't come back here!' Gollowitz said, getting unsteadily to his feet. 'Did anyone see you? Don't you know there's a warrant out for your arrest?'

'What's he doing here?' Maurer repeated, his voice deadly.

'He – he's come to take care of the girl – the Coleman girl,' Gollowitz spluttered.

'Did you send for him?' Maurer asked.

'The Syndicate thought . . .'

'— the Syndicate! Did you send for him?'

'What else could I do?' Gollowitz wailed. He had a horrible feeling that Maurer was going to shoot him. 'We had to get Weiner and the girl. He was the only one who could get at them!'

Maurer glared at Gollowitz, his mouth working.

'You goddamn fool! Couldn't you handle a little thing like that without calling in outside help?'

'It wasn't possible.'

McCann said quietly, 'Take it easy, Mr. Maurer. You shouldn't have come back. Every cop in town's on the look-out for you. Forest has cooked up a cast-iron case against you.'

'Yeah,' Maurer snarled, 'thanks to the bungling way you three have handled it.' He didn't include Ferrari in the wave of his hand. 'I've come back to handle it myself! For the first time in fifteen years there's a warrant out for me! The first time in fifteen years! That's what happens when I take my hand off the helm!'

'We did what we could,' Gollowitz said earnestly. He felt the danger was receding. 'We got Weiner. Now we're going to get the girl. It'll be okay, Jack, only you must keep out of this.'

'I'm not keeping out of it,' Maurer said, and walked to the desk.

Gollowitz hurriedly stepped away, and Maurer took his place behind the desk. He sat down.

Gollowitz pulled up a chair and took his place with the others. Sweat beads covered his forehead. He was sick with frustrated rage and fear. To be suddenly shoved aside to lose his authority in a few seconds, to be deprived of his position which he had believed to be unassailable for a long time, was a devastating blow to his pride.

Ferrari caught Maurer's eye. The two men looked at each other. Seigel, an interested spectator, was startled to see what could have been uneasy fear in Maurer's eyes. Ferrari was completely unruffled and indifferent.

'Hello, Maurer,' he said softly.

Maurer shifted his eyes away.

'Hello, Ferrari.'

'Big Joe sends his love,' Ferrari said, and smiled.

Maurer nodded. He knew how dangerous Ferrari was, and he was dismayed to find him here. He had to make an effort to get a grip on the situation.

'What the hell have you three been playing at?' he demanded. 'Why haven't you got rid of the girl? It's three weeks since I've been away. She should have been hit days ago.'

'Not so easy,' Seigel said. 'We don't know where she is, for a start.'

'You knew where she was!' Maurer snarled. 'Why didn't you hit her then?'

'We took Weiner first,' Gollowitz said quickly. 'He was the easiest.'

'The easiest! Don't you realize she is the dangerous one? With her out of the way Weiner's evidence wouldn't have amounted to a thing! You should have taken her first!'

Gollowitz had long ago realized his mistake of killing Weiner instead of Frances, and it bothered him that Maurer had so quickly spotted the weakness of his strategy.

'You know she's talked?' McCann said. 'She claims to have seen you knock off the Arnot woman. That's why there's a warrant out for you.'

Maurer's face turned a dusky red.

'Then she's lying! I didn't touch June!'

'They have pretty solid evidence,' McCann said slowly.

'Enough to convince any jury.'

Maurer looked at Gollowitz.

'What evidence?'

Gollowitz told him of Frances's statement and about the gold pencil.

'We tried to get the pencil,' he concluded, 'but they beat us to it.'

Maurer stiffened.

'What do you mean – beat you to it?'

'Seigel went out there with a bunch of boys and surprised Conrad and a couple of coppers who were digging up the pencil. There was a gun fight, and before Seigel could clinch it, a bunch of cops took them in the rear. We lost five of our boys.'

Maurer looked as if he were going to burst with fury.

'Was that one of your stunts?' he snarled, leaning across the desk and glaring at Gollowitz. 'You crazy fool! You should have left it alone. I knew about that pencil. I had a story to cover it. Five of our men killed! You must be out of your head!'

Gollowitz dropped back in his chair, his face ashen. He felt Ferrari's eyes on him, and in a moment of sick despair he realized that the story of his failure would get back to the Syndicate.

'You not only throw lives away, but you underline the importance of the pencil,' Maurer went on. 'I dropped that pencil down the drain two days before June was killed.'

'But there was her blood on it,' McCann said sharply.

Maurer's little eyes gleamed.

'It was my blood. I cut my hand on a bottle. The blood smeared the pencil and as I was wiping it clean it dropped out of my hand and fell down the drain.'

'That won't do,' McCann said curtly. 'Sorry, Mr. Maurer, but it won't do. The blood on the pencil belongs to Miss Arnot's blood group, and it happens to be a fairly rare group at that.'

Maurer jutted out his chin.

'What group is it?'

'B group.'

'Would it surprise you if I told you I'm also in B group? I had a Wasserman a few years ago, and I was told I was in B group. How do you like that?' He swung around and glared at Gollowitz. 'If you hadn't tried to be so goddamn tough, this would have been a soft touch if it ever came to a trial.'

Gollowitz wiped his face. He looked suddenly old and very tired.

'I didn't know.'

Maurer looked at him contemptuously, then turned away with a shrug of his shoulder.

'Where's the girl?' he asked McCann.

'I wish I knew,' McCann returned. 'Forest has hidden her somewhere, and no one knows where.'

'Don't *you*?' Maurer snarled. 'Goddamn it! You're still

Captain of Police, aren't you?'

'No one knows except the D.A., Conrad and twenty of my best men, who are guarding the girl. Conrad took her away the night Weiner died. Forest tells me no one but his office is to know where she is until the trial.'

Maurer clenched his fist and thumped on the desk.

'We've got to find her and wipe her out!' He looked over at Seigel. 'That's your job! I want to know where she is the day after tomorrow. Understand? If you slip up on this I'll damn well see you don't slip up on anything else!'

Seigel started to protest, but the murderous gleam in Maurer's eyes stopped him. He turned white and glanced over at Gollowitz, appealing to him for help, but Gollowitz had all the trouble he could handle and he didn't even look at Seigel.

'Okay,' Maurer said, and stood up. 'There's nothing more we can do until Seigel reports where she is. We'll meet here the day after tomorrow at eleven o'clock and decide on a plan to hit this girl.'

'You won't find her,' McCann said shortly, as he got to his feet. 'I knew how important it was not to lose sight of her, and I've been searching for her. She's vanished. If you ask me, they've got her out of town.'

'Seigel will find her,' Maurer said grimly. 'He damn well better find her!'

McCann shrugged and moved over to the door.

'Watch yourself, Mr. Maurer. This town's hotter than a red-hot stove for you, and if one of my men pick you up, there's nothing I can do for you.'

'Don't worry about me,' Maurer said curtly. 'I can take care of myself.'

Seigel, looking white and shaken, followed McCann out of the room.

Ferrari continued to sit in his armchair. He stroked his bony nose and watched Maurer with alert interest.

'Okay, Ferrari,' Maurer said, softening his tone slightly. 'Much obliged for taking care of Weiner. I can handle the girl. You can get back to New York.' He looked over at Gollowitz. 'Have you paid him?'

Gollowitz nodded.

'Well, so long, Ferrari. Remember me to Big Joe.'

Ferrari got out of the armchair, stretched his short arms, took a couple of steps towards the door, then paused.

'I guess I'll stick around for a couple of days,' he said. 'You might need me. You never know.'

'I won't need you,' Maurer said, trying to speak quietly.

'You never know,' Ferrari repeated. 'Big Joe said I was to see this thing through. If you want me to get out, maybe you'd better have a word with him first.'

Maurer glared at Ferrari. Their eyes locked, and Maurer's

was the first to give ground.

'Well, okay, if you want to waste your time,' Maurer said indifferently. 'But I don't need you to handle this. Please yourself what you do.'

'I'll stick,' Ferrari said, smiled, and went silently out of the room.

Maurer turned and looked at Gollowitz.

'Pleased with yourself, Abe?' he asked softly. 'Are you happy you've got that little snake into my organization? How have you liked being the boss around here? Think you've done well?'

Gollowitz didn't say anything. He sat staring down at the carpet, his face slack, his hands twitching in his lap.

'Do you imagine the Syndicate thinks much of you?' Maurer went on in the same deadly quiet voice. 'An idiot child couldn't have done worse. Everything you've touched up to now has been bungled. Everything! I know you've been hoping to take over the organization. I know you've been planning to take Dolores too. Do you think I'm not on to you? You couldn't take over a flea circus let alone a set-up like this, and as for Dolores, you can have her if you want her. I'm through with her!' He leaned forward and suddenly raised his voice. 'Why, you stupid, spineless, yellow-gutted punk! You make me sick to look at you. Get out of my sight!'

Gollowitz got up. He walked slowly to the door. His feet dragged and his shoulders drooped like those of a man carrying an impossible weight. He went out and shut the door.

Maurer sat down abruptly. He knew the danger he was in. If he didn't handle this right, the Syndicate would decide he must go. He wasn't ready to go just yet. He knew why Ferrari was staying in town. He was waiting for orders.

For the first time in his vicious, ruthless career, Maurer felt afraid.

IV

It wasn't until the afternoon of the following day that Seigel thought of Janey Conrad.

He had feverishly organized a search for Frances when he had realized Maurer would show him no mercy if he failed to locate her. He had sent out every available man to tap the underworld for news of her, but so far he had drawn a blank.

He was getting desperate when he remembered Janey Conrad. Immediately he cursed himself for being such a fool as not to have thought of her before.

He hadn't seen Janey now for two weeks. He had found her charms a little disappointing. She hadn't lived up to her promising looks. Seigel had a high standard, and besides, there were any amount of pretty girls who were more than willing to accommodate him. He could afford to be choosy, and when he found that Janey wouldn't tolerate some of his finer points of technique, he came to the conclusion that she wasn't worth his time or his money.

It was possible, he now reasoned, that Conrad had told her where Frances was, or at least let her know where she could get into touch with him, and he regretted having dropped her so quickly.

He decided it wouldn't be safe to call on her until it was dark, and he hoped she would be in. He had an idea that if he telephoned her he would get a rebuff, and he preferred not to warn her he intended to see her that night.

To make certain he didn't lose touch with her, he detailed one of his men to watch the house, and when darkness came, he was relieved to learn she was at home.

He left his car at the end of the street and walked down to the house. It was a dark night, with a hint of rain in the air, and he passed no one on the way.

There was a light on in one of the upstairs rooms, but the rest of the house was in darkness.

His man had reported that the coloured maid had left about half an hour ago, and Seigel was satisfied that Janey was in the house alone.

He dug his thumb into the bell-push and waited.

After a delay, he heard her running down the stairs, then the front door opened and she was staring up at him.

She was wearing a yellow silk wrap, and her hair was loose around her shoulders. She looked pretty and desirable, but she raised no desire in Seigel.

'Hello, baby,' he said, and stepped forward, riding her back into the hall, closing the front door with his foot.

Janey's eyes flashed angrily as she recognized him.

'You can't come in here! Have you gone crazy?'

'Why not? you're alone, aren't you? I've been lonely for you, baby.'

'You must go at once!'

'That's a nice way to talk to me,' he said, smiling at her, turning on a charm that had never failed him as yet. 'Don't be that way. It's all right. No one saw me come in.'

'It isn't all right.'

He side-stepped her and walked into the sitting-room, switching on the lights.

'Gee! This is nice. How do you like being left all alone? Weren't you lonesome for me?'

Janey followed him in. She was flustered and angry.

'If Paul came back . . .'

'Why should he?' Seigel dropped into an armchair and smiled up at her. 'Relax. He's gone away, hasn't he?'

'Yes, but he might come back. You can't stay here, Louis.'

He reached up and caught her hand.

'Where is he then?' he asked, pulling her towards him. She

struggled for a moment, then reluctantly let him draw her down on to his knees. 'That's better,' he went on. 'Gee! I've missed you. Haven't you missed me?'

'Well, I have. You might have ... Why haven't I seen you before this?' Janey asked angrily.

Seigel laughed.

'I bet you thought I'd thrown you over. You did, didn't you?'

'What if I did?' Janey snapped, sitting bolt upright on his knees. 'Do you think I care? There are plenty of other fish in the sea.'

'That's right, so there are.' He ran his finger down her spine, and grinned as she shivered in ecstasy, pulling away from him.

'Don't do that!'

'I'll do something more than that in a moment.'

'You won't!' She got off his lap. 'You must go.'

'Okay, but you're coming with me. I have my car at the end of the street. We'll go to Hank's Bar and have a sea-food dinner and champagne.'

'No.'

But there was no conviction in her voice.

'Go and put on your prettiest dress. I'll wait here.'

'I don't think I should.'

He got up.

'Do you want me to carry you upstairs?'

'You'll do nothing of the kind!'

'That's fighting talk, baby.'

He swept her off her feet, holding her against him as she struggled and kicked.

'Let me down this minute!'

'We're going upstairs.'

He carried her into the hall and started up the stairs.

'Louis! You're not to! I'll get angry. You must put me down!'

'All in good time.'

He reached the head of the stairs, spotted a light coming under a door, pushed the door open with his foot and walked into a big, airy bedroom with twin beds, one of which was cluttered up with dresses, coats and underwear.

He set her down, his arm still around her, holding her against him.

'You get out of here!' Janey said angrily. 'I'm not standing any more of this nonsense!'

Seigel had trouble in keeping his temper. He never allowed his women to talk to him like this, but he decided it was too soon to get tough with her.

'I must always keep you angry, baby,' he said softly. 'You look even prettier when your eyes flash like that.'

Janey softened a little. She never could resist a compliment.

'Now, please, Louis, go downstairs. If Paul comes back ...'

Seigel sat on the bed.

'Where is he?'

'That's none of your business. Now run along and wait for me downstairs.'

'Don't you know, then?'

'Of course I know, but it's none of your business.'

Seigel grinned.

'Seriously, is he likely to come back tonight?'

'I don't suppose he is, but I'm not taking any chances. Now please go downstairs.'

He got up and went over to her, putting his arms round her.

'Kiss me, Janey.'

She hesitated, then lifted her face to his. He crushed his mouth down on hers, and for a long moment he held her like that, his body hard against hers, his arms tight in the small of her back.

She tried to resist him, but he held her easily, and slowly he felt the resistance go out of her.

'Oh, Louis . . .' she sighed, leaning against him.

He manoeuvred her over to the bed, and she shook her head, but the resistance had gone completely out of her. She lay flat on her back, looking up at him, her eyes cloudy, her face flushed. 'We shouldn't . . .'

'Where is he, Janey?' he asked, bending over her.

'Where is who?' she asked, frowning.

'Your husband. Where is he?'

The cloudy look went out of her eyes.

'Why are you so interested?' Then she sat up abruptly, pushing him away. 'Of course! What a fool I am! Of course!'

He eyed her warily.

'Of course – what?'

'So that's why you're suddenly interested in me again,' she said, her eyes furious. 'You want to know where that Coleman woman is, don't you? Of course! Paul said you were one of Maurer's thugs. What a stupid fool I've been!' She jumped to her feet. 'Get out! Get out before I call the police!'

Seigel grinned at her. His smooth charm had gone, and the cold, ferocious expression in his eyes frightened her.

'Take it easy, baby,' he said softly. 'Don't start anything you can't finish. You know where he is, and you're going to tell me, or I'll damn well beat it out of you! Where is he?'

Janey backed away, quaking.

'I don't know. Get out!'

Seigel stood up.

As Janey opened her mouth to scream he crossed over to her with two quick strides and hit her across her face with his open hand so heavily that she went down on hands and knees, momentarily stunned.

He bent over her, dragged her upright and holding her by

165

her elbows he shook her, rocketing her head backwards and forwards. Then he gave her a violent shove that sent her reeling across the room to fall flat on the bed. She lay gasping, feeling as if she had been caught by the blast of a bomb.

He went over to her, knelt on the bed, caught her wrist and turned her over on her face. He twisted her arm, driving it up and screwing her wrist as he did so.

She screamed frantically, but his left hand pushed her face into the bedclothes, drowning her scream.

'Where is he?'

Janey wasn't cut out for a heroine. The pain in her arm made her feel faint. She began to cry.

He wrenched her arm back again.

'No! Don't! I'll tell you!' Janey screamed.

'Well, come on, damn you! Where is he?'

'I don't know where he is, but I've got his telephone number,' Janey sobbed.

He turned her and stared down at her white stricken face.

'What is it?'

'Barwood 99780.

'If you're lying it'll be the last lie you tell, baby!'

'Leave me alone,' she sobbed. 'Oh, you've hurt me, you beast!'

'We'll go downstairs and you'll call that number. You'll talk to him. Tell him you're lonely: tell him anything so long as I know for sure he's there.'

'I'll do it,' Janey gasped, so eagerly Seigel knew at once she had been telling the truth.

'Come on,' he snarled, jerking her to her feet.

She staggered across the room to the door, holding her aching arm. He followed her along the short passage to the head of the long flight of stairs. He was just behind her as she put her hand on the banister rail, and he braced himself as she groped for the first stair. Then he lifted his foot, aiming at the small of her back, and drove his leg forward with all his strength.

The flat of his foot hit her like a battering-ram, projecting her violently into space. Her wild, terrified scream as she hurtled down the stairs, set his nerves on edge.

Her body twisted around as she fell, and he caught a glimpse of her terrified eyes and wide open mouth before she crashed to the floor below, landing on the back of her head with a thud that shook the house.

CHAPTER TEN

TEN days had passed since Janey's death, and by now Conrad had absorbed the first shock. At first it had seemed unbelievable that she was dead, and it was only at the funeral that he finally realized the unhappy partnership was ended.

The Coroner had returned a verdict of death by misadventure. The high heel of one of Janey's slippers had been found to have caught in the hem of her wrap. It was obvious to the Coroner that as she was descending the stairs she had tripped and had fallen heavily, breaking her neck.

Conrad had left all the arrangements to Janey's father, and had stayed with Frances in the new hide-out. There was nothing he could do for Janey now, and the responsibility of Frances's safety lay on him like a dead weight.

He had puzzled over O'Brien's last cryptic words: *It wasn't an accident. Ferrari ... my kid ...*

Conrad, like every other police officer in the country, knew of Vito Ferrari. Had O'Brien meant that Weiner had been murdered and that Ferrari had been responsible? Conrad had warned McCann that Ferrari might be in town, and had asked him to alert his men, but McCann had reported back that there was no sign of the Syndicate's executioner.

Conrad worried about this. If Ferrari had been responsible for Weiner's death, then Frances was in serious danger. He took every possible precaution to guard her.

He had moved her to the Ocean Hotel at Barwood, a small town fifteen miles from Pacific City. The hotel was a ten-storey building, built on the edge of the cliffs, overlooking the sea.

Forest had taken over the whole of the top floor of the hotel. A special steel door now sealed off the approach to the top floor, and twenty of McCann's picked men were on constant patrol on the landing and in the grounds.

As Conrad improved the defences, he slowly satisfied himself that it was virtually impossible for anyone to get at Frances.

Madge Fielding and two police women never let Frances out of their sight, and it was agreed that until the trial, she should not leave her room.

During the past days, Conrad had seen Frances constantly. The more he saw her the more in love with her he became, and he was encouraged when he found she looked forward to his visits, and seemed disappointed when other duties made him late or prevented him from making his regular daily visit.

Although they found an easy companionship together and impersonal conversation came without effort, Conrad was conscious of a barrier that excluded any intimacy between them.

It was her father's terrible record that stood between them, and it was this barrier Conrad knew he had to break down before he could hope to give her the personal protection he so much wanted to give her.

Madge had told her of Janey's death, and Frances's few words of sympathy had made Conrad uncomfortable.

'It's been a great shock to me,' he told her seriously, 'but Janey and I didn't get along together. Our marriage would have broken up sooner or later. It's not the same as losing someone one really loves, is it? I'm sorry for her. She enjoyed life so much, but I'm not sorry for myself.'

On the evening of the tenth day of Janey's death, Conrad found the opportunity of making the first move towards a more intimate understanding between Frances and himself.

He had been to Pacific City to give evidence in a case he had worked on before June Arnot's murder, and had been away from Barwood for a day and a night. He had left Van Roche in charge, and was quite easy in his mind that Van would look after Frances as well as he could look after her himself.

He returned to the hotel soon after seven o'clock and went immediately to the top floor.

Madge was off duty, and she came to his room.

'No alarms?' he asked, as he unpacked his over-night case.

'No,' Madge said, 'but I'm worried about her, Paul. She's very unhappy, and I think she's getting frightened.'

He paused in putting away his handbag and looked at her sharply.

'Frightened?'

She nodded.

'Yes. She doesn't say anything, but since you've been away she seems depressed and nervy. If anyone knocks on the door, she nearly jumps out of her skin. She's been brooding too, and she doesn't seem to settle to anything. I've noticed it before, but I think it's getting worse.'

Conrad lit a cigarette.

'It's pretty extraordinary she's been as calm as she has been. Time's running out. She has a horrible experience before her.'

'Yes, of course she has, but I think there's more to it than that. I think she's brooding about Weiner. She was never completely convinced that he died accidentally.'

'I thought she had got over that.'

'I'm afraid she hasn't.'

'Who's with her now?'

'Van.'

'I'll talk to her,' Conrad said, realizing this might be the opportunity he was waiting for. If he could only break down the barrier. If he could only get her on his side and keep her there.

He went along to Frances's room, noting the alertness of the four guards who paced the long corridor. He paused outside the door, tapped and entered.

Van and the two police women were reading novels. Frances stood before the open bay window that overlooked the sea.

She didn't look around when Conrad came in. He made a sign to the others to leave. When they had gone, he shut the door and joined Frances at the window.

Far below was the rock-strewn beach. The tide was going out and the stretch of sand was golden in the sunshine.

'I bet you'd give anything for a swim,' he said quietly. 'It worries me that you have to be cooped up here. Are you getting restless?'

She shook her head, not looking at him.

'No, I don't mind,' she said indifferently.

'I've been thinking about you, Frankie,' he said after a long pause. 'Have you thought at all what you are going to do after the trial?'

'There doesn't seem much point in thinking about that,' she returned in a flat tired voice.

'Why do you say that?'

'It's obvious, isn't it? Pete said they would never let me give evidence, so why should I bother to think of the future?'

He stared at her.

'For goodness sake, Frankie! You mustn't talk like that! You're safe here. No one can get near you, and you'll be safe at the trial.'

'Am I safe?' she asked, leaning out of the window to look down at the golden sands. 'You said Pete would be safe, and yet he's dead.'

'I wouldn't be talking to you the way I am talking if I thought for one moment you weren't safe,' he said quietly.

She looked round quickly, her eyes searching his face.

'I don't understand . . .'

'No, I guess you don't.' He moved away from her. 'I promise you no one will touch you. I give you my word.'

She turned so her back was to the window and watched him as he moved slowly about the room. There was an interested and puzzled expression in her eyes.

'You've got to get this idea that Maurer is a superman out of your mind,' Conrad went on. 'I don't say he won't try to get at you, he will, but I assure you he won't succeed. This place is too well guarded. There's nothing I haven't thought of.' He stopped and faced her. 'You don't know how I've sweated on this thing. Don't you feel safe?'

'No.'

'Tell me why you don't.'

'I can't forget what Pete said.' She sat down abruptly. 'I wish now I hadn't told you what happened. Pete said no power on earth could save me if I told you. He said no power on earth could save him either, and he's dead.' An hysterical note crept into her voice. 'Pete said his time was running out. My time's running out too! He said Maurer could buy any of the policemen who guarded him. How do I know Maurer hasn't bought those women who stay with me?'

Conrad was both startled and shocked to learn how her mind was working.

'You must stop talking like this.' He went to her and caught hold of her arms. 'Look at me, Frankie. I love you. Can't you see I love you? I promise you you're safe. I promise you there's nothing to worry about.'

She was staring at him.

'You love me? You? I didn't think . . . I had no idea.'

'I don't suppose you had,' Conrad said quietly. 'I didn't intend to tell you, but I can't have you thinking you're not safe. You're more precious to me than my own life. You don't have to be scared of Madge or the other two. They're all right. Honest, they won't let anyone near you, nor will I.'

She pulled away from him.

'But how can you love me?' she said, half to herself. 'You know about me. You can't love me.'

'Now look, Frankie, you've got to stop this nonsense. You're not to blame for what your father did, and you've got to stop believing you are.'

She looked at him, her eyes shadowy with bitterness.

'So easy to talk,' she said. 'So very easy to talk. You don't know what it is like to have people point at you, to whisper about you, to pull their children out of your way. You don't know what it is like to be hunted by a screaming, infuriated mob as I was hunted the night they killed my father. And now it's going to start all over again. What a fool I was to have told you anything! What a stupid fool I was!'

He knelt beside her.

'Frankie, if you'll let me, I'll take care of you. I've got it all figured out. I'll take you away when the trial's over. We can start a new life together. I want you to marry me. No one will know who you are where we'll go. We'll go to England. I have a friend who wants me to sink some money in his farm. He wants me to be his partner. There's a house for us, and no one will know you. Will you let me take care of you? Will you let me build a new future for you?'

She got up abruptly and without looking at him, she went over to the window.

'Future?' she said. 'But I haven't a future. I know I haven't.' She stared at the red ball of the setting sun as it slowly sank below the horizon, casting a red glow over the sea. 'My time's running out, Paul. There's no future for me, only a very immediate present.'

'It's got to look like an accident, Jack,' Gollowitz said. 'It's got to. If there's the slightest suspicion of murder, we're finished. A full-scale inquiry would put us out of business. Someone is bound to talk once the pressure's on. It's got to look like an accident.'

Maurer sat hunched up over his desk, his small eyes gleaming angrily. For ten days now he had racked his brains for a way to get at Frances, but the solid wall of defence that Conrad had erected baffled him.

'She's got to die!' he snarled. 'The only way to get at her is to set fire to the hotel. Then when they bring her out, we'll swarm all over them.'

Gollowitz spread out his fat hands pleadingly.

'We've got to think of another way. We can't do it like that. It'd finish us.'

Maurer got up and began to pace the floor.

'What other way? Goddamn it! There is no other way! How are we to get at her unless we smoke her out? How the hell can we make it look like an accident?'

Gollowitz wiped his glistening face. The past ten days had been dangerous and difficult for him. It had come as a great relief when Maurer had sent for him and had told him to forget what he had said at their last meeting. He realized now Maurer couldn't do without him. The problem was too big for Maurer to handle himself.

'Ferrari could do it,' Gollowitz said. 'I'm sure he could.'

Maurer paused to stare at Gollowitz.

'Is he still in town?'

Gollowitz, who had expected an explosion, nodded eagerly.

'He's in the bar right now.'

'We're admitting failure by using him, Abe,' Maurer said. 'You realize that?'

'We have failed. I wouldn't have brought him in if we hadn't failed to get Weiner. I know you blame me, but there was no alternative as there is no alternative now. If anyone can get at that girl, Ferrari can.'

Maurer came back to his desk and sat down. He stared down at his snowy blotter, his forehead furrowed, his eyes narrowed. He sat like that for some minutes. Then he picked up the receiver.

'Louis? Ask Ferrari to come to my office. He's in the bar.'

Gollowitz sat back. It was a moment of triumph for him. He felt vindicated. Maurer was now doing what he had had to do.

'You're playing this right, Jack,' he said. 'It's the only way.'

Maurer looked up.

'You're kidding yourself, Abe,' he said softly. 'You think I'm playing it your way, but I'm not. Ferrari is going to take care of the girl, then I'll take care of Ferrari. That's the difference between running this organization and letting the organization run you!'

Gollowitz stiffened.

'Take care of Ferrari? What do you mean?'

Maurer showed his teeth in a grin that made him look like a wolf.

'Wait and see, Abe.'

They sat looking at each other for several long minutes, then the door opened and Ferrari came in. He walked silently across the room, climbed into an armchair, wriggled back until he was comfortable and looked at Maurer with alert bright eyes.

'About this girl,' Maurer said. 'It's got me beat. Abe says you can handle it. Can you?'

Ferrari lifted his eyebrows.

'Of course. It's my job to handle it.'

Maurer's eyes snapped, but his face remained impassive.

'I'll pay ten grand.'

Ferrari shook his head.

'Twenty. If it was worth only ten grand you'd be able to do it yourself.'

Maurer shrugged.

'Okay, I don't haggle. Twenty, then. What makes you so sure you can handle it?'

'I've never failed, and I don't intend to fail now,' Ferrari said. 'You look for difficulties, I look for solutions.'

'It's got to look like an accident.'

Ferrari nodded.

'It will be an accident.'

Maurer's face turned a purple red.

'You don't even know where she is! You don't know a thing about the set-up. How the hell can you talk like this?'

Ferrari gave him a sneering little smile.

'She's at the Ocean Hotel, Barwood. She's on the top floor, facing the sea. There are twenty guards; five of them in the grounds, five guarding the top floor, five in the three rooms below her windows, and five off duty. No one can enter the hotel without a security check. No one is allowed near the top floor. The elevators only travel to the ninth floor. Three police women remain with her day and night and never let her out of their sight. When she takes a bath the door is left open and one of the police women sits just outside. She isn't allowed to leave her room. There is no means of climbing up to her window as the windows below are guarded. The roof is perpendicular, and the only skylight to it is guarded day and night. What makes you think I don't know the set-up?'

Maurer felt a cold chill run down his back. He stared at

Ferrari as if he had been suddenly transformed into a snake.

'You're lying! How the hell do you know all this? I've had the place watched for days and I haven't even found her room!'

Ferrari smiled.

'But then you are an amateur, and I am a professional.'

Maurer swallowed this insult as he felt it was justified.

'But how do you know?'

'I've been up to the tenth floor. I've listened and I've watched. I've even seen her.'

Maurer gaped at him.

'You've been up there! How did you get there?'

'That's my secret,' Ferrari returned.

There was a long pause, then Maurer said, 'Well, okay, then tell me how she's to die accidentally.'

Ferrari crossed one short leg over the other. He yawned, stretched, then folded his hands in his lap.

'It's an interesting problem, not impossible, but difficult. I believe I am the only man in the world who can do it.'

'You really can do it?'

'I stake my reputation on it. If I fail, you don't pay me a dime. That's fair enough, isn't it? But you'll pay me. I don't intend to fail.'

'But how will it be done?'

'That you must leave to me. I never discuss my plans. There are two things I need. I haven't the time to bother with them myself. Maybe you can take care of them for me?'

'What things?'

'I'll need an aircraft and a stunt flyer.'

Maurer's eyes bulged.

'A stunt flyer? You're not suggesting he should land on the roof, are you?'

Ferrari smiled.

'Nothing so obvious. I merely want him to divert attention. The trick is really very simple. You have seen a good conjuror? When he does a trick he makes sure the audience is looking at something else and not at what he is doing. The stunt flyer will do just that and give me my chance to strike.'

'I'll get you an aircraft and a stunt flyer. When do you want them?' Maurer asked.

'Today is Wednesday. Shall we say Friday? I must talk to him. There are certain things I have to tell him.'

'When does she get hit?' Maurer demanded.

'Saturday night. It is a good night. The hotel laundry is delivered on Saturday night.' Ferrari slid out of his chair. 'Another useful piece of information I picked up.'

'The laundry? What's that to do with this business?' Maurer asked blankly.

'It has everything to do with it,' Ferrari returned and walked over to the door. 'I'll be here Saturday morning. Have the flyer for me to talk to.'

He went out and shut the door.

Maurer drew in a long deep breath.

'What do you think, Abe?'

'He'll do it,' Gollowitz said.

Maurer nodded.

'I guess that's right. Smart little snake, isn't he?' He got up. 'I've got things to do, Abe. Ask Louis to come here, will you?'

Gollowitz gave him a hard, searching look, but gathered nothing from Maurer's deadpan expression. He went out.

Maurer began to pace up and down.

After a few minutes Seigel came in.

'You wanted me, boss?'

'Yeah,' Maurer said. 'Sit down, Louis.'

Seigel sat down. He looked at Maurer nervously.

'I've got a job for you, Louis,' Maurer said softly. 'Ferrari's going out to the Ocean Hotel, Barwood, on Saturday night. You're going out there too. On his way back, you're going to run into him. You're going to take care of him for me.'

Seigel stared at Maurer.

'Ferrari?'

'That's right.'

'You want me to hit him?'

'That's what I said.'

'For God's sake, Mr. Maurer . . . !'

'That's what I said,' Maurer repeated. 'It's either he or you Louis. Please yourself.'

III

The Ocean Hotel was always crowded at the week-ends, and on this Saturday afternoon the bathing-pool and the vast stretch of lawn was packed solid with people who had come down from San Francisco and up from Los Angeles for a week-end of swimming and lounging in the sun.

Conrad sat in a tub chair under a shady tree and watched the crowd as it played, lounged and gossiped around the swimming-pool. He kept an eye on the long drive that led to the hotel, watching for Forest's car.

Around four-thirty, he spotted the car coming up the drive. He stood up and waved. The car slowed down and stopped. Forest got out, said something to his chauffeur, then came across the lawn towards Conrad. The car went on towards the hotel.

Forest wended his way through the sun-bathers until he reached Conrad's isolated shade under the tree.

'Hello, there, Paul,' he said. 'Seems you've picked yourself a good spot. Plenty of pretty girls and plenty to keep your eyes busy.'

'Too much,' Conrad said, pulling up another tub chair. 'I

had no idea this place got so crowded over the week-end. My boys are going crazy trying to keep a check on everyone.'

'Are they doing it?'

'Out here it's hopeless, but no one enters the hotel without being scrutinized.'

Forest sat down.

'How's it going?'

Conrad pulled a face.

'She's safe enough, but she's getting depressed. I'm afraid Weiner sowed a lot of seeds of doubt in her mind. Now she has had time to get over the shock of his death, she's regretting having talked. We may have trouble with her later. She may even try to back out of giving evidence.'

'Have you got her statement signed yet?'

Conrad shook his head.

'No. She won't sign it. She thinks so long as she doesn't sign the statement Maurer won't go for her. It's cockeyed reasoning, of course. Maurer is far more likely to try to get at her before she signs the statement than after she's signed it. I've told her that until I'm blue in the face, but I guess she isn't in a reasonable mood. The fact is she's getting scared. She talks about waiting to die. I wish you would see her and see if you can put some sense into her. I can't.'

Forest looked at Conrad quickly, then he leaned forward and tapped Conrad on his knee.

'Does this girl mean anything to you, Paul?'

'That's pretty cute of you, sir,' Conrad said with a wry smile. 'Well, you may as well know. She does mean a hell of a lot to me. I've asked her to marry me. I'm crazy about her.'

Forest nodded, took off his hat and wiped his forehead with his handkerchief.

'Is she as crazy about you?'

Conrad shook his head.

'I guess not. She's not in the mood to think of me. She insists she has no future.'

Forest stared across the lawn at a tall, slim girl in a white swim-suit who was lying on her back, her eyes closed.

'There are plenty of pretty girls to choose from, Paul. I wouldn't like you to make a mess of your life. Miss Coleman's not exactly a happy choice.'

'You mean because of her father?'

'Yes; because of her father. I have a high opinion of you, Paul. One of these days you'll be a D.A. If you saddle yourself with a wife whose past doesn't stand scrutiny, you won't get far in a career.'

Conrad stirred restlessly.

'I know you're thinking of my interests, sir, and I appreciate it, but a career doesn't seem to me to be all that important when it comes to picking a girl you want to spend the rest of your days with. The career's got to go. That's how I see it.'

Forest selected a cigar, bit off the end and lit it.

'Well, okay, that's up to you, Paul. What are your plans, then?'

'I haven't any at the moment, I had hoped to take her to England after the trial. I've had a talk with her about going there, but she just won't get her mind on the future. She says all she has left is a very immediate present. She won't give up this morbid obsession that she's going to die.'

'I can't say I blame her,' Forest said quietly. 'She's bucking the most dangerous organization in the country. Her evidence will smash a billion-dollar racket, and Maurer's not going to let go of a kingdom that big if he can help it. Frankly, Paul, I wouldn't give her more than an even chance of surviving.'

Conrad clenched his fists.

'They can't get at her here. The real danger will be when she goes to the court-house.'

'Are you quite sure she's safe here?'

Conrad nodded.

'Yes.' I'm sure. For a start they don't know she's here.'

'Are you sure of that too?'

Conrad stiffened and looked at Forest.

'What's on your mind, sir? Do you think they know where she is?'

Forest lifted his heavy shoulders.

'I don't know, but Maurer's no fool. Did Janey know about this hotel, Paul?'

'Janey? Why do you ask that?'

'Did she know about the hotel?'

'I had to give her the telephone number. She was all on her own, sir. I didn't want her to think she was completely cut off from me. I impressed on her how secret it was.'

'So she had only to call the number to find out it was the Ocean Hotel,' Forest said, blowing smoke into the still, hot air.

'I don't get your drift,' Conrad said sharply. 'For all her faults, Janey would never have talked about anything connected with my work.'

'I'm just warning you, Paul. We mustn't assume anything if we want to keep this girl safe. Your wife was seen at the Paradise Club, Maurer's headquarters. She knew where Miss Coleman was hidden, and now she's dead. I may be talking nonsense, but for goodness sake don't let yourself be lulled into a sense of false security. Security doesn't exist so long as Maurer's running the organization.'

'I know the danger,' Conrad said. 'But you can count Janey out. Her death was an accident. I've warned her a dozen times about the hem of her wrap. She was always treading on it and tearing it, but she could never be bothered to mend it. I am quite sure, too, she would never give this place away. I can't do more than I have done to keep Frances safe. There isn't anything more I can do. You'll see for yourself when you get upstairs, but if you do think I've slipped up on something, then I'll put it right.'

Forest grunted. He watched a large white van coming up the drive. Across the side of the van, picked out in chromium letters, was the legend:

BARWOOD HYGIENIC LAUNDRY SERVICE

'If you're satisfied, then I'm sure I will be,' he said. 'But it worries me sometimes when I think how much depends on this girl's evidence. This is the first time since Maurer got into the saddle that we've had the ghost of a chance of bringing him to trial.'

Conrad followed the direction Forest was looking in, and he, too, idly stared at the laundry van as it turned the bend in the drive and disappeared around to the back of the hotel.

'We're taking a hell of a time to catch him, aren't we?' he said. 'So long as he's at large, we'll have to keep Frances here.'

'Every ship at sea is on the look-out for him,' Forest returned. 'The sea's a big place in which to hide, Paul. But sooner or later he'll have to put in somewhere for provisions, and then we'll have him.' He stood up. 'Well, let's look your defences over, Paul. I'll see if I can pick a hole in them.'

Conrad got to his feet, and together the two men walked towards the hotel.

IV

Around six-thirty the passages, kitchens and still rooms of the Ocean Hotel were noisy with bustling activity as the staff prepared dinner for over five hundred guests.

Unlike the glittering, luxurious restaurant, the staff quarters were dark, damp and cramped. The kitchen staff, already sweating from the heat of the ovens, cursed the long line of laundry hampers that were stacked along the wall, narrowing the passage to and from the kitchens to the preparation room.

The hampers wouldn't be moved until the following morning when they would be unpacked and the laundry sorted and taken upstairs; in the meantime they were unwelcomed obstructions.

Vito Ferrari lay curled up in one of the top hampers. He listened to the activity going on around him and watched through a chink in the wicker-work the staff scurrying backwards and forwards.

In half an hour the activity would be transferred to the kitchens and the restaurant. In the meantime he waited.

Waiting was no hardship to Ferrari. Patience was the greatest asset to a professional killer, and Ferrari's patience was without limit.

It had cost him twenty dollars to be smuggled into the hotel basement in the laundry hamper. The delivery man had accepted Ferrari's story of an illicit love-affair between himself and the wife of the head chef. The delivery man thought it was pretty funny for a dwarf to be in love to the extent of paying out good money just for a chance of seeing the chef's wife through a hole in the laundry hamper.

It had been simple enough for him to carry Ferrari in the hamper down to the basement. Ferrari didn't weigh much more than ninety pounds, and the delivery man had handled heavier weights than that.

So Ferrari waited in his hamper, and the hands of his strap-watch crawled on. By ten minutes after seven, the rushing to and fro began to dwindle. By seven-thirty the long passage between the kitchen and the preparation room was silent and deserted.

Cautiously Ferrari lifted the lid of the hamper and peered up and down the dimly lit passage. He listened, then hearing only the uproar coming from the kitchens, he slid out of the hamper, closed the lid and keeping close to the darkest side of the wall, he went silently and swiftly down the passage, away from the kitchens towards the storerooms and the staff elevators. He arrived at the end of the passage which opened out into another big lobby stacked with cases of beer.

He heard an elevator on the move and he ducked behind the cases of beer.

The elevator bumped to rest and the door slid back. Two waiters, manoeuvring a trolley, came out and went away along the passage, leaving the elevator doors open.

In a matter of seconds, Ferrari was in the elevator and had pressed the button to the ninth floor. The elevator took him smoothly and quickly upwards.

He leaned against the wall and picked his teeth with a splinter of wood. He was as calm and as unruffled as a bishop at a tea-party.

The elevator stopped.

Ferrari knew this was his first dangerous moment. If someone happened to be in the passage when he opened the elevator doors his plans might easily be ruined. It was a risk he had to take. In any plan, no matter how carefully thought out, there were always two or three unavoidable risks. They were risks Ferrari accepted, knowing that up to now his luck had been extraordinary. He saw no reason why his luck should desert him at this moment.

He didn't hesitate. As he pressed the button to open the doors, his hand slid inside his coat and closed on the butt of his gun.

The corridor was deserted.

He left the elevator, slid across the corridor and behind a curtain that screened one of the big windows overlooking the sea. The curtain had barely fallen into place when he heard someone coming, and he grinned to himself. His luck hadn't deserted him.

He peered through a chink in the curtain and nodded to himself.

A big burly man who had 'cop' written all over him, came slowly along the corridor. He passed Ferrari's hiding-place and went on, disappearing around the bend of the corridor.

Ferrari immediately left his hiding-place, and walked swiftly in the opposite direction.

The long corridor stretched ahead of him, and after he had walked fifty yards or so, he again ducked behind a window curtain. He remained there, listening and watching.

A door opened suddenly a few yards from him, and a girl appeared. She was wearing a low-cut, off-the-shoulder evening gown, and Ferrari looked at her creamy neck and shoulders with an approving eye. She closed the door, but left the key in the lock. He watched her walk slowly to the elevator. She pressed the button and waited, humming under her breath.

The big cop came back along the corridor. He touched his hat to the girl who smiled brightly at him, and he went on, not looking back.

The elevator door opened and the girl entered the cage.

Ferrari waited.

After a few minutes the cop came back. He passed close to where Ferrari was hiding, and once more disappeared around the bend in the corridor.

Ferrari stepped out from behind the curtains, crossed over to the door of the room the girl had just left, opened it softly and looked in.

The room was in darkness. He took out the key, stepped into the room, closed the door and shot the bolt. Then he snapped on the lights.

The bed had been turned down and the room was tidy, Ferrari decided the floor maid had already visited the room, and with any luck he wouldn't be disturbed for at least an hour. He turned out the light and went over to the window, drawing back the curtains.

The window overlooked the swimming-pool and the lawn. He could see the bright lights, the crowds still swimming or lounging around the pool while waiters in white jackets hurried to and fro carrying trays of drinks.

Frances's room, Ferrari knew, was at the back of the hotel, facing the sea. He knew, too, that all the windows on the tenth floor on that side of the hotel were guarded. To reach her window, he would have to climb up the roof, lower himself over the ridge and then climb down the other side.

It would be a dangerous and difficult climb, one of the most dangerous climbs he had ever undertaken, but it didn't worry him. He had studied the roof for a long time through a pair of powerful field glasses, and had decided on the route to take.

He pulled the curtain and sat on the window ledge and watched the crowd below. It wasn't dark enough to make an attempt just yet. In another half hour the darkness would hide him from anyone who happened to look up towards the roof.

He sat staring down at the lighted bathing-pool, his mind a blank, his muscles relaxed. The hands of his strap-watch crawled on and the sky slowly darkened. At a few minutes past nine o'clock he decided it was dark enough.

From under his coat he produced a long coil of silk rope that he had wound round and round his thin body. At one end of the rope was a rubber-covered hook, and at the other end a heavily padded ring.

He stepped out on to the window sill and looked up. Above him was the balcony of one of the bedrooms on the tenth floor. He tossed up the hook which caught in a stone projection and held.

He climbed up the rope as effortlessly and as quickly as a monkey runs up a tree. He reached the balcony, swung himself over the balustrade and dropped on to hands and knees.

He peered through the window into an empty room, then he looked over the balustrade and stood watching the activity below until he had satisfied himself no one from the ground had seen him.

He climbed up on to the balustrade and looked up at the perpendicular roof some twenty feet or so above him. A stout rain gutter ran the length of the roof, and he tossed up his hook again. The hook caught in the gutter, and he pulled, testing the gutter's strength. It neither bent nor creaked under his persistent pulling, and without more ado he launched himself into space and went swarming up the rope until his claw-like hands got a grip on the gutter.

He pulled himself up as far as his waist above the gutter, shifted his hand-holds, got one leg up and along the gutter, his foot in the gutter. There he remained while he adjusted his balance.

The steep roof towered above him. Far below, the bright floodlights, the blue water of the swimming-pool and the continual arrival of cars, looked like a child's toy laid out on a green carpet.

Ferrari began to lean forward very slowly, and at the same time he drew up his other leg and got that along the gutter. He was now balanced only on his hands, and the slightest error of judgment would pitch him backwards into the black gulf below.

He was quite calm, but he knew his danger.

When he had told Maurer he believed he was the only man in the world who could do this job he had been sincere. This moment of balancing was the hardest task he had ever attempted. He wasn't frightened, but he did wonder if he hadn't overestimated his skill.

He leaned forward a trifle, then began to draw his legs along the gutter towards him. As he began to bend his knees he suddenly felt his balance go, and for a split second the weight of his body swayed outwards.

His fingers dug into the cold hard guttering, and he dropped his head down on to his chest. The shifting weight of his head corrected his balance, bringing him slightly forward again.

He remained motionless for over a minute while sweat ran down his face and his breath came from his emaciated chest in great rasping gasps. He had been but a heart-beat away from death, and he was momentarily shaken.

When he had recovered sufficiently he again leaned forward and keeping his head down, he again began to draw up his legs. This time he succeeded in getting his feet under him, his knees bent up to his chin. He looked like a tiny black ball perched precariously on the edge of the gutter. Then still leaning forward, he slowly straightened his legs, thrusting his body forward and upright. He had to let go of the gutter, and his hands reached out and flattened on the tiles of the roof.

He was standing upright now, his toes in the gutter, his body flat against the roof, his head still bent down. He remained in that position until his breathing had returned to normal.

Then he slowly freed the rope which he had hung around his neck and tossed the hook upwards towards the apex of the roof.

He had to make four casts before the hook caught, and once in his anxiety to make a better cast he again nearly over-balanced.

But as soon as he was satisfied the hook had a hold, he was once more his confident self. Taking hold of the rope in both hands and leaning well out, he walked up the perpendicular roof and got astride the apex.

He could now look down at the sea, calmly washing over the rocks some two hundred feet below him. Somewhere just below the edge of the roof was Frances's room.

He could see the reflected lights from the windows just below, and could hear music from a radio. He fixed the ring at the end of the rope around his ankle, then holding on to the rope he lowered himself down until his heels wedged into the gutter. On this side, the roof was much less steep and he had no difficulty in sitting against the tiles.

Silently he lowered himself over the edge of the roof, turning upside down as he did so. He released the rope and swung head downwards, held only by his ankle. His head and shoulders came just level with the open window and he looked into a big, airy bedroom.

For a moment he couldn't believe his good luck. He had hit on Frances's room at his first attempt!

There were three people in the room. Two police women and Frances.

The two police women were sitting away from the window;

one was reading, the other was knitting.

Frances sat before a dressing-table. She was brushing her hair.

He hung upside down in the darkness and watched her. After a minute or so, she laid down the hair-brush and stood up. She was wearing a pale-blue silk wrap that accentuated her paleness. She wandered over to an armchair near the window and sat down.

Ferrari swung himself upwards, catching hold of the rope and hauling himself back on to the gutter. He looked at his watch. The time was now half-past nine. He had half an hour to wait.

He waited.

v

Conrad looked up as Forest came into his room.

Forest had had dinner and had taken a stroll around the grounds before coming up to Conrad's room. He sank into a deep armchair with the air of a man both relaxed and satisfied.

'That wasn't a bad dinner,' he said. 'They do you well here, don't they?'

'Oh, sure,' Conrad said indifferently. He hadn't even noticed what he had had for dinner. 'Well, sir, what do you think of her?'

'A nice girl; a damned pretty girl, too,' Forest said, stretching out his legs. 'I had a long talk with her and I think I've persuaded her to sign the statement. Of course she's scared of Maurer. Weiner did a good job, putting the fear of Maurer into her, but she promises to let me know one way or the other tomorrow morning.' He looked up. 'I put in a word for you, Paul.'

'You did? How did she react?' Conrad asked, sitting forward.

'She seems a little stunned that you should want to marry her. She's got a lot of complexes, and that's not to be wondered at. You'll have to be patient, Paul. It may take a long time. I told her if she will sign the statement, we'll finance a trip to Europe for you and you and Miss Fielding for a couple of months immediately after the trial. She seemed to like the idea.'

'Did she? That's pretty good of you, sir. How about the financial angle? The Treasury won't finance her, will it?'

'Not a hope,' Forest said, and laughed. 'That's up to you, Paul. I'll give you leave for a couple of months, but you'll have to stand the racket.'

'I'll stand it. Did she say where she would like to go?'

'I made a suggestion,' Forest returned, rubbing the side of his nose and looking artful. 'I told her she should see Venice. If you can't cook up a little romance in a gondola, then you're not the man I think you are. Ever been to Venice? I took my wife there on our honeymoon. No place like it in the world.'

'I'll take your word for it,' Conrad said, smiling. 'Well, that's something to think about for the future, but right now we've got to think of getting her safely over the trial. What do you think of my precautions?'

'Excellent,' Forest returned. 'I'm as satisfied as you are they can't get at her here now I've seen for myself. This is a good spot, Paul. What are your plans for taking her to the court-house?' He glanced up sharply. 'That plane sounds damned low.'

The sudden whoosh of air and the roar of an aircraft engine had startled them both.

'There's a night trip from Pacific City to Los Angeles that passes about this time,' Conrad said, glancing at his watch. It was just ten o'clock. 'I think the best thing we can do is to take her from here in an armoured car with an escort of cycle cops. We'll keep her in the court-house. There're some rooms in the basement she can have. They're not particularly pleasant, but it'll only be for a week or so. There're no windows and only one entrance.'

'Yes,' Forest said, 'but we've got to catch Maurer first.'

'Still no news?'

'Bardin was on the phone about ten minutes ago. He says there's a rumour going around that Maurer's back. They're checking now.'

Conrad sat up.

'Back? Who started the rumour?'

'There's that plane again,' Forest said, as the aircraft, flying very low, roared past the window. He got up and went to the window. 'Goddamn it! Look at this, Paul.'

Conrad joined him at the window.

Flying out to sea was a small, single-winged aircraft, lit up by red neon lights. It looked like some strange bird of paradise as it swept around in a tight circle and came back towards the hotel.

'Some advertising stunt,' Conrad said, watching the plane without interest. His mind was busy thinking about Frances. The idea of taking her to Venice made his heart beat faster. The trip would give him a chance to try and straighten out her mind.

'Looks pretty good,' Forest said, leaning out of the window to see more of the plane as it came around the hotel and swept downwards towards the sea. 'What's he advertising, I wonder? Hey! Look at that, Paul.'

A little irritated by Forest's childish interest, Conrad moved closer to the open window.

The plane was now flying just below the cliffs and practically level with the hotel gardens. A figure, lit up by red and blue fairy lights, was standing on one of the wings. It waved as the plane roared past the hotel.

'The reckless fool,' Conrad grunted. 'The things people will do for money.'

'When I was a kid,' Forest said, 'I wanted to be a wing-walker. That guy's certainly got a nerve. Look at him!'

The plane was returning now, still flying low. The wing-walker was standing on his hands, balanced precariously on the edge of the wing.

Faintly above the roar of the engine, Conrad could hear the excited cries of the people in the garden as they waved to the plane.

'Here he comes,' Forest said, leaning farther out of the window. 'He's hanging on with one hand . . .'

Conrad felt the rug they were standing on shift suddenly as Forest leaned still farther out of the window. He saw Forest lurch forward and grab frantically for the window sill. Conrad snatched at Forest's coat, braced himself as he felt Forest over-balance. For one horrible moment he thought the coat was going to be wrenched out of his grip, then Forest managed to get a hold on the window-frame and heave himself back into the room.

'For God's sake . . .' Conrad gasped.

Forest was white-faced and shaken.

'Thanks, Paul,' he said huskily. 'Hell! I nearly went out. That's a long way down. Phew! I guess the rug slipped. . . .'

Conrad stood rooted, his face white. Above the returning roar of the aircraft both men heard a wild, terrified scream that chilled their blood.

'What's that?' Forest exclaimed.

Conrad flung himself across the room, wrenched open the door and ran blindly down the corridor to Frances's room.

Two of the guards were coming from the opposite direction. Conrad beat them to the door and threw it open.

The two police women were standing away from the open window, white-faced and like statues.

Madge Fielding was wringing her hands, her face ashen.

There was no sign of Frances.

'Madge! What's happened?' Conrad asked, in a strangled voice.

'She's gone! She was leaning out of the window, looking at the plane when suddenly she screamed. I rushed to her, but I was too late. She seemed to be pulled out of the window. She was struggling, then the rug slipped from under her and she went out . . .'

Forest pushed past Conrad and went over to the window. He looked out.

Two hundred feet below him, looking like a small, broken doll, Frances lay stretched out on the moonlit sands.

He looked down at her for a long moment, then he stepped back as Conrad walked unsteadily to a chair and sat down.

'Well, that's it,' Forest said in a low savage voice. 'Goddamn it! There goes my case against Maurer – like her – out of the window.'

The aircraft swooped once more over the hotel, then its neon lighting went out, and like a departing spirit it flew swiftly out to sea.

CHAPTER ELEVEN

AT ten o'clock the following morning, Jack Maurer, accompanied by his attorney, Abe Gollowitz, and four hard-faced, alert bodyguards, arrived in a blue and silver Cadillac outside the City Hall.

A half an hour previously every newspaper in town had been tipped off that Maurer was on his way to surrender to the District Attorney. There was a big crowd of newspaper men, camera men, television cameras and three movie cameras to greet him.

Maurer got out of the car, a broad smile on his swarthy face, and waved towards the television camera. Maurer was a television fan, and he liked the thought that his face was being watched at this very moment by three-quarters of a million people.

The reporters converged on him, but his four bodyguards formed a protective wall around him and waved them aside.

'Have a little patience, boys,' Maurer said from behind his screen. 'I'll have something to say to you when I come out. Just stick around until I've had a talk with the D.A.'

'What makes you think you're coming out?' one of the reporters bawled, his face red with anger.'

Maurer gave him a wide friendly smile, and still surrounded by his bodyguards, he mounted the steps to the entrance of the City Hall and disappeared through its portals.

'The fat sonofabitch,' the reporter said. 'He won't talk himself out of this rap. They've got him where it'll hurt most.'

'Yeah?' the *Pacific Herald* reporter sneered. 'Do you imagine a bastard like Maurer would surrender unless he knew he could beat the rap? I bet you ten dollars to a dime he comes out of there in ten minutes as free as the air.'

'You've got yourself a bet, son,' the other reporter said pityingly. 'I happen to know what Forest has got on him.'

'Do you happen to know the only witness he had to clinch the case fell out of a window last night?' the *Pacific Herald* reporter asked. 'You've got to hand it to that oily snake. He's never let anyone give evidence against him, and he never will.'

'That was an accident,' the other reporter said hotly. 'I've talked to Conrad. That guy knows what he's talking about. She fell out of the window accidentally.'

'Like Weiner got drowned in his bath accidentally? Yeah? If you believe that crap, you're the only one besides Conrad who does.'

They were still arguing ten minutes later when there was a sudden hush from the crowd, and looking up, they saw the four hard-faced men coming through the doors with Maurer in the middle of them.

Maurer was beaming. He paused at the top of the steps and looked down at the battery of cameras and the hostile faces of the reporters.

Abe Gollowitz, a little pale and very tired-looking, stood to his right. His fat face was expressionless, but his eyes were the eyes of a man without hope or without a future.

'Well, boys,' Maurer said breathlessly, 'seems it was all a mistake.'

'Hey, wait a minute, Mr. Maurer,' the television interviewer shouted excitedly. 'Will you step down here and speak into the mike? Will you give us a statement?'

'Sure,' Maurer said. 'I promised you a statement and I never go back on my promises.'

He walked down to the battery of microphones.

'It's not untimely,' he said, speaking directly into the microphones, 'at this moment to thank all my well-wishers for their encouragement and their support during this absurd, but none the less awkward, situation that arose entirely through a misunderstanding between the police force and the District Attorney's office.

'As you all know a warrant was issued for my arrest. I was accused of murdering Miss June Arnot, who happened to be a very dear friend of mine.' Maurer was finding it a little difficult to retain his wide, sincere smile under the scrutiny of the cynical eyes of the *Pacific Herald's* reporter who had wormed his way to the forefront and was staring at Maurer with unconcealed contempt. Maurer made a mental note to see that this young reporter should get a beating at the quickest and most convenient moment.

'A very dear friend,' he repeated, shifting his eyes away from the *Pacific Herald's* reporter. 'The District Attorney is an honest man; a man I admire; a man who is above the everyday corruption of the present administration. He sincerely believed he had a case against me, and I say here and now that he did his duty by issuing the warrant for my arrest.' Maurer lowered his voice, widened his smile and kept his eyes away from the staring eyes that surrounded him. He concentrated on the television cameras. After all, these cameras were taking his speech and his face into the homes of thousands of suckers who played his gambling tables, used his whores, paid the Union dues to him, drank his rot-gut champagne, and elected his men into public office. The least they deserved was his best smile. 'On the face of the evidence he was presented with, he had no alternative but to issue the warrant. But on closer examination it was found the evidence he had against me was no evidence at all.' He waved his white fat hands. 'Don't think for a moment the District Attorney has been irresponsible. He hasn't. The evidence was there. If I had been in this fine city instead of at sea, the warrant would never have been issued, for I could have explained away the evidence as I have just explained it away.' He smiled into the television camera. 'I have said June Arnot was a very dear friend of mine,' he went on. 'She was. I would never have done her any harm; I never did do her any harm. Her death was a great shock to me. As soon as I knew of the warrant for my arrest I came back to refute the charge. Gentlemen, the District Attorney has withdrawn the warrant. He has even been good enough to apologize for any inconvenience he has caused me . . .'

The *Herald* reporter broke in violently, 'Isn't it a fact the District Attorney's case against you has collapsed because his only two witnesses have met convenient and apparently accidental deaths?'

Maurer looked at him sorrowfully. This sonofabitch would find himself in a barrelful of cement at the bottom of the sea before he was much older, he thought, as he shook his head at him.

'Mr. Forest didn't take me into his confidence about any of his witnesses. I know nothing about them except what I read in some newspapers this morning. I am told that a gold pencil which belonged to me was found near the swimming-pool of my dear friend June Arnot. The pencil had my finger-prints and a smear of blood on it. The blood appeared to belong to Miss Arnot's group, and the police jumped to the conclusion that because there was no blood in the place where the pencil was found I must have murdered her. That was the flimsy evidence on which the police based their case. It so happened the previous day when I was with Miss Arnot I cut my finger and blood got on the pencil. I dropped the pencil down a drain. It so happens I am not a poor man and I have other gold pencils, so I left it down the drain.' He paused, then added with a smile that could have been a snarl, 'Can I help it if my blood group and Miss Arnot's blood group happen to be the same?'

He gave a signal and immediately the four bodyguards moved forward, shoving the reporters aside, and Maurer walked quickly down the steps and ducked into his car.

Gollowitz scrambled in after him, while the bodyguards kept the reporters from mobbing the car.

The car drove away fast.

As soon as they were clear of the gaping crowds, Maurer threw back his head and gave a short, barking laugh.

'Very funny, Abe. I wouldn't have missed seeing that punk Forest's face when you handled him, for all the money in town. Hell! We put it across him, didn't we?' He slapped Gollowitz's fat thigh. 'Now I can get down to business. Listen, Abe, here's what I want you to do. I want you to draw me up a list of all money and securities I own: every dollar; ready cash I'm talking about. I want also a list of stocks and bonds I hold, and the present market prices.'

Gollowitz gave him a quick, suspicious look.

'What's the idea, Jack?'

'Never mind. I may be pulling out. I've got all the dough I want. I'm fed up with the Syndicate. If they want to run California, let them get on with it.'

'I thought you were going to take care of Ferrari,' Gollowitz said sharply.

Maurer smiled, but his eyes were like ice.

'That's right; that was the idea. Seigel bungled it. I had an idea he might. He bungled every damn thing he touched. He was no good except with a woman; no good for anything else.'

Gollowitz looked at Maurer, his face paling.

'What happened to him?'

'Ferrari was too quick for him, that's what happened. It was a big gamble that didn't come off. I've talked to Big Joe. I explained it was nothing to do with me. He seemed amused that anyone should even try to rub Ferrari out; very amused.'

The big Cadillac swung through the open gates of Maurer's estate and drove rapidly up the drive. In the bright morning sunshine, Gollowitz noticed a number of men moving about the grounds.

'Who are these guys?' he asked. 'What are they doing here?'

'Just a precaution,' Maurer returned. 'I don't believe in taking risks. If Ferrari tries any of his tricks on me it'll be just too bad for him.'

Gollowitz didn't say anything, but he felt a chill run down his fat spine. Did Maurer really believe these gunmen could protect him from Ferrari if Ferrari once made up his mind to kill him, he wondered. Was he such a blind, arrogant fool?

The car pulled up outside the imposing entrance.

'Okay, Abe, get those lists for me, and be here for lunch. The yacht's standing by. I may be leaving tonight,' Maurer said, as he heaved himself out of the car.

'Jack,' Gollowitz said huskily, 'what's going to happen to me if you go away?'

Maurer stared at him as if he wasn't sure if he had heard aright.

'You?' he said, and frowned. 'Well, I guess you'll manage. Maybe Big Joe will find something for you. Maybe he'll give you my job. You're big enough to look after yourself, aren't you?' He grinned wolfishly. 'Maybe I might have an idea or two for you when you come back for lunch.'

He walked into the house, leaving Gollowitz sitting in a fat hopeless heap in the car.

Three hard-faced gunmen lounged in the hall. They stiffened to attention when they saw Maurer.

'Stick around, you guys,' Maurer said, 'and keep your eyes open.'

'Sure, boss,' one of the men said. 'There won't be no trouble.'

'There'd better not be,' Maurer grunted, and walked into the big sunny lounge.

Dolores stood by the open casement window. She looked slim and lovely in a simple black dress. There were shadows under her eyes, and she was pale.

'Hello, Jack.'

'There you are, Dolly,' Maurer said. 'Get me a drink, will you?'

He joined her at the window and looked down the long terraced garden. Guards stood about on the terraces, some of them cradled rifles under their arms.

'Seigel tried to knock off Ferrari,' Maurer said, as Dolores poured a stiff highball. He sank into an armchair, his back to the window. 'Ferrari stuck a knife into him. I'm taking a few precautions until Ferrari leaves town.'

Dolores didn't say anything. She brought the drink over to Maurer and set it on a small table near him.

'Well, Dolly, this is the last drink I'll have with you. I'm leaving town for good.'

'Are you?' she said, in a flat disinterested voice.

'Yes. I'm going to Florida,' Maurer said. 'I'm kissing the Syndicate good-bye. There are a lot of opportunities for a man with my abilities, money and organization in Florida. I shall have to decide what to do with you.'

'You don't have to worry about me,' Dolores said, not looking at him. She moved over to the window.

'Oh, I'm not going to worry about you, Dolly,' Maurer said, and laughed. 'I don't think Abe will make you a good husband. Abe's rather gone to pieces. I think he might meet with a little accident some time to-day. Would you be sorry?'

'No.'

'I thought you were hoping he'd take you over, Dolly.'

'I wonder what gave you that idea?' Dolores said.

She looked down the long flight of steps that linked one terrace with another. Coming up the steps was a small figure in a black suit and black hat. It was Ferrari. He walked slowly and softly. His hands in his pockets, his face raised, his eyes fixed on the casement windows, he appeared completely unaware of the guards who stood motionless, watching him coming.

He passed one guard, then another. Neither of the men moved. They just stared at him. He came slowly, a tiny menacing figure, moving like a ghost.

'Then I'm wrong?' Maurer said. 'Was it Seigel you had your eyes on?'

'No.' She came away from the window and walked slowly across the room to the door. 'You won't want me to come with you, Jack?'

He looked at her, smiling.

'You won't be going anywhere, Dolly – nowhere at all.'

She looked at him thoughtfully, and he was a little surprised to see there was no fear in her exciting eyes.

'I see,' she said, opened the door and went into the hall.

There were no guards in the hall.

As she walked slowly up the stairs to her room, she wondered when Big Joe had taken over the organization. He must have moved fast. She wondered, too, what her life would be like with Ferrari.

She went into her bedroom and sat down. Because she had lived with Maurer for four long years, sharing his bed with him, taking his gifts as well as his insults, she felt sick and cold.

She closed her eyes and waited for the sound that would tell her that she was Ferrari's chattel and Maurer's widow.

The sudden crash of gunfire from downstairs struck her like a physical blow. She leaned forward, her hands covering her face, and for the first time for many years she wept.

She wasn't weeping for Maurer. She was weeping for herself.